Soul Whispers

JULIA WILD

Heartline
Books

First published in the United Kingdom in 2001
by Heartline Books Limited.

Heartline Books Limited
PO Box 22598, London W8 7GB

Heartline Books Ltd. Reg No: 03986653

ISBN 1-903867-03-7

Designed by Oxford Designers & Illustrators

Printed and bound in Great Britain by
Cox & Wyman, Reading, Berkshire

JULIA WILD

Although Julia Wild says her entire life has been spent leaping from one scrape to another, she is always happiest when she's writing. In 1989, after reading a particularly 'bland' book, Julia decided she could do better and started writing in earnest. She believed that all she had to do was write a book, send it off and it would be published!

Several manuscripts and a drawerful of rejections later, Julia realised it wasn't that easy and enrolled on a creative writing course. In 1997, Julia received the news that not only was an editor interested in publishing her novel DARK CANVAS, but that it had also won that year's Romantic Novelist Association New Writers' Award.

prologue

The first time they met, Jordan Elliot took one look at Megan Lacey and threw away a lifetime of caution where women were concerned.

He arrived late at his friend Ray Blackmore's party. Tie skewed and hair tousled from a wild afternoon on the terraces at Chelsea football club.

He was perfectly calm until a mass of vibrant, copper hair, voluptuous breasts and legs that were perfection, all wrapped up in a waitress's outfit met him at the door of the club. 'This is a private party, sir.' She smiled. It was a first – the first smile that had ever hit him in the solar plexus. 'I'm afraid you can't come in without an invitation.'

'What if I have an invitation?' He smiled right back at her, one of his 'knock 'em over' smiles; but it didn't affect her. She just responded politely. 'If you have an invitation, you can come in, sir.'

'My name's Jordan.'

'Fine.'

Laughing, he pulled the invitation from his jacket pocket. 'This is where you're supposed to tell me your name.'

'Miss is fine, sir.' She turned away from him to skewer the invitation on a sharp spike. 'If you'd like to follow me, I'll get you a glass of champagne.'

'Sure.' He followed her to the reception table and couldn't take his eyes off her legs; couldn't rid his mind of how they'd feel wrapped around him, and felt weird because he'd never had such a powerful, instantaneous reaction to a woman before. It wasn't one thing about her that caught his attention – it was everything. And it was very,

very sexual – yet more than that. For the first time ever, he felt the emotional pull of a woman. She scared the hell out of him! What if she was married? What if she had ten children?

He gulped the champagne – good stuff – and panicked when she moved away from the table to attend to someone else. Instinctively his hand shot out to stop her; and when she turned, still smiling, still polite, he couldn't think of what to say.

'Would you like some more to drink, sir?' The gorgeous red-head raised the bottle. 'Or something else?'

'Ah-umm.' Somewhere in the last seconds, he'd lost the power of speech, felt something move inside him when her soft, forest-green eyes, connected briefly with his.

'Do help yourself to the buffet. We'll refill your glass at the table.'

She had a sprinkle of freckles across the bridge of her nose, her mouth was to die for. 'Thank you,' was all he'd managed to say, when his friend Ray appeared from nowhere and draped an arm along her slender shoulders.

'Ah, Mr Blackmore,' she took hold of his fingers and extracted herself from his hold. 'All your guests are here now.'

As Megan walked towards the buffet table, Ray winked at Jordan. 'Fifty quid says I'll score with Megan Lacey before the end of the evening.'

So her name was Megan – it suited her. 'You'll lose,' Jordan responded lightly, knowing that if Ray thought he was interested in the waitress, his friend would redouble his efforts to conquer her.

Jordan watched the warm glow of the candlelight against Megan's pale skin and vibrant hair. She was laughing and it moved his heart. He felt as he'd never felt before; he wanted to know everything about her – *everything*! Were those soft green eyes really as gentle as they looked? Did she always laugh that way? What kind of films did she like? Flowers…? Perfume…? How the hell would she cope if Ray came on to her really strongly?

He shook his head and turned away to lean against the bar. He must be sickening for something – he was thinking things he'd never thought before.

Hearing a shocked gasp, he swung back towards the room. Ray had clearly drunk too much, and had Megan Lacey pinned against one of the tables.

As Jordan moved towards them, so did a burly barman. Both of them winced out loud when Megan brought her knee up – hard – to Ray's groin. Ray groaned louder than both of them and stumbled backwards into the barman and Jordan, swearing coarsely.

'Can you take care of him,' the barman asked Jordan, who had no choice other than to agree.

'Thanks. I'll check on Megan.'

Jordan looked across at her as he supported Ray. He smiled. She didn't. Those soft green eyes were now sparkling, blazing emeralds – and for a space of a few seconds he was stunned to stillness. As Ray moaned, calling Megan all the names under the sun, Jordan broke eye contact with her as she assured the barman she was fine.

'Most men know how much drink they can take by that age.' She shot Jordan one last accusing look, then said, 'I'll be just a minute. I need to freshen up.'

'Come on, man – sit down.' Jordan practically dragged Ray to the other side of the room.

Ray moaned. 'I'm gonna kill her.'

'No you're not. You shouldn't have done that to her. She's doing her job – she's not here for you to grope.' He signalled to the barman. 'Can I get a couple of black coffees and some water over here, please?'

'I paid enough for this damn party!'

'Yeah, but I'll bet it didn't say anything in the brochure about a harem being provided for your entertainment! Ray, you're drunk and behaving like a total jerk.'

Half an hour later, after a couple of cups of coffee and a bottle of water, apart from a slight limp Ray was back to his old self. 'I want some dessert, man.'

He noisily hailed Megan. 'Hey, *Copper-knob*! How about serving me and my mate here, just to show there's no hard feelings?'

The deep chuckle under Ray's breath annoyed Jordan. 'Leave it alone, Ray.'

'There's fifty quid at stake, man. I don't give up easy.'

'And I told you there was no bet.'

Megan arrived at the table with a heavily-laden trolley, wearing a fixed smile and no sign of her earlier anger. And she continued to smile as she asked Ray which dessert he'd like.

'What's that on the bottom shelf again?' Ray pushed his chair back from the table and Jordan groaned inwardly. For a highly intelligent man, Ray was a complete idiot when he drank too much.

'You'd like the trifle, Mr Blackmore?'

'Yes, please.' As she leaned across Jordan to serve him, Ray slid his hand straight up the inside of Megan's long shapely leg. For a second she froze, then spun to face Jordan.

'I don't appreciate being manhandled, *sir!*' Jordan almost fell of his chair when Megan emptied the entire contents of the trifle bowl into his tuxedo-clad lap. She thought *he'd* touched her! Her eyes where really blazing this time. Jordan was angry too. With Ray – and with Megan. She should get her facts right! He knew then why Ray had pushed his chair so close to the trolley, so Megan would think it was Jordan touching her. The lousy bastard!

'If *I'd* touched you, Ms Lacey – believe me, you'd have known all about it!'

As soon as the words were out, he regretted them. How the heck was he supposed to get to know her after this?

Ray was almost choking with laughter as Megan, bright colour rising in her cheeks, challenged Jordan directly with those incredible emerald eyes.

'Would sir like a spoon?' She dropped a dessert spoon noisily on the table in front of him and marched off, her head held high.

'Things never look as bad in the morning,' Jordan told himself as he entered his Docklands flat, convinced that after a good night's sleep, the woman with the copper curls, amazing eyes and feisty attitude would be out of his system.

Unfortunately, she wasn't. She woke him three times – each time moving closer to him, with that gorgeous smile on her lips. Her perfume filling his senses and rendering him a gibbering wreck.

At four a.m. he sat bolt upright, the memory of her closeness and the touch of her soft skin, sending him leaping out of bed, cursing violently under his breath. Nothing in his life so far had prepared him for Megan Lacey. For the first time, he didn't know what to do about the situation. Rubbing his eyes he walked over to his desk, flipped on the light and started writing on one of his business cards.

Dear Ms Lacey, I'm sorry about both my own and my friend's behaviour. There was no excuse for it. Please forgive me. If you'd like to see me again, give me a call.

The moment it was light, he went along to the flower seller at the station. Buying the entire contents of the bemused woman's stall, he staggered round to Megan Lacey's business address, where he left the mass of flowers and his card at the front door.

Jordan did the same thing for the next three mornings. On

the fourth, he arrived at dawn with a huge bouquet of red roses, to find a note tied to the railings.

Please don't bring me any more flowers. I have no more vases – nor do my friends, colleagues, neighbours – or the milkman!

Jordan laughed out loud, slipped the note from the railings and wrote on it: *Sounds like most of London has enough flowers. Am I forgiven? Will you come out with me... soon?* He tucked the note into the roses and left them on her doorstep.

Next morning there was small envelope attached to the railings. Anticipating the worst, he tore it open. The small card inside bore one word in a curly, feminine hand: *Yes*.

Jordan punched the air in triumph and set off to arrange their date...

That weekend, Megan was driving along the M25 on her way to arrange an intimate dinner for two on the Thames. If she was upset that Jordan hadn't bothered to contact her after she'd accepted his invitation, she wouldn't admit it. He and his stupid friend, Ray, had obviously had another bet as to which of them would make her give in first. The trouble was, Jordan had seemed different. Of all the men she'd met, it was Jordan her soul had whispered to. It just shows, she told herself, that it's always smartest to let your head rule your heart. So let's concentrate on work.

Although the party was a small one, her friend and colleague Alexa had told her that the host, Mr Ellis, wanted no detail spared. He must love his wife a lot to go to all this trouble, she thought with a sigh.

Three hours later, Megan stood in the spacious, yet cosy main cabin of the luxury cruiser and rubbed her hands together in anticipation.

Two fat, luscious bunches of grapes – one deep purple, the other fresh green – lay plump and tempting on the table and she flicked a little water on them to add sparkle, before tipping nuts and nibbles into little blue bowls. Polishing the wafer-thin champagne flutes, Megan glanced at her watch, noting that she had ten minutes in hand to deal with unpacking the seafood, cheeses, salmon steaks and warm up the crispy rolls.

In the bathroom, she hung her overall behind the door, brushed her copper curls into a gleaming mass and put in her pearl earrings. She checked her outfit in front of the mirror. 'Amazing the effect a few bits of glitter can have,' she told her reflection. She giggled at her sea-green outfit. The skirt was calf-length, but made up of several panels which parted as she moved to reveal the length of her slender, tanned legs. Gold and green stars meandered like a river down the pale green sleeveless top and ran down the skirt. A sudden pang of longing that Jordan could see her now clutched at her heart, before she forced her mind back to the job in hand.

Hearing movement up on deck, Megan hurried out to greet the couple. She had a vision of what they would look like: a charming, grey-haired gentleman, and a wife who would be gracious, buxom and cuddly.

'Hello there.' She smiled, but the sun was bright and her eyes didn't adjust immediately after the mellow light of the cabin. 'I'm Megan Lacey. Welcome aboard.' She extended her hand, and felt her fingertips tingle as a shadow fell across her. At first, all she could see was the faded blue jeans and T-shirt, and then...

'J-Jordan...!' she gasped in astonishment as he smiled down at her, noting the slash of a dimple indenting one sculptured cheek; the golden butter colour of his soft blond hair and his startling, deep blue eyes which seemed to reflect the water.

'So you're Mr Ellis? Are we picking your wife up somewhere along the way?'

'A lady friend.' He shielded his eyes from the sun, and

smiled again. 'And it's Elliot. Jordan Elliot.'

Megan tried to keep smiling. 'Do you want to see what I've done to the cabin?'

'Sure. I'd love to.' He gestured for her to enter before him. Megan beamed with delight when he whistled, 'I don't believe it! This is exactly what I had in mind. But a hundred times better.'

'Great!' Megan burbled. 'Do you think she'll like it?'

A frown touched his brow. 'Who?'

'Your lady friend?'

'Do you?'

Stunned Megan glanced around at the mermaid's bower she'd arranged on 'Mr Ellis' instructions.

'You were wrong, Ms Lacey. We're not picking anyone else up.'

She was angry. But her fury only lasted for less than ten seconds, before she erupted into laughter. 'Are you saying that all this is for me?'

'For me, too!'

'But…I…how, I mean …'

He put his finger across her lips. 'Every time I rang your office you were busy. So I figured that I'd buy you some free time. I couldn't think of any other way to get you away from your business for more than a couple of hours.'

'You've got a bloody nerve!'

'Alexa told me that you'd say that!'

'Alexa was in on this?'

'Well, you don't think she'd let you go off, on your own, with some man she'd only spoken to over the 'phone? I had to let her into the secret of who I was and what I was up to. But I didn't dare call myself 'Elliot' in case you'd changed your mind about me.'

'I get the picture.' Megan winced. 'I can't believe my best friend set me up like this!' she grumbled, before suddenly realising how petty she was being. She *liked* Jordan.

She liked the way he spoke, the way he looked – the way he just *was*. So why shouldn't she relax for once and enjoy herself?

'Jordan, I can tell you right now that I'm not prepared to sleep with you. Just because you've brought me to this lovely boat, arranged the food and…and…'

'Bought you jewellery?' His hand slid into the hold-all he'd placed on one of the seats and produced two black velvet cases.

'You can't…' She held up her hands.

'There are no rules today,' he told her firmly, flipping open the lid of one box to display a twisted strand of gold decorated with green stones. 'You spend your whole life creating fantasies for other people, Megan, so I decided it was time someone made a few dreams come true for you.' He raised his hands, fastening the slender chain about her throat.

She gasped, shaking her head in disbelief, her fingers spreading over the beautiful, delicate necklace. Unexpectedly, tears filled her eyes. 'Oh Jordan,' she breathed. 'I can't let you do this.'

Again he put his finger across her lips. 'Yes, you can.' Deftly unfastening the smaller box, he slipped a bracelet on to her wrist, 'There's something else you can do too.'

The emerald and gold bracelet turned to rainbows through the tears in her eyes. She couldn't look at him, speak or move, save for a hoarse, 'What?'

'Stop worrying! If you want to make love, that's fine. If you don't, we won't. I just want to get to know you.'

Tears spilled down Megan's cheeks, but she couldn't help it; it was as if something was unravelling inside her. Jordan handed her a tissue and encouraged her to sit down.

'I've got to tell you, Megan, I've never had this reaction to offering a woman all her own way before.'

She tried to speak, but couldn't.

He handed her another tissue. And another.

'I'm being ridiculous,' she finally managed to gasp, wiping the mascara from her cheeks with the back of her hand. 'I'm sorry about this.'

'So am I,' he laughed wryly. 'I wanted to make you happy. Maybe I'm not cut out for this romantic stuff. Maybe I'm getting it all wrong?'

'No, you're not.' Megan looked up into his handsome features. 'I'm so touched by all the trouble you've gone to.' She sniffed. 'Jordan, I feel such a fool. You've spent all this money, and I'm blubbering like an idiot.'

He dismissed that. 'Just how long is it since you've had a break?'

'About four years.'

'How long for?'

She grimaced. 'Only a long weekend. I was shattered. I'd become run-down or something. I'm OK now.'

'What's going to happen if you take a couple of days off, Megan? The world won't end, you know.'

'I couldn't manage.'

'There are ways. You could get someone to invest in Lacey's, then you'd be able to afford more staff. Put your prices up, too. If all else fails, I'll have to keep buying your time.'

'No! You're not paying for any more of my time.' She'd find it somehow. 'You know what's really tough about this?' she added. 'I'm so used to organising things for others, that it's really hard to…well, to "take" from other people.'

'Just smile and say thanks. It's easy.' He grinned and Megan's stomach flipped over.

She smiled. 'Thanks for the advice!'

'You might want to go and wash your face – you look like Dracula's Bride!' He laughed when she flushed with embarrassment. 'Go on – I'll put on some music.'

When she returned from washing the mascara from

her cheeks, Jordan handed her a flute of champagne. 'I don't know if Brides of Dracula are allowed to drink this.' She laughed.

Jordan tipped the glass towards her lips and said, 'Well, let's try an experiment!'

Half-a-bottle of bubbly later, Jordan filled plates with two of everything, then stretched out on a wide seat in the lounge.

To Megan everything tasted twice as good as it should, and she relaxed against the cushions giggling. 'I never realised how much fun my parties are!'

She felt herself growing sleepy. 'Jordan, I think I need some air. I'm going to fall asleep in a minute.'

He shrugged, 'So sleep. I told you, there are no rules today.'

'Are you serious? I thought you wanted to talk.'

'We'll talk later.'

'Mmm…' It washed over her just how liberating it was to have someone else making decisions, after she'd spent six years constantly juggling money and time. Eight years, if she included working to support her mother after the death of her father. Maybe, just for this one day, it would be OK to hand over control to someone else.

'Come here.' His response to Megan's slow smile was to pull her against his hard, muscular frame.

She was completely unprepared for the sizzling sensation coursing through her body at the contact. Staring into his smouldering eyes, Megan knew that she was prepared to give everything to this man. Something which she'd known since the day of Ray's party, when she'd immediately recognised the fact that their 'souls' had seemed to 'whisper' to one another. But she hadn't allowed herself to admit as much.

'Jordan,' she murmured. 'I want you.' But he frowned lightly as she pressed her lips to his cheek, nudging her thigh between his denim-clad ones.

'Megan..? Are you sure about this?' he asked, holding her firmly away by the shoulders as he stared intently into her green eyes.

Megan wriggled closer so that her body aligned with his. Spreading her fingers at his neck, delicious anticipation shimmering through her nerve ends, she could feel her stomach lurch as Jordan's eyes darkened before his mouth covered hers. A soft moan broke from her throat as he buried his fingers in her long hair, and Meg seemed unable to prevent her own hands from roaming boldly, slowly, over his beautifully firm body; swamped by feeling of desire that she'd never felt for a man – until now.

Jordan's tongue was warm and tantalising, his mouth so firm on her lips; yet his hands – the hands she ached to feel crushing her against him – moved only in her hair, on her neck. He was driving her crazy.

She broke the kiss just long enough to whisper, 'Jordan, touch me...!' And then she wanted to weep because he seemed to ignored her – but only for a moment. Slowly, his hand moved to caress her breast through the thin fabric of her top. She could feel his hand trembling slightly, and sensed from his body's reaction to her closeness that it was deliberate restraint, not lack of desire, that lay behind his response. Because he held back, Megan was infused with delicious boldness.

She wriggled astride his hips so that she nestled his denim-clad hardness against her, pulled his T-shirt free of his jeans and spread her fingers over his hard, flat stomach, all the time staring into his glittering blue eyes.

'Megan...'

'Relax,' she murmured with a smile. 'I'm taking advantage of you, not the other way round.'

'You say that now.' His cheeks flushed with something close to anger. 'But tomorrow, this will be seen as my fault.'

'No, it's mine.' She shook her head, lay flat on top of him, kissed him, teasing his mouth apart with her tongue, felt his sharp intake of breath. 'If you don't fancy me, just say so.'

'Are you kidding?'

'No.' She lifted one shoulder. 'I thought you said that I could have my own way today…?' she teased.

A sexy grin slanted his mouth. 'You're quite right. I did say that.'

She unsnapped his jeans. Sliding her fingers into the waistband. 'And what I want – is you!'

'Well, slow down! This isn't an Olympic event.'

She laughed when he rolled her on to her back. 'You'll be able to tell all your friends you've slept with Dracula's Bride,' she told him huskily.

'Lady, I won't be telling my friends *anything*!' he muttered thickly, his fingers and mouth exploring her sensitised skin, leaving no part of her unkissed or untouched. Her top, bra and pants hit the floor sometime during Jordan's love-making, just the wispy little skirt remaining a tantalising barrier between them as he quickly removed his denim jeans – his mouth remaining firmly in contact with her own as she felt the material rasping against her inner thighs.

Instinctively, she wrapped her legs around his hips as he entered her, pressing her lips to his shoulder to stifle her gasp of pleasure. Then his mouth turned demanding, his movements urgent as he pressed her harder against him.

A sweet, swift need held Megan. She called out, her incredible pleasure refusing to be stifled any longer, and Jordan, in response, filled her. Sweat slicked their skin as he grated, 'Sweet heaven, Megan..!'

'You're squashing me,' she laughed softy against his ear, still gripped by rippling spasms of pleasure. But, as he began to shift his long, powerful body away from her, she slid her arms about his neck. 'No, don't move, it feels too good.'

'Hmm,' he nibbled her ear and Megan almost shot off the couch with excitement.

'Getting squashed seems pretty good to me!' she murmured, snuggling closer and feeling completely happy, if a little dazed.

'Megan, you should have told me.' Something in Jordan's tone made her raise her sleepy head.

'Umm? Told you what?'

'I'd no idea that you were a virgin.'

'So, now you know.' She gazed into his deep blue eyes. 'And now I'm not.' She grinned as his brow rose slightly. 'What did you expect? Someone more experienced?'

'I guess I did.'

'And now you're disappointed?'

'*No!*' He grasped hold of her shoulders, pressing her down on the thick cushions. 'I'm shocked. There aren't many virgins of your age around. Besides, you look so – I don't know – alluring.'

'All those men in the world – and I get the one with a conscience!' Megan raised her head to plant a kiss on the smiling curve of his mouth.

'I don't suppose you'll understand,' she added with a small shrug. 'But I've never met anyone, before you came along, who made me think, "I'll just *die* if I don't have that man!" And when you have to take care of a mother who's gone completely off the rails, it doesn't leave time for much of a personal life. Besides…' She grinned. 'If you'd met me in winter, you wouldn't call me alluring. I dress like the Michelin Man.'

'You're just saying that to turn me on.' Jordan's eyes glinted, his hands savouring the delicious curves of her body. 'As far as I'm concerned, it wouldn't matter if you were wearing a sack.'

For the rest of the evening and night, they ate and made love, laughed and Megan answered all Jordan's questions about her life.

'So, how did the idea for your company come about?'

'I was eighteen. My mother had been over-dosing on alcohol as usual, and I was working at this night-club to pay our bills. I had this mad moment – I must have gone crazy. Because, at the end of one of those awful catered parties they used to hold in the night-club, I stood on the table and announced that I could do better. And, to make good my boast – I invited them all back to my house for a party the following night!'

'So, how did you go about catering for the party?'

'Well, I begged half-a-dozen bottles of fizz from my boss, and decided to cook all the food myself,' she explained. 'We lived in a huge house then. The trouble was,' Megan added with a grimace, 'When I got home, Mum had lost it. She'd finally read the letter I'd been trying to get her to look at for ages – the one that said the bailiffs were coming the following week to evict us. She'd trashed all the furniture, ripped down the curtains – you name it, she'd done it. I managed to get her to bed and called for the doctor.'

'What happened?'

'She was admitted to a drying-out clinic.'

'Then what?'

'Unfortunately, despite once having been very wealthy, Mum and I were by now flat broke – mainly due to Dad's gambling problem. He kept expecting his luck to change and it never did. He'd re-mortgaged the house, and sold just about everything. He'd told my mother, but when he died suddenly of a heart attack, she couldn't cope. I don't think she ever really grasped the fact that we had absolutely *nothing*. That's why she drank. And that's why I had to go out to work at sixteen.'

'So you had no money, the bailiffs were coming, and you had a party to organise?' Jordan's arms tightened comfortingly about her.

'In a wrecked house.'

'What the hell did you do next?'

'The party was easy. I covered everything in spray-on cobwebs and dust, lit loads of candles and called it a 'haunted house' party. The punters loved it!'

Jordan kissed her tenderly on the brow, but let her go on talking.

'It was while I was in the attic looking for props that I found this old box file. It was full of some tatty company share certificates, which turned out to be worth something. Not a fortune, of course, but enough to pay off the worst of our debts and buy the mews house where my office is now.'

'What happened after the party?'

'I took enough bookings to start up the company, and it sort of snowballed from there.'

'And your mother, Megan? What happened to her?'

'Well, they dried her out that time, but I don't think she could bear her life. No matter how many times I told her that I loved her – or how hard I worked and however much money I saved – it was never enough. She started drinking again and…and it killed her in the end. When I was twenty-one.'

'Oh my darling, how I wish I'd been there to help you.' Jordan dabbed at Megan's tear-filled eyes. 'So, I'm guessing that the reason you work so hard is that you're still paying off your debts?'

'It left me feeling so scared. One minute we were so secure and so happy – and the next minute our lives were completely shattered. It made me realise I couldn't rely on anyone but myself.'

'Yes, I can see that.'

'And now maybe you can see why I can't get involved with you?'

'You're already involved.' A potent promise glittered in his blue eyes as he gently drew her towards him, making love to her until dawn broke in the sky.

Jordan's eyes glinted as he kissed her awake the next morning. 'Do you know what I'll fantasise about from now on, whenever I have to stay in a hotel?'

Megan shook her head, closing her eyes with pleasure as Jordan's fingertip traced the line of her mouth. 'Tell me?'

'When I order room service,' his eyes were dark, 'I'll imagine what it'd be like if you came into the room pushing the trolley.'

'What am I wearing?' Megan touched his neck.

'A short, tightly-fitting maid's uniform.'

'What colour?'

'White. And you're not wearing any shoes.'

'I'll have to see what I can do.' She kissed him and he groaned in surrender...

chapter one

'Yoo-hoo! Megan?' Loud rapping on the door pulled Megan from her bittersweet trance.

'Just a moment!' She pushed the miniature photo album into her handbag, blinked the mist from her eyes and flew downstairs. Ten months since Jordan's desertion, and still Megan hid anger and clawing agony from sympathetic eyes.

'Hi, Alexa – all set to go?' Megan whisked open the door and grimaced as her partner sneezed over the entrance buttons. 'Oh, yuk!'

'I've got a stinker, Megan.' Alexa's eyes were watery, her nose red, short honey-brown hair dishevelled and she shivered despite the early morning sunshine, 'I don't believe it – this cold hit me like a sledgehammer while I was ironing the uniforms an hour ago.'

'Would you like a hot drink?' Megan opened the door wide, as the other woman nodded into her handkerchief.

'Here you go,' Megan said minutes later, setting a box of tissues down at Alexa's elbow, along with a cup of coffee as both women sank into comfy, overstuffed chairs.

'I can't serve food with a cold like this. Which means that I can't do the party, Megan. I'm sorry.'

'Don't worry.' Megan sipped her tea. 'It's not your fault. And as long as you can help me get everything there, I'm sure we'll be fine.'

The little wedding album poking out of Megan's bag caught her eye. The photographs had been taken almost a year ago. For too long she'd been saying, 'I need to keep drumming up new business…' as a good reason to always stay close to home. They were doing pretty well. In fact,

Lacey's hard-earned reputation for flexibility and reliability was at last opening some obstinate doors.

'It's only a one-day job, so I might as well do it.'

'Good idea.' Alexa blew her nose. 'It will get you out of London for a bit. You could maybe go on to Paris – and do a bit of sightseeing afterwards. If this cold clears up, I can join you there on Sunday.'

'Maybe.' Megan rose from the chair, gazing out of the window over the pretty mews-style street down below; all window boxes and cobblestones, wrought iron railings and steep basement steps. A miniature haven of a tiny back street, just minutes from Regent's Park.

Some days it was tough hiding devastation. Some days, the pain of Jordan's disappearance pushed so close to the surface, she thought that it would explode from her.

Maybe the party on board the boat was just what she needed? OK – it was work, not pleasure, but it would be a change. At least it would be one day when she'd know for certain Jordan wasn't going to appear any moment and reel off a perfectly sound explanation of why he'd disappeared into thin air, after just two months of marriage. If nothing else, it would be Megan's way of proving to herself that she'd finally accepted that he wasn't coming home.

Perching on the edge of the window sill, Megan smiled to cover the awful, gnawing pain. 'If you'll handle things here till next week, I'll oversee The Dream's catering. Do you want me to bring anything back from Calais?'

'*Atchoo..*!' Alexa sneezed, her eyes watering. 'Yes, that would be great. I'll make a list.'

After Alexa left, Megan sank down on to the bed and picked up the little photograph album. Her fingertip traced the image of her own and Jordan's first married kiss…

Confetti starred her wild copper hair, her eyes were just closing, Jordan's beautiful, sensual mouth was just about to capture hers. She could hear him whispering against her mouth, 'How much longer till we can leave, Megan? I can't wait to get you alone.' They'd only just stepped out of the church.

It would be hours before they could be alone, but Megan forgot the question as Jordan pulled her lace-dressed form up against his dark-grey suited figure, kissing her until she trembled all over. Talk about a blushing bride!

With a heavy sigh, she turned to the second photograph, which showed the bride and groom waving out the back of a beribboned pony and trap. She recalled how, just seconds later, Jordan's mouth was covering her shoulders with kisses, laughing against her skin as he wickedly suggested, 'Let's skip the reception. No one will notice.'

'You'd end up on Alexa's hit list.' Megan brushed her fingers through his straight, blond hair. 'And my name would be mud for all eternity.'

Jordan's blue eyes had darkened with need. 'I'd risk anything for you, my darling,' he murmured, the sexy slash of dimple appearing in his cheek. 'Anything – except Alexa's hit list!'

'Idiot!' She'd smiled tantalising at him, a wicked light in her green eyes as she placed her hand on her new husband's long, firmly-muscled thigh. 'I was going to ask the driver to swing by my place!' Of course she'd been teasing, but a second later Jordan had instructed the liveried coachman to take a detour to the mews...

The loud noise of a horn suddenly broke into her thoughts. Megan ran to the window and waved down at Alexa, quickly picking up her travel bag and preparing to join her friend. And then, just as she was about to leave the room, she swiftly grabbed the small photo album and stuffed it into her handbag, before removing her rings – a choked sob breaking the silence as she dropped them into a little Wedgwood pot on her bedroom dressing-table. Never...

never in even her craziest nightmares, had Megan expected to spend her first wedding anniversary alone, at sea.

The Dream was vast. A one-hundred-and-fifty foot luxury yacht, it gleamed millionaire-white in the May sunshine; a vast mounted radar system at the highest point of its super-structure.

A uniformed Purser greeted staff at the bottom of the boarding steps, ticking off security pass numbers and assigning cabins to the regular crew members who'd be staying on board for the onward journey from Calais to the West Indies. He frowned at Megan and her unfamiliar entourage as they spilled out of the mini-bus.

'We're from Themes and Dreams,' Megan told him. 'I'm helping with the catering as far as Calais. The rest of my group are leaving after tonight's party.'

'Ah, yes. "Megan Lacey and staff",' he said, making a note on his clipboard. 'Your group can use the large cabin on the lower deck to change, Ms Lacey.'

'Lower deck? That's where all the slaves go!' Alexa grumbled as they made their way up one set of steps, then down another into the bowels of the luxurious vessel.

'Stop moaning,' Megan told her shortly. 'If we want the money, we have to work for it.'

Alexa sighed. 'Do you know what's wrong with you these days, Megan?'

'Yes.' Lights flickered on automatically in the narrow corridor, illuminating thick, deep russet carpet. 'I'm bitter and twisted and disillusioned – and I'm no fun any more.'

'I mean, besides all that.' Alexa swiped her card in the reader on the thick, blond wood door, pushing it open with her shoulder. 'You seem to have totally lost your sense of humour.'

'Along with my gorgeous home, and my "It will last

forever", lying husband? Hell! How dare I lose my sense of humour too?'

'Oh, Megan – lighten up! It's time you got over him, and admitted that he's not coming back to you.'

One of the other women gasped at Alexa's bluntness, before they all began talking at once to fill in the awkward moment.

'I know.' Megan took a deep breath, suddenly realising that it was exactly a year ago – to the hour – that she'd exchanged marriage vows with Jordan. 'It's over. I've taken off my rings, and this…' She pulled the photo album from her handbag. '*This* is going to be thrown into the deepest part of the English Channel!'

'I'm sorry…'

So am I, she responded silently as she went into the bathroom to change into her working clothes – the traditional uniform of black dress and white apron, black stockings and court shoes.

'OK, everyone – I'll catch up with you up in the stateroom. I'm going to start setting up,' Megan announced as she emerged from the bathroom.

Alexa was squinting at herself in the mirror, putting on her make-up. 'Are you OK?' she asked Megan when the other assistants had left. 'I mean *really* OK? Because I truly didn't mean to be rotten.' Alexa grimaced. 'I just want my crazy, funny friend back.'

'Nothing wrong with being honest.' Megan shrugged. 'I'm going to see if I can find a spare sense of humour anywhere on board this floating palace.'

Megan could have sworn she saw tears spring into Alexa's eyes – but didn't wait around long enough to be sure. She could cope with anything – except sympathy.

Three hours later, silver bowls held pyramids of caviar, decorated crackers nestled on ornate plates, a whole salmon lay languid and pretty on a large platter; truffles snuggled in silver dishes, huge salad bowls and mountains of delicious sandwiches supplemented the more extravagant nibbles. Champagne rested in silver ice buckets, and while stewards hung tiny fairy lights around the cabin interior, Megan and her team set small bowls of flowers in the centre of the round tables.

'Thanks for your help, Alexa,' Megan smiled broadly as her friend prepared to leave the boat. 'I'll see you in Paris on Sunday?'

'Don't worry – I'll definitely be there, Megan. And don't get too depressed about Jordan. After all, there is still a chance that he could come back, with a good explanation of where he's been and what he's been doing.'

'Ten months is long enough. It's taken some time, but I've finally got the message,' Megan told her grimly.

'Well,' Alexa said quietly. 'I suppose that's fair enough. But wherever he is, I'll bet Jordan still thinks about you.'

Looking across the brand new marina-cum-water sports centre, with the sun sparkling on the water, Megan shook her head. 'It would have been our first anniversary today. If Jordan had any thoughts at all about me, he'd have contacted me by now.'

Waving goodbye to her friend, Megan was gripped by a familiar sadness. 'It's time to let go,' she muttered to herself, before catching sight, in the distance, of dark shining limousines driving slowly down the road to the marina. It looked as if the guests were beginning to arrive.

'Can I get you something to eat or drink?' Automatically repeating the words, Megan and the other waitresses circulated amongst the guests, filling and refilling plates and glasses, while reporters and photographers had a field day with the celebrities on board. There must be enough impromptu interviews and 'photos with the famous' being taken for a year's worth of Sunday magazines, Megan told herself with a grin. Despite having to keep smiling while having her bottom pinched, being splashed with champagne or playfully having the strings of her apron unfastened, she still felt a deep sense of satisfaction. Because, her company's first, high profile showbiz party, was clearly a great success.

Her spirits rose another notch when Matt Duprey, The Dream's millionaire owner, made himself known to her.

'Your company has done very well, Miss Lacey,' he said. Megan's delight at his words being captured by a photo-journalist. 'I will be happy to recommend your services.' His smile and handshake were warm and sincere, his bearded features fatherly.

'Thank you.' Megan's smile swung right off the dazzle-meter. 'I hope the rest of your journey goes as well.'

He laughed. 'Don't be fooled by this party. It will be all work and meetings from now on, until we reach the Caribbean.'

It wasn't until she heard the sound of a horn, and heard the Captain reminding all those who weren't travelling on board The Dream that it was time to leave the ship, that Megan realised just how much her feet were aching.

Security men mingled with revellers, helping those ashore who could hardly walk – courtesy of too much champagne – and discreetly checking the identity of those remaining on board; most of whom had already left the saloon for their cabins, in order to change for dinner.

'If you can clear-up the stateroom, we'll clean the floors, OK?' Philip, the head steward said, busy stacking chairs as Megan cleared the tables.

Finished – at last! Megan told herself with relief, looking around at the gleaming stainless steel surfaces in the galley, before glancing down at her watch. Ten minutes later, having waved the rest of her staff off on to the dockside, and promised that she'd be OK on her own until the yacht reached Calais, she returned to the galley kitchen.

Boy – it was hot in here! She expected The Dream's own kitchen staff to come and hurry her along at any moment, in order to get the pre-prepared dinner into the ovens.

As she waited, her eyes were drawn to the large walk-in fridge, which looked cool and inviting, Megan opened the door and sighed with bliss as icy-cold tentacles whispered around her. Feeling a slight lurch of the yacht, she realised that the Captain and crew must be getting ready to cast off. Quickly checking over her shoulder that she was alone, she smiled guiltily as she pulled the door closer to her back. Just a few more minutes of delicious coolness, then she'd go back to the stateroom and start setting up for dinner.

The Dream lurched again, sending the fridge door swinging away from her fingertips. A reminder, if she needed one, that it was time she went back to work.

Closing the fridge, Megan walked down to the far end of the galley, towards the swing doors which led to the stateroom.

chapter two

'Oh my God…*No*!' Megan cried. Surely her eyes *had* to be playing tricks…?

Totally stunned, she stared at the expressions of fear and horror reflected on upturned white faces. With their hands on head and fingers interlaced, the yacht's guests and crew were gazing with terror-focused eyes at the armed men surrounding them; the masked, dark figures spaced at equal distance around the perimeter of the spacious, luxurious stateroom.

The silence following her shocked outburst seemed to last forever. *Hijacked? The Dream had been hijacked…*?

'You said everyone was here!' A savage voice snapped, and the Captain's head jerked back as a gun poked at his neck. Megan's mouth dropped open. The antagonist was dressed like a man, yet it was a woman who'd spoken – her accent thick and deep.

Megan felt the eyes of all those darkly-clad, masked forms fix on her, then swing to the Captain for an explanation. She froze. Was this some kind of joke? An elaborate publicity stunt? This couldn't be happening. No. It couldn't. *Definitely not*!

Cushioned in a bubble of unreality, Megan slipped backwards through the kitchen swing doors, her mind in a daze as she struggled to get a grip. Maybe she was in the middle of a nightmare?

'Get in here!' A bulky black form suddenly gripped her elbows, swinging her around and back into the main room. She staggered and snapped, 'Get off me!'

Those words earned her a jab from the butt of a gun

between her shoulder blades. 'Sit! Be silent!'

'Buzz off!' Oh, lord – maybe it was real…?

Immediately, fingers circled her chin, holding her face upwards and roughly distorting her mouth. 'Feisty, eh?' He also had a heavy, foreign accent. 'I like spirit in a woman.'

Instinctively, Megan shook her head to loosen the man's grip. 'Let go of me. I'll sit down.'

'What is your name?' He fired the words at her. 'What are you doing on board this vessel?'

'I'm the bloody Captain…what do you think?'

That earned her a sharp push. When she'd stopped reeling, blinking away dancing black spots in front of her eyes, Megan's temper completely exploded.

'You're some tough guy, aren't you?' Her terror-driven temper erupted. 'You're nothing but a bully in a stupid mask. You'd be useless without your toy gun!'

Fury emanated from the man. A shot exploded, hit the ceiling, splinters cascaded, screams filled the cabin, making it small, claustrophobic.

'What is your name?' he repeated, 'What is your role on this vessel?'

'What difference does that make?'

'Answer me.'

'I was hired to do the catering.' She glanced down and rubbed her ringless finger. 'My name is Megan Lacey.'

'Miss or Mrs?' Deliberately, he flicked a long tendril of escaped copper hair with the muzzle of his gun.

'Miss.' Even though fear was swelling inside her, some strange instinct said she mustn't let it show.

'Where is your cabin?'

'Why?'

'Answer me!'

Megan bit hard on her lips, revulsion squirmed in her stomach.

'Hades! Stop throwing your weight around.'

Megan's head snapped around to face another of the darkly-clad figures. He was taller than the rest, and leaning casually against one of the Grecian-style pillars. As everyone twisted around to look at him, she noted that his voice was rough and deep.

'I need somewhere to sleep,' Hades responded. 'And I like a woman with fire in her blood.' Again, he flicked the ends of Megan's hair with his gun, his grin obscene beneath its woollen shroud, eyes bulging inside round eye-holes.

Megan wanted to scream.

'I want this woman.'

'*No*!' Megan's composure fragmented, she flailed against the man when he clamped his hand around her waist, pulled her bodily backwards against the front of him, 'Get off me, you…you slimeball!'

'You heard the lady. Let her go!'

It was the man leaning casually up against the pillar who'd spoken – and, somehow, he was more frightening than the burly buffoon holding on to her. More frightening, more menacing, and far more powerful.

'Ha! She has no rights! She is merely a hostage,' Hades retorted. As he jerked Megan against him, she stamped down hard on the arch of his foot with her high heel, feeling his body stiffen angrily and his sharp intake of breath as he took another swipe at her. But his fist didn't have chance to connect with her cheek before he was toppled by the other man.

'You are correct. She doesn't have "rights". However, *I* do.'

'What?' Hades scrambled to his feet, brushing his palms down his black sweater; something in his stance betraying the fact that he was wary of the taller man.

'Leave the woman alone. I'm pulling rank over you.'

Relief swamped Megan. At least one of these jerks had some decency.

'What difference does it make to you, if I want to fool around with her?' Hades rubbed his cheek where the other man had hit him.

Dark eyes settled on Megan, and any relief she might have felt quickly disintegrating as Zeus put a gloved fore-finger under her chin, and met her blazing green eyes with chilling arrogance. 'I want this one for myself.'

Harsh laughter filled the room. It was the female leader. 'At last, Zeus. I had begun to think that your appetites had faded!' She smiled at him, a gesture distorted beneath her woollen mask 'However, you must wait. We have work to do.'

She snapped out orders in another language and one of the darkly-dressed forms moved towards the Captain and demanded, 'Come with me.'

The Captain had no choice but to leave with the man as she continued, 'Hades, Kronos – deal with the cargo.'

There was a murmuring amongst the passengers, and many sympathetic glances cast in Megan's direction, until the female leader demanded, 'Quiet!'

'Deal with what cargo?' Megan frowned at the woman.

A large hand grasped her forearm, pulled her to the edge of the room, gesturing that she sit against a pillar.

'No questions, Lacey! Just do as you are told.'

Megan shot him a look of disgust, but remained silent. What was the horrible Hades 'dealing' with? What would happen to them all? Had the authorities been told that this lovely yacht had been taken over by a bunch of nutters using the names of Greek gods? Oh, Lord – what would she do if this black-eyed man touched her? A great shudder wracked her body and she felt ill; desperately sick with fear.

'Zeus – search the woman,' the leader snapped at the tall man still standing beside Megan. 'Everyone else has been searched. We do not want her stabbing you while your back is turned.'

What a good idea Megan thought. There were plenty of knives in the kitchen.

'Stand up!' Zeus stood in front of her, tucking his gun in his leather shoulder holster. Megan sensed all eyes on her again, tried to make it to her feet, but her limbs were trembling and useless. Only her mind worked with frightening clarity.

'Stand!'

'I'm trying…'

Unexpectedly, his palms closed under her arms, raised her up and propped her against the white marble pillar, her back to the room.

She closed her eyes against his searching hands as they covered every inch of her through her clothes. Palms flat and thorough against her back, yanking open her uniform dress to expose her breasts and probing inside her bra. He was taking so long, touching…under her arms, then down her ribs. Megan held on to the thought that every other passenger on board had probably submitted to this disgusting intrusion; it was her turn and it would soon be over. It didn't stop her shuddering.

'Fasten your dress,' he commanded over her shiver.

Megan, fighting to control fingers that seemed as fat and flabby as defrosted sausages, couldn't get the press studs to bite; gasping with horror when his fingers delved inside her stocking tops, down her thighs and over sheer stockings that couldn't possibly hide anything. Then his fingers circled her ankle, slipped off her shoe, searched it thoroughly, replaced it beside her foot and repeated the movement with her other foot. Her damp palms clung to the marble column, deeply grateful that she had her back to this man and everyone else. Nervous perspiration broke from every pore; first soaking and then chilling her.

Jordan, she thought, pressing her cheek against the cool, pale marble. *Oh, Jordan – where are you*? I'll never forgive you for leaving me to submit to this…this pig! We should have been toasting a year of marriage. We should have been holding one another, should have been celebrating and…

'Sit down, Lacey.'

If she let go of the pillar, she would drop to the ground; her uniform buttons were still undone, breasts pushing up where Zeus had disturbed her underwear. She pressed her forehead against the marble. She must remember that they'd done this to all the passengers – mauled them, taken their dignity, made them into captives. If she turned around now, they would see the tears on her cheeks. Every pulse in her body was jumping and thundering.

'I'm going to be sick.'

'Take her to the washroom!' the woman terrorist snapped. 'And make her clean up any mess she makes.'

The woman swore in her own tongue as Megan staggered blindly; Zeus half-dragging, half-carrying her into the luxurious bathroom off the stateroom.

The tall minder watched impassively through black eyes as she leant against the sink for a long time, trying to pull her scrambled mind into order. There was nothing here to attack the man with. But there would be. It was just a matter of keeping her eyes open and biding her time.

In the mirror above the sink, her eyes were huge, hair dishevelled, dress undone, whiter-than-white skin gleaming under muted strip lights. She looked…what? Wanton…? The thought made her glance up at Zeus, before turning quickly away from his black, careful eyes. Again, she tried to fasten her dress, but the studs were strong, needed force to press them together.

Silently, Zeus pushed her hands aside, deftly fastened the large, metal press studs. 'Where is your cabin?'

'I…I already share.'

'With me.'

'No!'

'Then you prefer Hades?' He shrugged, 'He is not gentle with women.'

'And you are?'

'I would not kill you when making love to you.'

'*Oh, God*!' Somewhere deep inside, rising up through bleak horror, the mind-bending fear, a sense of self-preservation kicked in. '*Please* don't let Hades near me!'

'That is your worst fear?'

'Yes.'

'Do as I say and you will live.' A second's pause, then, 'Take me to your cabin.'

'Now…? But…'

'No matter. Now.'

Was he going to do anything to her now? Surely not? But if she didn't submit? Hades might…

Despite walking slowly, stumbling, hesitating and pretending she didn't know which room she was in, Megan eventually ran out of corridor on the lowest deck.

'Move to the far wall.'

Megan frowned at the command, but went where he said, sinking down on to a small dressing table chair inside her cabin. In seconds, he'd emptied all her belongings into a pile on the carpet, deftly separating manicure items and anything sharp or remotely useful as a weapon. He swept everything into a hold-all, which he slung outside the cabin door, and kicked the rest to one side of the cabin.

'Could I…could I brush my teeth?'

He gave a nod. 'I'll come with you.'

Zeus removed all the spray bottles from the bathroom whilst Megan brushed her teeth. It had been a long shot anyway.

'I'm going to make love to you, very soon.' His gloved hand touched her forearm. Megan shuddered.

'My husband will kill you!'

'I thought you were unmarried, Miss Lacey.'

'Lacey's my working name.'

'You have no ring.'

Plunging her hand into her bag, Megan produced her wedding album. 'Here!'

But the man's black eyes merely glanced at the photos. 'He will thank me.'

'You low-life!'

'We need to get back.'

'Fine.'

'A word of advice.' Zeus kept his hand around her wrist as they moved along the corridor, up the steps towards the main hall. 'Do not inflame Hades with your "fire". I doubt he will touch you now – not without my permission. But he may still prove troublesome if you push him too far.'

'Why the hell should I believe anything you say?'

She lurched forward to escape his grip, but he held her tightly, swinging her around to face him, before pinning her against the corridor wall.

'Because you want to live.' His deep, gravelly voice offered no comfort, just the bald truth. 'If you want to survive – you'd be well advised to be sensible.'

She could feel the heat of his body close to the shocked, chilled skin of her own; wondered if a running leap over the side of The Dream was an option. Maybe if she appeared to acquiesce, she'd have more chance to fight back…?

'I want to live.' Green eyes met black ones directly, she didn't flinch when his palm touched her breast and his leather-clad fingers spread over her softness. 'But I'll not willingly let you maul me.'

'Don't fight me.'

'Or what?'

'Don't fight me, Megan Lacey – that will be enough.'

Megan's green eyes burned with hatred, she turned her face aside; hating Zeus, terrified of what she might have to do to survive, but knowing that whatever happened she *would* survive. If only to bring these terrorists to justice.

All eyes turned to her, questioning, afraid, as Megan was escorted back into the main lounge.

'Ah!' It was the woman. 'There you are, Zeus.'

He pushed Megan against the pillar, jerked his thumb to the floor and gave the leader his full attention. 'Artemis?'

'You have been a while. Have you been enjoying yourself with that girl?'

'Not yet.' He shrugged. 'There's no point in wasting my time if she's no good.'

Artemis laughed, then snapped, 'Take her to the kitchen. I want supper prepared. But watch her!' she added warningly.

Zeus shrugged, pulled Megan to her feet by her elbow. 'You heard.'

'One moment!' Artemis again, 'That girl of yours has missed hearing our ground rules.' The leader waited whilst Megan turned at the swing door and faced her, the man beside her holding her elbow.

'If any one of you, passengers or staff alike, do anything stupid, you will be punished.' She eased her tall, slender form from a stool and emphasised her words with a sweep of her pistol. 'Not the brave or the stupid – but any other two amongst you. And as for you…,' she added, turning to Megan. 'If you even think about poisoning our food, or "playing with knives", your companions will die.'

Megan could feel the blood draining from her face. At that moment, she knew that she'd do anything…anything she had to – if not for herself – then for her fellow hostages.

'Do you understand?' It was the second time Artemis had asked the question, the first lost in a wash of painful heartbeats and impotence.

'Yes. I understand,' Megan muttered.

'Zeus?' His feline leader prompted.

Megan frowned as Zeus took her chin in his palm, his eyes probing into hers. 'Are you sure you understand?' His strange black eyes and deep, gravelly voice searched inside her for the truth.

'Of course, I'm sure!'

Artemis gave a slight nod of dismissal and Zeus opened the swing door. As he gave Megan a push into the kitchen, she looked around her thinking that there HAD to be something she could do!

As if reading her mind with perfect precision, Zeus said, 'There is nothing you can do.' He yanked the menu from the wall clip, handed it to her. 'Carry on as though you have extra passengers.'

'I need help – I can't do it alone,' Megan told him, realising that she had to try to get someone else to help her in the kitchen. She glanced quickly upward at the racks of food, and the underside of the decking.

'Supper. Drinks. That is all you are required to do tonight. And you will do it alone.'

Turning her back on Zeus, Megan filled a silver trolley with mugs and heated jugs of milk, water, tea, coffee and drinking chocolate.

Angry, frustrated at her captor's insight, Megan clenched her teeth and turned to face him. 'Would the Greek gods like biscuits? Or do I have to sacrifice a cow?'

'Do what you would normally do.' Those dangerous eyes trapped her for an instant, 'And, if you know what's good for you – you'll keep that busy tongue of yours under control.'

Megan flung the wafer-thin china mug in her hand – only realising what she'd done in blind fury when it smashed on the wall beside him. The sound of splintering china, echoing as loudly as the shattering of a plate-glass window, saw the inevitable entry of yet another black clad form. It was Hades.

Megan shuddered with revulsion and turned her eyes helplessly to the tall man beside her.

'It was just an accident,' Zeus told the other man with a shrug. 'She will be out in a minute, Hades.'

The big, muscled, mean man looked disappointed. 'An accident?' He didn't believe his comrade. But Zeus nodded, held the door for the other man to move back outside. 'Nothing for you to worry about.'

The threat – not only that someone else would be punished if Megan tried to disable anyone, but that this man would leave her to the tender mercies of Hades if she didn't comply – swirled around in her blood, mixed with overriding fear. She knew a surge of gratitude to Zeus as he saw the other man out, sharing some inaudible joke. Megan stood rigid, waiting for his anger or some kind of retribution as the door slapped shut.

'I…' Megan couldn't bring herself to apologise.

'Yes?'

'Please keep him away from me…'

'Clean this up.' He jabbed a finger at the broken china.

Keen eyes watched her put every last piece of china into the waste disposal system. Megan thought Zeus probably knew just how badly she wanted to keep a slither of the sharp porcelain with which to defend herself; was probably laughing up his sleeve at the futile gesture. Yet there was one sharp shard, just by her knee. If she could whisk it into her apron pocket…

'And that piece, as well.' He sounded very impatient. 'Now!'

'You can't punish my thoughts.' Megan picked the white slither of sharpness up between her finger and thumb and disposed of it.

'No more chances. Do you understand?'

'I've a temper.' She shrugged helplessly. 'Sometimes it takes over.'

It was the wrong thing to say. Megan watched his frame tense as she busied herself finishing off the supper refreshments. He didn't speak, merely watched her every move, and Megan thought she'd better become a model hostage – and quick – or the fate she saw in this man's eyes would be worse than being thrown to Hades.

One by one, Megan waited on the passengers and The Dream's employees alike. In their eyes she saw a wish they could help her, but begged her to understand that they were as helpless as she.

'We'll be fine,' Megan whispered, fingers trembling as she passed around biscuits and cocoa, then reeled as Artemis cuffed her round the head.

'No talking!' She spun to Zeus. 'This woman is trouble. You must make it clear to her that we will tolerate no talking. No communication!'

Fearing for her companions, Megan burst out, 'I'm sorry!' Tears swelled up in her green eyes, her palms open towards Zeus. 'I'm sorry…' She caught at her bottom lip to keep it from quivering. No more chances, he'd said. 'Please don't hurt them.' She was shaking, her eyes fixed on Zeus as he spoke quietly with Artemis at the edge of the room. 'Please!'

Artemis laughed at something Zeus said. She gripped his shoulders and pushed herself squarely against him, kissing him briefly. 'Then I shall leave it to you.'

Megan prayed no one would separate her from the others. She had never prayed so hard, silently promising herself that she'd do just about anything, so long as all the others could be spared.

'Then I shall leave it to you,' Artemis' words echoed in Megan's mind, tormenting her to within an inch of hysteria. Clever – because not knowing what her punishment would be was infinitely worse than facing up to the reality.

As she collected plates and cups, Megan's eyes filled with

tears. She couldn't seem to focus and could barely hold on to the crockery with cold, shaky fingers.

As a hand at her elbow jerked her away from the sink, Megan bit down a squeal of terror. Those black eyes frowning down at her, he gestured towards the corridor door.

Zeus didn't speak, didn't touch her, but followed her to the cabin. Once there, he pulled her into the tiny bathroom. 'Strip.'

She could no longer meet his eyes with defiance. Too much depended on her reaction now. Once again her shaky fingers didn't seem able to pull apart the poppers until, with a great effort, she managed to tear the sides of her black uniform dress apart. Tightly gripping hold of the shower curtain, she trembled as his hands pulled the tie of her white, lace-edged apron so that it fell on her feet before he reached forward to turn on the water.

Slowly, while still keeping her back to him, Megan removed her shoes and stockings; her bra still twisted from his earlier search. As her hands reached behind to unfasten the clasp, his fingers pushed hers aside, allowing her last bit of protection to fall down on to the tiled floor.

Only Jordan had seen her like this – naked. Only Jordan, whom she'd loved so deeply, had ever touched her bare body. As glove-clad palms rested on her shoulders, turning her to face him, Megan blanked her expression before looking up at Zeus.

Oh, he wanted her. She could tell by the heat in his black eyes. But, whatever happened, Megan was determined hold her memories of Jordan around her like a snugly-lined cape; an intangible but necessary barrier to keep her sanity intact.

She closed her eyes, strained and tense as she waited for Zeus to touch her. When he didn't, Megan opened her eyes. Resisting the need to cross her arms over her chest, she stared straight back into the man's gaze.

'Shower.' He pulled the shower curtain aside, 'Then get

into your bed.'

Megan immediately stepped into the shower, gulping with relief when he pulled the curtain across between them.

Dazed, with warm water splashing over cold skin, she moved her stiff limbs; washing herself and her hair, and trying to keep her thoughts to the 'here and now', for however short a time she had on her own. Megan was determined to spend that time in her mind with Jordan. Whatever Zeus might do, she wouldn't let him inside her mind.

She turned off the shower. Some things it was better to get over and done with. The unknown – teetering on a knife edge in case Zeus made his move – was much worse.

Voices…there were voices beyond the bathroom door. Zeus and Artemis…?

'Kronos has the cargo safe. I am pleased.'

Cargo? Wasn't this a passenger ship, owned by Matt Duprey? The self-made man who had everything? The kind, charismatic elderly man who'd taken the trouble to thank her earlier in the day.

She rubbed a towel over her hair, conscious of lowered tones beyond the bathroom door.

'The other passengers are concerned and afraid for the woman Lacey. Keep her here until midday tomorrow. One of the other fools can take care of the food.' Artemis gave a harsh laugh. 'It will help our guests to realise they must behave or face the consequences.'

The others were all right! Relief was almost painful as Megan gripped the edge of the tiny sink. Oh, thank God!

Zeus made some deeply-spoken response Megan didn't catch, before she heard Artemis say, 'Just be sure that Lacey looks as though you have her well-disciplined – and I don't mean all smiles and fluttering eyes.'

'She won't be doing any of that.'

Damn right! Megan told herself grimly. The steel was now back in her soul, holding her upright.

'Knock her around a little. Yes?'

Zeus merely laughed. Megan heard him close the door, before saying in a loud voice, 'You can stop eavesdropping and come out now, Lacey.'

She opened the door, darkened wet hair falling over her shoulders and down over her breasts.

'You heard what Artemis said about your friends?'

Nodding, Megan whispered, 'I heard.'

'Their fate is still dependent on you.'

'I understand.' She looked him levelly in the eyes and saw his eyebrows raised a little beneath his woollen mask. Megan wanted nothing more than to dive under the sheets and pull them tightly around her, yet resisted. 'I can't promise not to cry. I've never been "knocked around" by a man.' She raised her chin, just short of defiance. 'My husband is a gentle man.'

Strong, but gentle. And she was sure that Alexa was right – wherever he was, he *would* still be thinking about her. Although, whether it was true or not didn't really matter. Megan just needed something to hold on to.

'Get into bed.' He turned from her. 'I have work to do. You will be here alone for an hour. Try to leave, and you know the consequences.'

An hour? Alone? It seemed too good to be true. Megan hardly dared move into the bed in case Zeus changed his mind.

'You hesitate?' Zeus looked towards the bed.

'I'm afraid.'

'Yes.' Dark eyes stared narrowly at her for a moment, before he turned and left the room.

Whimpering with relief, Megan quickly pulled the tiny photo album from her handbag, and then dived beneath under the neatly-arranged bedding.

'Jordan…,' she whispered his name, her trembling fingers gently touching the photographic image of her beloved husband as she remembered their wedding day, her eyes filling with tears as she gazed at his beautiful, chiselled features, wreathed in happiness.

He'd lifted her out of the horse-drawn carriage, refusing to put her down so that she could walk into the hotel that they'd chosen for their reception.

Gazing at herself in the photo, her head thrown back, hair streaming down her back, Megan could still hear her own laughter. 'Not here..! You're supposed to carry me over the threshold of our own *home*, Jordan!'

'I'm taking you straight upstairs to our room.'

'Alexa's hit list…?'

'OK, OK. I love you, so I'd better keep your friends happy.'

'Tell you what…' Megan, upright at last, had drawn her fingers down his slashed cheek. 'How about coming upstairs with me when I change out of this "meringue"?'

His mouth was on hers then, a photograph taken in the provocative pose.

'Megan, do you have any idea what you do to me?' Jordan's deep voice unsteady as he'd finally broken away from her, clear blue eyes stealing her breath, before his mouth had curved into a sensual smile. 'Am I supposed to eat this "meringue" off you?'

Heat had flushed her cheeks. 'No, just what's underneath it.'

And then it had been Jordan's turn to colour. She'd seen the beads of moisture on his forehead beneath his soft dark blond hair, his eyes turning from blue to almost completely black. Long, strong fingers struggling to loosen his tie.

'Jordan!' His best man had slapped him on the back, shaking his hand, 'You'll have time for all that later. Now, it's *my* turn to kiss the bride.'

With that, Ray Blackmore had kissed Megan soundly on

the lips, laughing at her shocked response before shaking Jordan's hand again. 'Think I'll…ah…leave it at that, Megan. I'd love a dance later, but Jordan's got a jealous streak wider than England when it comes to you.'

Jealous? She'd smiled politely, past brushes with Blackmore having made her wary. And she was relieved when Jordan pulled her to his side. 'You're not still jealous? He was kidding, right?'

'Nope.' They laughed together, turned towards the double glass doors to join the reception. Unexpectedly, Jordan had stopped, drawn her gently into a flower-framed alcove and taken hold of her hands.

'What Ray said, Megan, about me being jealous?'

'Oh, I'd forgotten about that.' Megan had shrugged as if it was of no importance.

'It…it's hard for me to deal with. I've never had a problem with jealousy. Not until now.'

'It's not a problem now.' Megan frowned. 'Jordan, I'm not even a practised flirt – and I don't exactly encourage other men.'

'I know. But, when Ray kissed you…Megan, I'd normally trust that man with my life – but just now, I wanted to hit him!'

She'd been shocked by his admission, wanting to brush it aside, but Jordan had looked so troubled that she couldn't. 'I don't know what to say? Don't you trust me?'

'Yes, yes I do.' He'd loosened his tie further, brushing his hands roughly through his hair. 'Megan, I'm worried that I love you so much. I think maybe I'm obsessed with you.'

She'd shaken her head, shining copper waves shifting with the movement as she put a hand to his cheek.

'I've only ever been myself with you, Jordan.' She gave him a wry smile. 'If you can put up with my temper, I'll handle your jealousy.' She kissed his lips briefly. 'All you've got to do, is to tell me how you're feeling.'

Jordan had pulled her close, and kissed her long and hard.

'The way we feel about one another, Mr Elliot, it's nothing to be ashamed of,' she'd continued, searching her mind as she tried to find an explanation for his feelings. 'Maybe it's your job? Maybe you've seen too much?'

'Maybe.' He'd sighed. 'Maybe it *is* the job. I hated being away from you before. Now it's going to be far worse.'

'Well, buster, I wouldn't ask you to change your job – any more than you'd ask me to change mine.'

'Even if I have to go away?'

'I'll cry and try to blackmail you into staying – and I'll probably throw a temper tantrum like you've never seen,' she'd giggled. 'But I married you knowing that you were a civil engineer and would be forced to travel. I promise you, though, that I won't be flying into another man's arms, Jordan.' She'd wriggled against him, 'Yours feel too good for that.'

He smiled, tracing her lips with his forefinger; his touch sending shimmering waves of pleasure coursing through her body.

Turning to the next wedding photograph, taken when they'd been cutting the cake, it was obvious that the newly-weds hadn't been able to take their eyes off one another.

'Cor Blimey!' Ray had wafted close as he danced with the chief bridesmaid, Alexa. 'Are you going to let someone else have a look in with your missus?'

Blue eyes gazed fixedly down into hers as Jordan had replied, 'Only if they've a wooden leg and two left feet.' His mouth had slanted into a smile as she'd snuggled closer, sliding her arms inside his dark grey jacket. Megan had never felt so secure, or so loved…

And then, suddenly, she was abruptly dragged back to dangerous reality as the cabin door was thrown open.

Megan feigned sleep, leaving the album open on her pillow. Maybe Zeus would leave her alone if she appeared to be sleeping? Besides, he couldn't possibly expect her to stretch out sinuous fingers in his direction, beckoning him seductively towards her!

Through her closed eyelids, Megan was aware of him moving around in the cabin and hearing the sound of running water from the bathroom. She wished that she could miraculously fall asleep, but knew that strain and tension wouldn't let her. Was he really going to 'knock her about' as Artemis had suggested?

Strangely, on that thought, sheer exhaustion seemed to overtake her and she sank slowly away into a deep sleep. She was only vaguely aware of the album being removed from her fingertips, and of a deep, inaudible murmur; sleep gripping her so tightly that she was incapable of any response.

Megan dreamed of Jordan…his possessive hands moving over her calves, her thighs, encircling her waist and smoothing up her back, relaxing her tensed muscles. His lovely white teeth nibbled her shoulders, he laughed against her skin; and sure hands turned her on her back. His fingers teased her starving lips apart, touched her tongue and she gasped. That same finger laid a damp trail down her chin and neck, to her hardened nipples. His tongue flicked lightly, then more insistently against sensitive skin, sucking gently, drawing sighs of pleasure from Megan, those same sighs became a delicious chanting of his name when his mouth worked lower; moist lips against her soft-firm belly.

'Jordan…' she reached out to touch and just for a second, his silky soft hair met with her fingertips. 'Jordan…' But, he'd gone. The dream vanished and tears choked Megan, 'Jordan, where did you go?' she muttered incoherently.

Still more asleep than awake, she cried into her pillow, woke when its dampness chilled, her heart swamped with pain. She swung her legs out of bed, and dropped her head into her palms. Those vivid dreams…they'd plagued her every night for three months after he'd gone.

Every night Megan had woken like this. Devastated, her pillow wet from tears. She'd submerged herself in work. The recently radiant bride had drawn sidelong glances from concerned friends, who'd watched her pale skin turn paler, the mauve smudges beneath her eyes becoming deeper, her once cascading and vibrant hair now dull and lacklustre. The curves Jordan had loved fell victim to Megan's appalling diet of tea, coffee, toast and a state of suspended mourning and confusion. But she never spoke about him.

About then, love had half-turned to hatred, swinging wildly between the two. But it had helped to catapult Megan from her malaise. Anger, softened for weeks by grief, had surged to the fore, firing Megan into the kind of working frenzy that worried her friends almost as much as her previous melancholy.

Jordan Elliot wasn't going to wreck her life. Not one more minute of it! Married she may be, but when friends began guiding suitable men in her direction, Megan had gone out for meals and to the cinema. But it had stopped there, and she hadn't as much as exchanged a kiss with any one of them.

Still, the dream clung to her; the sensation of Jordan's touch lingered against her skin. Why now? Why, when she'd symbolically removed her rings, and intended throwing her wedding album into the deepest part of the ocean? Why did she have to suffer that dream again? As always, she'd only briefly touched him, before he disappeared, leaving her to wake with that dreadful sense of loss.

Megan shivered, her deep feelings of grief as intense as ever. And that other, sickening vision had been just as clear. Jordan, tall and handsome as always…with another woman in his arms!

Bile rising in her throat, she stumbled to the bathroom. *No, not again*! She mustn't sink into that desperate void, ever again!

'Are you ill?'

Zeus's deep, resonant voice barely made it through Megan's anguish; the realisation that she was no more over Jordan now, than the day when she'd heard that he'd been seeing another woman.

'Lacey?'

In that moment, Megan forgot to entertain fear or caution with Zeus. She even forgot that the man was a cruel bastard whose advances she dreaded.

'I'm OK.' Splashing her face with water, and brushing her teeth, Megan pushed the tangle of hair from her face; twisting it at her nape and straightening her arms for support against the sink. Naked, shivering, Megan forced herself to stand upright.

His thin woollen mask was a little crooked – hastily yanked on? Megan wondered. So he slept without it? Yet he slept fully clothed.

'Is it fear?' There was little emotion in his tone, yet Megan sensed something akin to a wisp of concern in his manner. 'Fear of me?'

Megan pulled a towel in front of her body, stared him straight in the eyes. It was only then that she remembered that this man and his colleagues were capable of inflicting terror with such ease.

'I'm not afraid of you. Anything you do to me, won't touch me.' Released from tentacles of the sensual dream was slowly bringing a return of fear – but she was damned if she'd let Zeus know that.

He folded his arms, leaning casually back against the doorframe. 'Someone named "Jordan" concerns you?'

Those words cut through her like an icy-cold wind. Once again, she forced herself to meet his eyes. 'Jordan is my husband.'

'So you say.'

'He is!'

'A husband whose ring you don't wear?'

'Not when I'm catering…'

'Whose name you don't use?'

'Lacey's the name of my business, my maiden name.'

His shoulders moved in a shrug. 'It doesn't sound like much of a marriage to me.'

'It's got nothing to do with you!' Unnerved by those black eyes that never broke contact with hers, Megan gave a derisive laugh. 'I don't suppose for one minute that you were born with the name "Zeus". By the same token, what I do with my name is my business.'

Through the woollen mask that revealed only eyes and mouth, she could sense his anger. And yet, foolishly, she couldn't stop herself from adding, 'Are you married, Zeus? Or is there a shortage of Greek goddesses these days?'

She saw the tension tighten every well-defined muscle beneath his black cotton sweater; his hands clenching into fists.

'Knock her about a bit…' Artemis's words rang in her head as Megan's raised her chin, her eyes flashed with rage.

'Why don't you strike me as your brave leader suggested, Zeus?' she cried, drumming her fists on his solid chest, his fingers catching hold of a wrist, clamping it tightly between their bodies. 'And afterwards, you can ask yourself – is that the act of a man whose chosen name represents order and justice?'

She jerked her hand away from his fingers. 'I'm half your size, you…you muscle-bound jerk!' she continued angrily. So, what's "just" about hurting me?'

'I warned you to keep your tongue under control, Lacey.'

His tone of voice was deep and dangerous, conjuring dreadful images of punishment. 'Whilst I may chose to be lenient sometimes, the others will never be. You'd be well advised to bear that in mind.'

A cold shiver skimmed over Megan's skin, and she closed

her eyes as his fingertips slipped over the top of her towel-covered breasts. It was not knowing what he was going to do…it was the dreadful suspense which pricked ceaselessly at her nerve ends. The reason why she now found herself foolishly challenging this man.

'Why don't you just get it over with?'

'Are you inviting me into your bed, Lacey?' As he spoke, he dropped his hand to his side.

'I'll do what I have to do, to keep us all safe,' Megan muttered, suddenly overwhelmed by such a torrent of shame and shock that she couldn't force herself to look up at him.

Shame, because mingling with fear was the utterly shameful, slight leap of her pulse. Which was completely inexplicable, especially since she'd allowed no man to touch her for the past ten months. And shock – total shock that she really *was* prepared to do anything this man demanded, in order to save the lives of everyone else on this boat.

He turned away. 'When I want you, I will have you.'

A stay of execution! Megan scrambled beneath the covers, pulled them tightly around her, wanting to ask Zeus what he'd done with her photo album, but not wishing to remind him that she was in the same cabin. Tomorrow, she'd look for it herself.

Moonlight was flooding through the port-hole and she could hear the slap of gentle waves against the hull. It seemed such a contrast: the peace of the night and the beauty of The Dream, at odds with the constant threat against all but six of her passengers. She turned, searching the darkness for the moment when Zeus would remove his mask. Because, when this was all over, she wanted to be able to identify him. To be sure that he'd rot in gaol, along with his companions.

The other bed was deep in shadow, and although Megan could hear him settling against the crisp sheets, she couldn't see anything on that side of the cabin. I'll stay awake, she told herself, forcing her eyelids open against the heavy temptation of sleep. She must stay awake… she must try and gain a glimpse of his face, before he pulled on his disguise in the morning. *He won't know that I've committed his features to my memory. And he'll pay…they'll all pay…*

She was laughing, running with Jordan along the edge of the crystal-clear water of Gran Canaria; the soft, dark, volcanic sand clinging to their feet. The beach was virtually deserted – evening sending visitors back to their hotel and apartments for meals and showers. Abruptly, Jordan was lifting Megan off her feet, swinging her around and around as drops of water dripped on to her skin from his hair. Brilliant blue eyes staring down into hers, darkening, smouldering as he pulled her body close to him; the salt water dampness of their skin more sensual than anything she'd ever known.

Evocative scents of tropical suntan lotions and warm, lazy days filled her senses. Gazing up into Jordan's blue eyes, she spread her fingertips over his strong shoulders, gasping with pure need as he drew her closer against his hard muscular body, letting her slide down against his arousal as he lowered her slowly to the ground. Deft fingers at her back unfastened the turquoise bikini top, freeing her softness to press against his hard torso.

'You can't know how much I love you,' he murmured, his voice husky with emotion, his hands moulding her hot damp body to his own.

Filled with such overwhelming love for her lover…her husband…Megan wanted him to throw her down on one of the cushioned blue sun beds – and make love to her there and then, whilst the setting sun's last rays threw the world into golden-pink relief. He was so solid, so honest, so unbelievably sexy…and endowed with the kind of masculine beauty that turned heads.

As a soft warm breeze wrapped around them, and with

warm sand at their feet, the outside world ceased to exist. Her green eyes smiled up into him, the air between their bodies sizzling with passion. 'I *do* know how much you love me, Jordan,' she whispered as his mouth touched hers. 'Because I feel exactly the same. Has anyone *ever* been this happy?'

'No.' Jordan shook his handsome head. 'It feels so good with you – it's got to be a crime!' It was all there in his eyes, the way he held her: all the love one woman could handle. His mouth neared hers, she raised her lips, hungry for his kiss…

'Wake up, Lacey.'

Still embraced by her powerful, sensual dream, Megan sighed sexily, rolled on her back, hair spilling over her shoulders, arms reaching out to hold Jordan, bring his mouth down on hers, 'Kiss me…' the soft murmur broke from her lips.

'When I have you, Lacey, I will not kiss you.'

No! The wrong voice jerked Megan into bleak wakefulness, the sound of her voice echoing in her ears. Sleep-misted vision cleared, and it wasn't Jordan close by – *it was Zeus*!

Her mouth was dry, her languid body still warm and aroused with the remnants of her dream.

'You were dreaming – noisily.'

'Leave me alone…' Megan could have wept at Zeus's timing – just to feel Jordan's mouth on hers, even in a dream, would have been wonderful. She felt cheated, bereft and totally disoriented. 'I hate you!'

'Be quiet!'

If anger was a visible thing, then it flashed white in the air between them. In the soft light of dawn he reached for the sheet around her, stilled as she wriggled away, clutching the cover, her knuckles white with tension.

'No!' She truly hated the dark figure that had dragged her from the dream of Jordan's arms. 'Leave me alone!'

'On this ship you are mine to do with as I wish. Understand?'

He didn't move a single muscle, merely stood between Megan and the light. No – not now, she prayed desperately. Please don't let him touch her now, when she'd just been dreaming of being in Jordan's arms.

Black eyes stared threateningly down and her mind whirled, fear trapping the air in her lungs. How could she face this?

Suddenly, she couldn't control her overwhelming fear and terror. 'Please leave me alone!' she cried, raw panic in her voice, tears glistening in her forest-green eyes. Her voice a whispered plea as she added helplessly, 'I need…I need time to get used to the situation.'

Trying to sound rational was about the hardest thing Megan had ever done, and she knew that she was failing miserably. As Zeus moved towards her, she knew her words had fallen on stony ground.

'Are…are you married?' she gasped, desperately hoping to prick his conscience as she wriggled away until her back was up against the cabin wall. Again, he paused, very briefly. 'You are married, aren't you?' Clutching the sheet, she struggled up into a sitting position.

'Be quiet!'

From the sudden tensing of his tall figure she knew that she'd hit a nerve. 'What's she like? Your wife? Do you love her?'

Megan lurched from the bed, dragging the sheet with her. 'You shouldn't be unfaithful, Zeus…!' Breathless, she twisted around, determined to escape into the bathroom. But her feet became tangled in the crisp linen and she toppled over, her cheek grazing the edge of the bedside table as she fell.

Zeus strode swiftly across the room, quickly picked her up and carefully adjusted the trailing sheet, enabling Megan to stalk into the bathroom with her head held high.

chapter three

Megan woke to find sunlight flooding in through the port-hole. 'Ah…' she muttered, forcing herself upright on the bed and squinted, shielding her eyes from the sun.

'Zeus!' Artemis called out, opening the door. 'I need you up with the others in an hour. Bring the woman with you.'

Appearing from the bathroom, adjusting his mask, Zeus jerked a thumb in Megan's direction. 'That might be diffi-cult.'

Artemis trained her cold gaze on Megan for the first time, laughing at the sight of the scratch on the copper-haired woman's face. 'I said knock her about "a bit", Zeus!' She laughed. 'But was it really necessary to go that far?'

Zeus merely responded with a casual shrug of his broad shoulders.

'I need your help,' the woman told him. 'The Captain is proving obstinate. I may have to shoot him.'

'We can speak outside.' He cast Megan a sidelong glance. 'Stay where you are.'

She clenched her teeth to still her gasp of horror as the door closed behind the two, all-powerful members of the terrorist gang as they spoke in lowered, foreign tones.

'As if I'm capable of throwing out a rope, and swimming a hundred miles in these seas!' Megan muttered grimly to herself, wrapping her arms around her ribs as she settled comfortably against the soft pillows.

Outside the cabin, she could hear the man's deep, rough voice speaking rapidly in a foreign tongue, his words inter-spersed with sharp responses from Artemis. Megan longed to sleep, longed to fight back against these ruthless captors, but the price was too great. Instinctively, she tensed when the cabin door opened.

'Shower and get dressed.'

Feigning sleep, Megan watched him walk over to the cabin window through shuttered eyes. Leave me alone, she begged silently. Please, just leave me alone!

Involuntarily, Megan's eyes opened when she sensed Zeus move towards the bed. 'Didn't you hear what I said?'

'I…I heard,' she whispered, her words catching in her throat as she let her hair fall forwards over her face, so that he wouldn't see her grimace as she pushed herself upright. Mindful of what happened the last time she tried to shield herself with the sheet, Megan raised it clear of the deck and wrapped it carefully around her.

In an almost gentlemanly gesture, Zeus turned on the shower before she managed to reach it, holding the shower curtain aside and taking the sheet from her. Some perverse part of her wanted to see shock in his eyes when he glimpsed her nakedness. But she knew that she wouldn't see anything, let alone remorse, in the eyes of such a man. He'd obviously seen too much, and inflicted too much fear in other human beings. So she turned her face away as she stepped into the steam-filled shower.

Once in the shower, she could only stand there beneath the spray of warm water, which soothed her heated flesh. She tried to raise her arms to soap her skin and wash her hair, but she was so dejected she couldn't seem to stop the tears from coursing down her pale cheeks.

'Wash yourself!' The gravelly command came from beyond the transparent curtain.

Gritting her teeth, she hissed, 'Do it for me if you're so keen!'

A thousand times in the next few minutes, Megan regretted those words. Careless that water sprayed out, both on to the cushioned soft flooring and himself, Zeus jerked back the plastic curtain, reaching beyond her for the soap. She shuddered, then stood still as a statue while strong, sure hands proceeded to wash her. Eyes closed against her own hatred and disgust, she endured Zeus's soapy hands whilst visualising kneeing him in the groin. But then, when he tipped cool, honeysuckle fragrance shampoo over her hair, her troubled thoughts shifted longingly to Jordan...remembering the first evening of their honeymoon...

A marble-floored apartment with doors that opened out onto a massive patio, and palms surrounding a swimming pool. When they'd finally returned from the beach – running, laughing and kissing, back to their accommodation, they'd turned on the shower and tantalised one another's needy bodies with soapy hands. Jordan spreading the fingers of one hand low across her stomach, while placing the other arm around her waist, holding her upright as her knees went weaker and weaker, water playing over them both as he drove Megan insane with need and took her again and again to the brink; until finally, lifting her against him, he'd guided her legs around his waist...

'Ah...' The erotic memory prompted an involuntary gasp to escape her lips before, seconds later, Zeus turned off the water.

As Zeus threw a large bath towel around her shoulders, Megan was shocked that whilst this man had soaped her, she'd so easily slipped into thinking about Jordan. Ashamed of her instinctive gasp of pleasure, she comforted herself with the thought that he would think it an expression of fear. And he'd enjoy that! Green eyes burned, angry and frightened into his broad back as he left the bathroom.

Try as she might – and maybe it was delayed shock – but Megan found her hands shaking so hard, that she was having difficulty in trying to dry herself. Honeysuckle-scented hair dripped, soaking the towel.

'Damn it!' Frustrated at her own stupidity, Megan wriggled, the towel falling into the wet shower basin. How on earth was she supposed to dry herself now?

'Lacey,' he held aside the shower curtain. 'Can you step out here?'

Damn and blast! She was naked again, and those black, dispassionate eyes raked over her. Wrapping herself in pride alone, Megan retorted grimly, 'Yes, of course I can.'

Still unable to control her shivering, trembling limbs, she might have crumpled outside the shower if his dry, leather-clad hand hadn't caught her elbow. 'You're a clumsy woman,' he drawled. He'd changed his clothes for dry ones – army fatigues this time.

His comment earned him a mulish glare. 'Something seems to have happened to me – maybe it's delayed shock? Or, maybe I don't like being bullied – although I can't think why?' she added with childish defiance.

'Get in there and dress!'

Megan had the uncontrollable urge to laugh, because Zeus could barely contain his mounting anger with her. 'If I can't wash, how on earth can I dress myself? You should leave me here. I'm just holding you up.'

'Lacey – you are becoming a pain in the neck!'

Exasperation oozed from every one of his taut muscles as he glared down at Megan for a moment, before spinning around to pick up her clean uniform and throwing it at her.

'Artemis wants you upstairs with the others.'

'I can't dress.' Affecting calmness she didn't feel, Megan kept her eyes on Zeus.

'Find a way, Lacey, or I will take you upstairs naked.'

Suddenly, his hands were under her arms. And as Megan blinked, trying to clear her vision and regain control, she was vaguely aware of Zeus hooking her bra over her arms, pulling it towards her. The thought of his hands fastening the garment had her quickly shaking her head.

'No,' she whispered helplessly.

He flung it to the floor.

'I presume you've no objection to wearing pants?' His anger vibrated in the inches between them. Zeus was crouched at her feet, dangling the slip of pretty cotton from his finger.

Megan was seized by an almost hysterical urge to laugh. Here was a masked, international criminal – and he was having to dress her like a helpless baby! But as he looped the underwear over her bare feet, before sliding the cotton up her legs, she couldn't prevent an involuntary shiver as she felt Zeus's breath against her thigh.

A moment later he was frowning down at her, his black gaze heated for a second before he turned away. 'Where are your stockings?'

'In the hold-all.' Megan clutched her fingers together, desperately trying to repress the continual shivering that gripped her.

She balanced on one leg, rested her palm on his shoulder whilst he pulled the sheer fabric on to her foot, then slowly, with a strange mixture of sensuality and practicality, Zeus slipped the soft stocking up Megan's shapely leg, his fingers lingering at the top of her thigh. He then repeated the process with her other stocking, but so slowly that her entire body seemed on fire.

Closing her eyes, she was seized by the memory of Jordan doing the self-same thing for her – but for pleasure, not necessity. 'Jor…' she bit back the word, grimaced when Zeus straightened and glared down at her.

'You are missing your husband.'

'Not enough to want you!' she retorted grimly.

'I don't care whether you want me or not, Lacey. Just don't fight me.' As he spoke, he pulled her uniform dress upwards, hooked the fabric on to her shoulders, pulling the two sides together, the black material straining over Megan's full breasts.

Scowling, she managed to top herself saying: *Yeah, right – I'll throw myself at your feet – you jerk!* But she clearly couldn't stay silent for too long.

'What would your wife say, if she could see you "pawing" me?' Megan demanded angrily. Of course, she didn't know if he was married or not. He hadn't answered her question the last time she'd asked it. But, on the other hand, he hadn't denied being married, had he? 'If my husband was here, he'd kill you,' she added angrily.

'Your husband…?' He caught her chin lightly in his fingertips, 'Your husband is stupid to allow you to travel alone.' His hand fell away. 'And my wife is my own concern.'

'Do you punish her for your amusement? Do you play sick games with her, like you're doing with me?'

'One day you will thank me.'

'*Thank you*?' Colour flooded Megan's cheeks, 'Believe me, Zeus, one day I'll see you *dead*.'

His detached manner didn't alter one iota. If anything, she detected amusement in his black eyes, and felt an ever-deepening hatred swelling inside her.

'I don't think so,' he drawled, the calm certainty in his voice seeped fearfully under her skin. 'Upstairs, now. And show respect – or you'll be punished.'

Because she could almost feel his tension, Megan dawdled as much as she dared. But he knew what she was doing. 'Would you rather I carried you?' he demanded curtly.

'No, I would not!'

'Then move a little faster,' he grated, and all too soon, they reached the stateroom.

Hold your head high! Megan told herself, forcing her chin up and brushing her hair back over her shoulder. Zeus, his hand on the door, turned and she thought he was going to say something, but he didn't. He did, however, hold the door open for her.

'The facade of gentlemanly rogue isn't going to fool any-one – not when you're only too ready to fire that gun of yours,' she ground out childishly; and the whole room heard her – everyone falling silent and turning to face the new arrivals.

A murmur of shock rippled through the hostages. It was Artemis who stepped towards Megan, her cold laughter silencing everyone.

'I presume you struggled with Zeus, Lacey?' She gave Megan no moment to respond as she turned to face the occu-pants of the room. 'You see?' She gestured at the long scratch on Megan's cheek. 'It is so much easier and far more pleasant for us all, if everyone does as they are told!'

The Captain was staring, eyes wide in an awful mixture of disbelief and horror at what he assumed Megan had expe-rienced with the tall terrorist. As he opened his mouth, Megan gave him a quick, fleeting shake of her head. Her stomach clenching with fear, she could only pray that the others would hold their tongues.

No one spoke, but Megan read the words, 'How *could* you?' in their eyes.

'I really think, Zeus,' Artemis flicked her fingers upwards, long, manicured fingernails catching the light. 'I do think that you should have left her to Hades.'

The tall man shrugged. 'She has a big mouth. It irritated me,' he added with a harsh bark of laughter.

'I need you to stay here, and take charge,' Artemis announced, smiling as she walked slowly over to him, plac-ing a hand possessively on his arm. 'Take another woman if you wish, and feed this one to the sharks. She is little use to you now.'

Although Zeus stood with his back to her, Megan could hear the note of amusement in his voice. 'On the contrary, she is surprisingly…' he paused, as though searching for the right word. 'She is surprisingly inventive, in bed.'

Megan heard groans of disgust. But she didn't care that Zeus was lying through his teeth. It suited her purpose – and it obviously suited him. Maybe he was gay and he didn't want his comrades to know the truth…?

'Watch her,' Artemis warned as she met Megan's gaze. 'I have a feeling she could be troublesome. I think that she would kill you, if she could.'

'Don't worry! She knows that she is only a step away from Hades.'

The foreign woman gave a high-pitched, manic laugh, before striding out of the salon.

A young, good-looking young crewman stood up. 'Excuse me…'

Zeus frowned, his cold black eyes on the man who said quickly, 'Megan…it looks as though she needs medical attention.'

'This woman?'

'Yes.' Colour stained the man's cheeks, he looked both uncomfortable and angry, 'I'm trained in First Aid. I could help.'

Megan felt like someone who needed help – a ton of it. Why couldn't the man just keep quiet? If she was any more trouble, Zeus would throw her to the sharks – or Hades. And she would prefer sharks.

'You are…?' Zeus moved closer, read the man's name badge, 'Philip Trevean, ship's steward?'

'Yes.'

'When I want your help, Trevean, I will ask for it.'

'Megan could have a punctured lung. She could die,' the young steward protested.

Could she? Megan felt bad, but not on her last legs…not yet, anyway. When she'd been younger, she'd often hurt herself by falling over, but she'd been OK the next day. She'd always had that kind of skin – bruise easy, mend quick. And it was her fault she'd got this nasty scratch on her face, anyway.

And then, for some, inexplicable reason, Megan suddenly felt faint, the room seeming to be circling around her dazed head before she found herself falling down on to the floor.

'Ms Lacey!' Philip ran to her side. Megan, returning to full consciousness, felt the man's fingers tuck something – paper? – between the studs of the belt at her waist. What *was* Trevean playing at? He'd get them all killed!

'Sit down!' Zeus growled. 'She is not injured. I suspect that she is merely suffering from faintness due to lack of food. The stupid woman probably didn't eat enough last night, and has had nothing to eat this morning.'

Food? Megan frowned. Was the fact that she'd been too frightened to face eating anything, the reason why she'd been feeling so light-headed? But she couldn't remain down here, on the floor, much longer. Just the thought of Zeus or Hades' leather-clad hands touching, prodding her whilst hauling her to her feet, was very disturbing.

It was different with her husband. Jordan used to touch her whilst she slept and she would waken, sleepy and smiling, because he freely admitted that when he couldn't sleep, he watched her; could never resist touching her. 'I want you all the time, Megan,' he'd said, his voice husky with love.

A loud, cracking sound made Megan jump. Hades' cruel laughter filled her ears, his toe pushed against her back. 'That woke her up!'

'Quite.' Zeus waited while she scrambled to her feet, before gesturing for Megan to move back to his side. And for once she didn't hesitate to obey his command.

It seemed that hours passed as she sat, leaning against the mock Grecian pillar with Zeus standing beside her. He, like the others, constantly scanned the hostages, preferred silence to chatter.

The Dream's six passengers consisted of three couples, all connected directly with the TV and film industry and dressed in expensive evening wear – a legacy of the dinner party.

Dick Melancamp was a film director whom Megan had no problem recognising from the glossy magazines which Alexa constantly leafed through; he was stout and broad, nice-looking in a 'retired-bouncer' kind of way. He obviously cared deeply for his younger, attractive wife, Melissa, whose dark-haired, silver-sequinned form had lain against him the whole journey so far. He was respectful to the hijackers, his greatest fear obviously for his wife. Megan could read the message in his brown eyes when he caught her gaze; clearly as if he had spoken: *For God's sake, just do as these lunatics ask. I want to live. Sleep with the lot of them, if you have to!*

A message reflected by Jack Hodges, in particular. For the past decade, Jack's golden looks had seen him star in one action-packed film after another. He was a man at the peak of his career on both sides of the Atlantic; sought after by producers and lusted after by audiences. His figure was lean and hard-looking, a typical 'hero' of the film world. But the famous killer grin and arrogant, 'I can have any woman I want' charisma now appeared to have sunk without trace.

His secretary/girlfriend, Suzanne, gave Megan a sympathetic smile, her hazel eyes clearly saying that she wished there was something she could do to help.

Smiling back at Suzanne, Megan swore silently to herself that if she ever had the chance, she'd let Suzanne know just how grateful she was for those few bolstering glances and smiles, before she turned her attention to the third couple.

Matt and Linda Duprey. At first, Megan had read sympathy and fear in both their eyes; especially those of Matt, the self-made millionaire to whose West Indies island The Dream was headed. Now, however, they were clearly absorbed with one another; their reportedly 'rocky marriage' strengthening visibly in the holding of hands, and the knowledge that one wrong move would see them without any use for all their money.

Megan 'eavesdropped' shamelessly on the silent glances between Matt and Linda. Glances that clearly said: *I'll never be unfaithful again, so long as we live through this. There will never there be anyone else.*

It would be nice to think that something good and true could come out of this dangerous situation. But, if she was honest, Megan couldn't help cynically wondering if – once they'd been rescued – whether Matt's eyes would begin roving again, and if Linda's legendary jealousy would see her wielding any weapon to keep Matt at her side?

Megan closed her eyes, letting her forehead sink to her palm and her sore cheek met with Zeus's lower leg. She drew a sharp breath, stifled the sound with her fingertips; felt Zeus adjust his stance beside her.

Stop it! Think of something else.

Maybe, she thought dispassionately, everyone here was absorbing the peculiar atmosphere in order to harness the fear and drama. Dick Melancamp could direct a hostage film starring Jack Hodges. Then Megan wondered peevishly what poor starlet they'd pay a fortune to play the part of Megan Lacey? The woman at whom everyone shot sympathetic glances, until they were convinced that she was tainted, corrupted by sex with the second-in-command?

It was only as the thought struck her, that Megan suddenly realised she was no longer 'one of them'; a hostage pure and simple. She was marked – maybe for ever in their eyes – as part of the ruthless gang. If not by choice, then by sleeping with their most powerful male member.

Oh, my God! Why hadn't she thought of that before now? After all, Zeus had virtually paraded her as a loose woman, whose '*inventiveness*' had delighted him. So, who would ever believe the truth? As long as they lived, every passenger would be convinced that she'd taken part in some kind of sordid sexual act with the tall terrorist.

They wouldn't consider that even if she had – which she hadn't – her choice would have been either to submit, or watch one of them die. Or – far worse, to have found herself in Hades' brutal clutches. No, they would remember her forever as a traitor. Megan didn't blame them for their shuttered glances. In their shoes, she might well have come to the same false conclusion.

At that moment, when despair seemed ready to swallow her whole, Megan glanced up to see Suzanne smiling at her. It was, as always, a wonderful boost to her morale. The other woman's smile seemed to say: *I know that you're doing this, for us all.* And, most eloquently, it also said: *Thank you!*

Megan's eyelids drooped. Lulled by the warmth and quiet of the cabin, with the cool pillar at her back, she gave in to the urge to close her eyes. Oblivious to Zeus's frown as sleep claimed her, she leaned against his lower leg, as well as the pillar for support…

'Megan..?' she was in the kitchen of the flat above her business, cooking for Jordan. They were each drinking a glass of red wine and he was fascinated by the speed with which she chopped and shaped vegetables. Standing behind her, he slipped an arm around her waist. 'Darling – someone must have told you about the fast track to a man's heart!'

Laughing, Megan sprinkled fresh vegetables into the chicken casserole, added coriander and pushed the dish into the small wood-burning stove. She rose on her tip-toes and briefly kissed his sensual mouth.

'So, you'll marry me?' He looked vulnerable and Jordan *never* looked vulnerable. It was only that strained, lost look that convinced Megan he wasn't kidding around.

'I…' She gazed at him, speechless with astonishment. Was Jordan proposing?

She shook her head, batting him on the chest with a plastic spoon. 'Aren't we OK as we are?'

A sexy smile curved his mouth. 'Just say "yes", and we'll get married tomorrow.'

'No chance, Buster!'

'Not ever?' He had that nervous, uncertain look again.

'Not tomorrow.' She reached up, threaded her fingers around his neck, tangled them with the hair brushing the collar of his white shirt. 'Maybe in a couple of months.'

'That's "yes"?'

'No, it's "maybe".'

'You know that I'm an expert in interrogation?'

'I know, *Detective* Elliot.'

'Do you love me?'

'You're definitely growing on me, Jordan.'

'You're evading the question!'

Megan shrugged, tingling crazily all over as his hand cupped her well-rounded breast.

'How does that make you feel?'

'Maybe I will marry you, after all!' She laughed against his mouth before he kissed her soundly.

'Do you love me?'

'Yes, Jordan, I love you. I thought you knew that?'

'If you don't like it, we can change it.' Jordan said a few moments later, placing a small maroon velvet box into the palm of her hand.

Slowly, delicious anticipation mounting, Megan opened the hinged lid to reveal an emerald surrounded by light-loving diamonds and set on a delicate gold band. Tears blurred her eyes as she gazed down at the delicate ring. 'It's exquisite!'

He slipped the ring on her finger. 'Marry me soon?'

'Oh, Jordan!'

'The thing is…' He paused, looking mildly uncomfortable. 'I've to go away on a case very soon.'

'For how long?' Megan was horrified.

'Not too long. A couple of weeks – maybe a month at most. I don't leave until next week.' Those clear, intense blue eyes soothed away the shock of his words, his kiss banished it further.

'I was going to wait till I got back. But I need you to know that I'm committed to you, Megan,' he continued, looking uncertain again as he grimaced and shoved his fingers through his hair. 'Hell, that's not it. The truth is that I don't want you hanging out with other blokes while I'm gone.'

'Other men? Me? You're *far* more likely to meet some exotic beauty while you're working away, and I won't see you for dust,' Megan teased. 'I'll be standing at the altar, and you'll be thousands of miles away thinking, "Wasn't I supposed to be somewhere today? This date rings a bell!"' Megan fiddled with his loosened tie, missing his frown as she gave a husky laugh. 'If you come back – we can think about it.'

'I don't need to think about it, Megan. I want to marry you – very soon.'

The urgency in his tone puzzled her, but Megan merely shook her head. 'I'd be hard pushed to organise a wedding in a couple of months.'

'Even a small one?'

'Even a tiny one.' Megan smiled, captivated by the light in Jordan's blue eyes.

'But you could do it?' The sexy smile slanting his mouth had Megan ready to agree to anything, but she shook her head decisively.

Jordan said hopefully, 'You know, we could always elope – and tell everyone afterwards?'

Megan was transfixed by the ring, so just smiled as she looked from it to Jordan. Laughing because he looked seriously bewildered, she shook her head. 'All brides expect their wedding day to be turned into a three-ring circus.'

'Megan, it's got to be what we both want. You decide – church or registry office?'

'Church.'

'Hotel or our new home? Maybe we could find some- where before we're married?'

'You could move in here.'

'With your business downstairs?' Jordan shook his head. 'No way.'

'I'm not selling this.'

'I don't want you to, love. And I don't want to move to the other side of the world. I just don't want the door bell going every time we want to be alone together.'

'No, I don't either,' Megan responded thoughtfully. 'If I could live anywhere in London – I'd love it to be in Dock- lands. One of those converted warehouses with big arched windows looking out over the Thames, where we could watch the traffic sailing up and down the river. If we stay in London, I'd like to live near water; it's soothing.'

'I could manage that.' A look of mild shock flickered in his eyes.

'Oh, don't worry, it's just a pipe dream,' Megan told him, well aware that they could never afford such a place. Cer- tainly not on what she earned! 'After all, Jordan – you're an engineer, not Rockefeller.'

One of his eyebrows twitched, his mouth curved up at one corner. 'You've heard of Elliot and Ponsonby Antiques?'

'That's like asking if I've heard of Marks and Spencer!' Megan laughed, her newly-engaged, somewhat woolly state of mind only slowly latching on to Jordan's inference – that he – or his family was the 'Elliot' in one of the largest and most reputable antique dealers in London. 'Is it really…?'

'My father and uncle.'

'Just tell me that you're not a parasitic son who's trying hard to blow "Daddy's" fortune.'

'Nope. I'm a lucky son who's always been encouraged to

do what I want. Dad settled a small fortune on me – in trust – and I've hardly touched it.' He named a figure that sounded more like a big lottery win than anything a fiancé of hers would have 'in trust'.

'Oh.'

'What do you mean, "Oh"?'

'Well, I don't know. It's a bit weird. I'd imagined us buying somewhere together, you know, struggling and all that stuff.'

He laughed. 'It would be as much yours as mine, Megan.' And then, seeing the uncertainty in her eyes, he added, 'We'd be married, for pity's sake!'

'What about what *you* want? Where do *you* want to live?'

'I couldn't care less. I just want to live with you!'

But Megan hesitated too long. The curve he'd thrown was just too much to take in. She didn't even know if she was glad or not that Jordan was stinking rich.

'Most women would be bloody pleased!'

'I'm just shocked – OK?'

'So shocked, that you're now not sure that you want to marry me?'

'Yes!' As soon as the word was out, Megan regretted it. She put her fingers flat against Jordan's chest, feeling his heartbeat thump against her hands. 'Jordan, I don't know. I mean, I love you – and that's *all* I know.'

'If I'd thought this was going to be a problem, I wouldn't have said anything.'

'I'm sorry – it's just – I've always handled my own finances, everything. I'm an independent woman, Jordan. I've had to be for years, and…'

'Look, I'm not offering you money to sleep with me,' he retorted harshly. 'All I said was that we can live wherever you want.'

'But you're so rich, you could have anyone…'

'I haven't even touched the bloody money! Megan,

doesn't that tell you anything?' At her light frown, he continued, 'I haven't shared my life, or my money, with anyone.'

So intense were his eyes, his anger and confusion – and yes, his hurt – that Megan cringed. What the hell was she doing? Would she marry Jordan if he was an ordinary Joe Bloggs? Of course she would! He was offering her the world on a beautiful plate – and she was hesitating?

'Why do you want me, when you have everything?'

His eyes darkened and Megan knew she'd said too much. 'Haven't you been listening to a word I've said?' he ground out angrily. 'Can't you see that without you, I don't have *anything*!'

Megan hugged herself, stared up at Jordan's hard, masculine features. Did he really mean that?

'I love you. I can't say it any other way,' he added firmly. 'If the fact that I have money changes everything, maybe I'd better come back tomorrow when you've had chance to take it all in?'

Maybe? When Megan didn't respond, Jordan shoved his fingers back through his silky dark blond hair and turned for the door. 'I'm still "me", you know!'

'Jordan…' she ran after him, catching hold of his arm. 'Please don't go.'

She felt his frame stiffen, heard a controlled breath leave him.

'Please stay. I just don't want money to change anything between us.' He didn't look at her until she added, 'I want us to choose somewhere together.'

'What's the real reason, Megan? The real reason you freaked out, just now, when you found out that I've got money?'

Megan recovered her nerve as Jordan's eyes softened and he put his hands on her shoulders. 'My mother had a fling with a rich guy…' she worried at her bottom lip with white, even teeth.

'It didn't work out?' Jordan frowned.

'No, it didn't,' Megan agreed sadly. 'She wasn't over my dad, so she wasn't exactly emotionally stable. But when the guy threw her over – he played around a lot and wasn't discreet – my mother tried to end her life.' Megan grimaced. 'Unfortunately, she also began drinking again.'

The remnants of confusion melted from Jordan's clear blue eyes. 'Megan, money doesn't make bastards out of all of us, you know.'

'Don't go,' she murmured helplessly.

A second later he was holding her tightly against his chest. 'I'll move in here, if that's what you want.'

When Megan looked up at him, and then around at her tiny flat, they both found themselves laughing. The dining area was completely given over to files, plants, a computer, bookshelves and the lounge was delightfully, outrageously sunny – but small.

'That single bed of yours will *have* to go!' he told her with a grin.

That amazing smile – the sensuality in his darkened eyes as he glanced at her bedroom door made Megan laugh again. 'Maybe your idea's best – there isn't room in there for a bigger bed. I'll definitely need an extension for you!'

'I don't care, we'll use your single one.' He kissed her then, and all Megan wanted to do was drag him in to her bedroom. 'Now?' She leant back in his arms, felt his heart race beneath her palm.

'What about the food?'

'It'll be half-an-hour before it's ready,' she murmured, wanting…needing Jordan to make love to her.

'OK?' she added huskily, wrapping her fingers around his neck, leaning her generous softness against his rock-hard chest and raising herself on her tip-toes to press her mouth to his.

He was already aroused, and his hardness increased as he

returned her kiss with such sensuality, that Megan shivered all over, gasping his name and trembling as his hands caressed the curves of her body. His breathing was ragged and shallow, and he drew a sharp breath when her hand found him through his clothes.

'Megan..!' Gently, he drew her hand away.

'I need you.'

He laughed, but not cruelly as he held her hands down at her side, 'Sweetheart, I'm proving something to you here. You're different. We can both wait.' A sexy grin slanted his mouth, 'Or, at least until you've locked the door!'

'Do you remember that night we first met?'

Jordan grimaced. 'I was smashed – you could've been a gorilla and I'd have tried it on.'

Megan broke into peals of laughter. 'I thought…I thought you were revolting! I didn't want to see you ever again!'

'Don't remind me.' He gave her a slightly embarrassed grin. 'When I sobered up, it took fifteen phone calls and all the flowers in London to get you back on the hook.'

'Why did you bother?' Megan tilted her head to one side, her hair tumbled and caught the soft evening light in its waves.

'I couldn't believe that you'd tipped trifle in my lap and told me to "go away"!' They both laughed – especially as they both knew that Megan's language had been much stronger.

'You'd been a real pain, all night. I was trying to serve food to you and your rowdy mates, and every time I came near you, you touched me!'

'That was Ray – although you do have beautiful legs.'

'Don't change the subject!'

'I fell in love with you there and then.'

Jordan pushed his fingers into her hair, leant down to kiss her and grabbed her hand. 'Come on – dinner can wait. I've got something to show you.'

Jordan's mouth touched hers again and Megan melted as his cool lips covered hers, the warmth of his tongue an exciting, sensually erotic contrast.

She'd completely forgotten where she was, until he said, 'We'd better go. And, when we get where we're going, I want you to close your eyes.'

'What, like – "here's a surprise, close your eyes"?' Megan said as she slid into his low car, laughing as she added, 'You're a nut-case, Jordan!'

When they arrived at their destination, she noted that the whole complex was surrounded by a low brick wall, topped with ornate wrought iron railings. A navy-uniformed security guard appeared, opening the electric wrought iron security gates and saluted. 'Good evening, Mr Elliot.'

'Hi, Sam.' Jordan smiled, before driving down the cobbled road to the waterfront.

'Close your eyes, Miss Lacey,' he said firmly, glancing sideways at Megan who obediently did as she was told.

He guided her from the car, his arm around her waist. 'OK, you can open your eyes now, Megan. Look up there.'

Green eyes widened, her mouth fell open. Up there, on the fourth floor of the converted warehouse, was the arched floor-to-ceiling window Megan had described, underlined by a wrought iron balcony decorated with early Spring flowers.

'Do you want to look inside?' He dangled a bunch of keys from his forefinger, grinning as he enjoyed Megan's speechless delight.

The view across the river, the dark red brick building – everything was *exactly* as she'd imagined it to be.

'This is totally unreal, Jordan. It's as though you've somehow completely read my mind!'

'No.' He leaned back on the railing, looking up at the property as he shook his head. 'It's much more bizarre than that.'

Megan looked at him quizzically, moving closer to take his hand. 'What do you mean?'

Jordan had rarely looked so serious – an expression that sent little shivers racing down her spine. 'When you described your ideal home, Megan – I was utterly shaken. Because, it was an *exact* description of where I live.'

Astonished, Megan could only stare at him in open-mouthed astonishment. 'You mean…you mean you have an apartment here?'

'Yep. Which is why I reckon you must be a witch!' His lips twitched with amusement. 'Not only are you torturing me with your sexy body, it looks as if you've taken over my mind and soul as well.' His strong fingers teased her luxuriant hair, gently pulling her closer to him.

'It's just a coincidence.' A playful light entered her eyes. 'But just in case I *do* have supernatural powers – don't go trying to keep any secrets from me in future, Mr Elliot!'

'Come on, I'll show you inside,' he said, but as he took her hand, Megan missed the slightly-troubled look in his eyes.

'Someone had better pinch me – and tell me that I'm not dreaming!' Megan knelt on the wide, cushion-covered windowsill, staring in awe at the fantastic view of the Thames and the lights of the city, sparkling like diamonds in the dusk.

'Wake up, Lacey!'

'Umm..?' Oh, Lord, the window seat was hard, and it was so hot and…

'Wake up!' A large hand was shaking her shoulder and reluctantly her eyes opened. It wasn't dusk in London. She was on board The Dream.

'Ah…!' She gave a gasp of emotional pain. Jordan wasn't there. *He was never bloody there*! And he *never* would be again.

The other hostages slept, and Megan guessed that she must have been sleeping for the best part of eight hours.

'Zeus, it's your turn go and get some rest – and take that woman with you,' Hades growled, jerking his thumb at the saloon doors.

Megan tensed herself, but as she stood up, something scraped against her stomach.

Oh, lord! It was the note which the young member of the crew had slipped into her uniform, earlier in the day. Immediately, Megan wrapped her arms around her stomach, pretending more pain than she felt in order to keep the note from dropping out. Zeus shot her an impatient look, gesturing for her to move out of the room before him.

'Zeus!' Hades shouted across the room. 'Let me know when you get tired of that woman. I might find a use for her!'

Revulsion surged through Megan. Instinctively, foolishly, she glanced to Zeus for some kind of reassurance. But his eyes were black and cold as ever. 'Move yourself!'

Her only aim was to reach the bathroom and read the note. It would have to be in the shower, with her back to Zeus. It was the only time she managed to escape his attention. Or whilst he slept. That was it, whilst he slept... But did he *ever* sleep?

She was suddenly overcome by a sudden longing for the husband who'd deserted her; to feel the comforting strength of his arms holding her firmly and protectively against his powerful chest. Which reminded her...

'Zeus?' she said as he slid the security card into the cabin door lock, and pushed the door open. 'You took my photo album. Can I please have it back?'

At first, she didn't think he'd heard her, because he moved across the cabin to gaze out across a moonlit sea. However, after a long silence, he asked, 'Why do you want it back?'

He didn't turn on the light, so Megan stood in the shadows, thinking what a stupid question that was. 'Why do you think?'

'I asked you.'

'I miss my husband. I want to look at his photograph.'

There was a pause. Two, three heartbeats, and then Zeus held out the album towards her.

'Thank you,' she whispered, and despite his mask, she sensed that the man was exhausted. Which suddenly had the effect of making her feel stronger and more alert. 'You're tired?'

He gave a slight nod, but didn't speak.

'Do you miss your wife?' Megan wasn't sure quite why she'd asked that question. Maybe because, somewhere in her subconscious, she needed to identify some kind of gentler emotion in the man. She didn't wait for his reply. Already she knew him well enough to know that he wouldn't give her one.

'It's strange being separated,' she continued in the face of his silence. 'It's like an aching, painful void that grows larger and deeper every day, unless you can somehow learn to patch up the hole.' Megan paused for a moment, before giving a heavy sigh. 'But, however hard you try, it's like being patched up with a gossamer-thin spider's web. It only takes one vivid memory; a subtle fragrance, or a song that reminds you of happier times – and you're all wide open again.'

She sat on the arm of the easy chair, about three feet from the man's back as she added in a husky voice, 'Every time I close my eyes, I dream about him. The worst part is, sometimes I hate him so much, I could kill him. And sometimes I love him so much, I just…I just ache.'

'He should not have allowed you to come on this cruise alone.'

Megan, about to correct him, fell silent. Zeus thought her

pain was for days of separation – not months. For her own safety and sanity, it would be better not to correct him.

'No one knows that The Dream has been taken over,' he added. 'So long as it remains that way, your husband won't worry about your safety.'

'He probably wouldn't worry anyway.' Megan closed her eyes on the truth of her words, then grimaced, hoping that Zeus hadn't heard.

Turning, he folded his arms. 'Why do you say that?'

A terrible weakness seemed to overcome Megan as she leaned against the back of the chair. Strangely, she forgot that this man was her enemy.

'He should be with me!' she muttered helplessly, only just managing to keep silent about the fact that Jordan had dumped her, and was probably on the far side of the globe with some beautiful woman in red leather pandering to his every need.

Even thinking about it was enough to almost make her gasp with agony. And suddenly she found herself snatching up the photograph album and slinging it violently across the cabin. 'Pig!'

As Zeus laughed, she yelled with frustration, launching herself at him, her clenched fists striking at his face and shoulders.

'You bastard!' she ground out thickly. 'It's not funny! You stinking, rotten bastard!'

Her eyes widened when he gripped her wrists and forced both her arms behind her back, raised her so her feet left the deck and gave her a jolt. 'It's not funny!' She kicked at his shins, watched black eyes narrow emotionlessly. 'Put me down!' Her hair flew around her shoulders as she flailed, strands flicking against his hard mouth.

He didn't put her down. He held her so they were nose to nose; Megan's temper at screaming pitch, while Zeus's cold amusement seemed to vibrate around the room.

'Whatever anger you feel for your husband, I suggest that you keep your temper to yourself,' he drawled menacingly. 'If you ask me, I reckon that temper of yours is probably the reason why he isn't here.'

'No! Put me down!' she gasped, attempting to wriggle from his iron grip. And then, quite suddenly, she was stunned and trembling as she felt his body harden against her.

Still holding her firmly with one hand, he raised the other to tear the uniform from her shivering figure; poppers straining and then breaking, spilling her full, creamy breasts against his cotton army shirt.

Megan was horrified, not only by his action, but also by her own body's response as a tide of deep crimson flooded over her cheeks.

'You have been without him too long,' Zeus said, never taking his cold black eyes from her.

'*No.*' she protested heatedly, although she knew that he was right. But...but she didn't want this!

Without warning, he lifted her, his hands gentle on the naked skin at the tops of her thighs. He pulled her legs around his waist, brought her full, firm breasts closer to his mouth. Warm breath broke on her skin – she tried to lurch away, but he was ready for that. His forearm angled up her back, forcing her to arch closer. And he caught her nipple with his lips.

Shuddering with revulsion, Megan put her palms on his shoulders, desperately trying to escape. Visions of Jordan making love to her flashed through her mind – and she hated *him*, too. She *must* get away from this man! But as she opened her eyes, the sight of his sculptured lips and tongue tormenting her breast confused everything inside her.

What on earth was she to do? Could she reach for his gun? Blow his brains out? But even the thought of doing so repulsed her. She might want to kill him, but Megan knew that she simply wasn't capable of cold-blooded murder. He's just a man, she told herself silently. Let him do this, and maybe you'll live. But no – *she couldn't*!

She jerked away from him, repulsed that she even for one, brief fleeting moment, had considered yielding without a fight. But, as she glanced frantically about her for some form of escape, she saw the tiny folded note that the young crew member had slipped inside her belt, and which was now lying on the floor by Zeus' foot. It glowed white in the dusk, mocking her. There was no way he could avoid seeing it, unless…unless she found some way to distract him.

Oh, God – please forgive me! she prayed fervently as she rested her hands on his shoulders, fingers reluctant, stiff, blanking her mind to everything except distracting Zeus as he caressed the soft curves of her body. As she forced herself to give a small, false sigh of pleasure, his dark eyes smouldered with sensuality – and triumph.

'Admit you have been without him too long.'

This time, Megan didn't deny it; instead, she twined her fingers around his neck, tried to bring his mouth to hers. The tiny note, visible in the corner of her eye, appeared to grow bigger every moment, until she was totally certain that the man couldn't fail to see it.

But he pulled back from her, didn't allow Megan to initiate a kiss. Too personal, she supposed. But without kissing her, would he see the note? 'I'd like to kiss you,' she whispered; her voice sounded hoarse with terror, not sultry as intended.

'Do not lie.' His chiselled mouth, the shadowy growth just peeping round the hole in his mask pulled into a taut line. 'I don't want you to fight me. But there is no necessity to lie.'

'I've never made love without kissing.'

'We will have sex. I "make love" to my wife.'

Normally, Megan would have jumped at the opportunity

to bring his wife into the picture and dig at his conscience. But she couldn't afford the risk this time. She had to keep his all-seeing eyes on *her*, and well away from the note on the floor.

'It's hot.' She breathed deeply again, pushed her hair back over one shoulder, but Zeus pressed his mouth to her skin again, the fingers of one of his supporting hands kneading the back of her thigh. She trapped a pleasurable sigh, but it turned to a deep growl in her throat and Megan grimaced. Black eyes flicked up to hers, and she glimpsed something like triumph? Amusement? Anger? Or all three?

Don't look down! She begged him silently. But she knew that she needed to do more than pray. He'd moved slightly, but not enough, and the note was still clearly visible on the burgundy carpet. Megan tried to think what Jordan enjoyed, and her fingers instinctively pushed into his shoulder muscles. She leaned back, letting her head fall to one side, hair streaming downwards, taking the chance that he would watch her and not look down at the floor. Her heart bumped for those seconds whilst she let her eyes close, forcing herself to give a low moan of pleasure.

'Megan..?'

Black eyes burned into her as she forced a breathy, 'Yes?'

'I didn't want you to fight me, but I'm puzzled by your response.'

Oh, Lord – she'd gone too far!

'What are you up to?' he demanded.

Megan's heart thumped with fear. 'N-Nothing,' she muttered, before adding quickly, 'Maybe, you're right? Maybe I've been too long without my husband.'

Blatant disbelief filled his eyes. 'Are you inviting me into your bed?'

He'd asked her that question before and Megan had so far managed to side-step it. Now, however, she would somehow have to control her screaming revulsion; stifle her instinctive denial. And all because of that little piece of paper, lying on the floor by his foot.

'Yes,' she lied, because she had no choice.

'I don't believe you.'

'I…I'm telling the truth.'

'No. There is something – a scheme? – in your eyes.'

'I did think about shooting you with your own gun,' Megan saw his gaze drop to her breasts as she wriggled against him. 'But unlike you, I'm not capable of murder.'

'And yet, it seems that you want me to believe you're capable of behaving like a loose woman?'

Megan bit down on her bottom lip. It wasn't easy trying to fool this man. He might want to believe her, but his all-seeing eyes seemed to gaze right through her; past the part she was playing and straight into her soul.

'Maybe…maybe I really am that sort of woman?' she said weakly, knowing that the words didn't sound convincing, but unable to think of anything else to say.

Derision mixed with dark lust in his eyes. He released the arm holding her hips to him and Megan dropped to her feet. Yes! The note was now safely hidden beneath her foot.

'Prove it!'

'What?' She gazed at him in bewilderment for a moment.

'If you want me to believe that you're a loose woman – you can prove it by taking off your clothes.'

Megan froze at his words. If she wasn't convincing now, she was going to be in deep trouble. Especially as he was already suspicious of her motives; clearly believing that she was playing some sort of game.

She let her hair fall forwards to hide her face and took a deep breath, before letting her uniform dress fall down into a dark pool at her feet. In a slight movement, she removed her foot delicately from the neck of the dress, relieved when the fabric fully concealed that vital piece of paper.

If nothing else, she told herself as she moved slowly towards him, as far as the safety of the other prisoners on the boat was concerned, she had to be making the right decision.

And then she realised that she had to…she must try and find some way to stop him hurting the others. And, unfortunately, she could only think of one way to ensure that… 'If…if you promise not to hurt anyone on board,' she whispered, placing her hands on his chest, 'I…I'll try to please you.'

Shocked. Yes, she'd shocked him with her words – *almost as much as she'd managed to shock herself*!

Yet he stood like a rock, didn't touch her, or move a muscle. He wasn't going to help her. Megan's fingers trembled as she unfastened the buttons of his thick cotton shirt with a devastating slowness that could be either reluctance, or sensuality. She felt him jolt as her cool fingers worked inside his shirt, spread across his powerful shoulders and she brought her near-naked body closer so that where a line of skin was bared, it touched hers.

Megan thought she was mentally prepared for what she must do; but she wasn't prepared for Zeus's body to burn against hers the way Jordan's did. She closed her eyes, about to slip into the sensual world she'd shared with her husband, but Zeus caught her wrists.

'Wait.'

Megan looked into those black eyes, frowned slightly, her heart pounding like a sledgehammer.

'Turn around.'

When she just stared, her mouth falling open on a gasp, he turned her so her naked back faced him. 'What…what are you doing?' she cried helplessly.

'Close your eyes,' he commanded roughly No sooner had he spoken than something soft and silky shimmered, then covered her eyes. A little light permeated the fabric, then none as Zeus knotted the blindfold at the back of her head.

His fingers touched the tips of Megan's. 'Where do you want to do this?'

Her mind spun helplessly, her brain struggling to comprehend what was happening to her. *I can't go through with this!* she screamed silently at the man she could no longer see. *I thought I could – but I can't!*

But even as the words formed in her mind, she knew that her own and the others' lives depended on her performance.

'M-my b-bed,' she stuttered, trembling like a leaf as he guided her across the room.

'Are you losing your nerve?'

'Yes…no…I don't know,' she whispered helplessly as he swung her up in his arms and placed her surprisingly gently down on the bed, before she felt the mattress give as he lay down beside her.

Desperation prompted Megan to frantically try and concentrate on Jordan's laughing, sensuous image. There's only one thing you can do, she told herself grimly. The only way you've a hope of surviving this, is to pretend that it's Jordan lying beside you – and not this dark, extremely dangerous stranger.

But giving herself good advice was one thing – trying to force herself to carry it out, was quite another. She shivered helplessly; cold sweat breaking out on her forehead as she felt his hard body turning towards her.

'Shush…' he murmured, gently stroking her body. Beneath the mastery of his touch, she found herself involuntarily relaxing, her fears dissolving in response to the throbbing intensity and pleasure engendered by his magical hands. And what Megan learned about herself in the dark hours that followed, she swore she'd never share with another living soul.

chapter four

Until she was certain that Zeus was deep in sleep, Megan didn't attempt to leave his side. The discarded silk scarf lay across the shared pillow; Zeus having pulled on his mask before unknotting the scarf from her eyes. She slid from beneath the warm covers, didn't dare look back in the moonlit cabin for fear of him wakening or of losing her nerve.

She grabbed up the uniform and the crumpled, folded note, and hurried into the bathroom. Fingers trembling, Megan unfolded the note, expecting Zeus to materialise through the closed door any second – and that would be it. Curtains!

From the fat fold of paper fell a painkiller. There was nothing written on the paper around it. '*No*!' Anger, disbelief, shame and reality hit Megan like a slap. She'd gone through all that...for a single, bloody painkiller! 'Oh, Jordan...' she whispered, throwing the pill and the paper down the toilet, and flushing them away.

She knew such anger, such frustration, and there was nowhere and no one to vent it on. A stream of whispered, growled curses broke from her; she shoved her fist into her mouth when a light tap sounded on the bathroom door.

'You have been long enough.'

'Just a minute...'

'Open the door.'

'In...in a minute...' A glance at her desperately dishevelled appearance, the wet tears on her cheeks saw a quick dash to the sink, to try and wash away her anger.

'Now, Lacey.'

'Oh, what the hell!' She unlocked the door, water still dripping from her hands and face, wrapped a bath sheet around her and immediately turned her back on Zeus.

'Do not lock this door at any time.'

'No.'

'Are you regretting the sex?'

Megan shook her head, gripped the towel more tightly around her. 'What difference does it make?'

'None.' A stolen glance in the mirror showed Zeus leaning against the doorframe, his shirt still unfastened. A terrible wave of sensual awareness threatened to drown her.

Despair licked like hot flames through her because she wanted Jordan to hold her, obliterate what she'd done with this man. She wanted to explain that all the time – especially in the darkness – it was Jordan she'd loved. Most of all, she wanted to turn back the clock and not know what she was capable of in order to survive.

'Come back to bed.' There was a thread of gentleness in his accented tone Megan hadn't heard before, it pulled at her, then knotted in awful confusion.

'I will,' she took a deep breath, gambling a little by telling the truth, 'I...I haven't been unfaithful to my husband before...' Megan glanced up, but saw no warmth in his eyes, no invitation to assuage her guilt. If she could get to know him better, would it make her feel less remorseful?

She slid beneath the covers, Zeus followed her. For a long time, she lay there with her eyes wide open, staring at nothing, blanking her mind against pleasure given and received.

Unexpectedly, Zeus turned to face her. 'You're not able to sleep?'

'I'm not tired.'

'Do you have any family?'

His question surprised Megan. She smiled, felt a bit better, that was what she needed – to talk to this man.

'No children. Just...just a husband.'

Wriggling to get comfortable against Zeus's solid shoulder, Megan tucked her hair behind her ear, caught her breath when his fingers pushed the thick bath sheet from her curves.

'I like to touch you, while you speak.'

'Ah…' her insides clenched in response as she rested her hand at his waist. 'My father died when I was sixteen…' she babbled, reaching for old anecdotes from a time gone by. 'Do you know what a soap opera is?'

The moonlight caught a flicker of amusement in black eyes; she giggled at his wry, 'I believe no country is safe from them.'

'There's this thing I do – it's kind of crazy.' His hand moved on her hip – a sexy, yet comforting gesture. 'Sometimes, I dramatise things that happen. You know, when I'm doing something mundane, like going to the bank, I might pretend…' Megan laughed softly against his shoulder. 'I'll pretend that the man in front is my long-lost uncle – and he's a millionaire!'

She tilted back her head, noting that there was a definite glint of amusement in those blacker-than-black eyes. 'It's all nonsense really. It just keeps me laughing when there's not a lot to laugh about. I come out with daft lines like, ''Don't worry, Megan. So what if your father's dead and your mother's an alcoholic, and you've got no money so you have to walk six miles to college. Not to mention the fact that your clothes are from a charity shop. And it doesn't matter that the family was once rich, or that…'

'Was it really that bad?'

Megan leant her cheek on her palm, clouds moved over the moon's bright face; the ensuing lack of light lending a normality to their conversation. In the dark, she couldn't see his mask, could only feel his body close to hers; the touch of his knowing fingers on her skin.

'No, I exaggerated a bit.' She grimaced. 'I just list all my disasters and they sound like the plot for a silly soap opera. And it makes me laugh even when I feel like crying.'

Zeus frowned. 'You are crazy, Lacey.'

'I know.'

There was a silence as she laid her head on his shoulder, and her other self sought to trivialise what had happened…was happening, with Zeus… *Oh, just have sex with him, don't worry about it – at least you're helping to keep the other passengers alive. You're a hostage, you have no choice,* she told herself as firmly as she could.

Outside her thoughts, Zeus's palm moved over her thigh, upwards to cup her breast. She closed her eyes in an attempt to deny that she found his touch arousing; the pit of her stomach fizzing when his lips found her nipple, teasing it to hardness.

No amount of denial would keep a soft sigh from escaping her; gentle – he was so gentle, then his hand moved to push her knees apart.

Megan's eyes flew open, 'No…!' She clamped her knees together despite the sensual languor stealing through her limbs.

'You forget your promise?'

What promise? Then she remembered as Zeus gently nudged her legs apart. In return for…for this, he'd promised not to hurt her fellow hostages.

'I…yes…no, I…I haven't forgotten.'

Deftly, Zeus fastened the blindfold over Megan's eyes as she lay half against him. 'Can't you leave it off?' she whispered. 'It's so dark. I can't see you.'

'No.' His finger briefly touched her lips. 'I cannot do that.'

Megan blanked her mind to the betrayal her body welcomed, bit his shoulder and neck to muffle rising sounds of pleasure.

As he moved against her, she shuddered on wave upon

wave of powerful enchantment, and nothing prepared Megan for the way he made her cry out…made her respond.

Zeus's breathing was ragged as he rolled away from her, 'Perhaps you are so hungry for sex, you should be serving *that* instead of food?'

Those words brought reality crashing into Megan's giddy euphoria. She gasped, catching her lip in her teeth. Reality became a deep, yawning hole as he ran his fingertips down the length of her body.

'*Bastard*!' she cried, her hand coming up to strike him. But he caught her wrist and pushed it hard down into the pillow.

'I promised not to hurt you, Lacey. So, don't try to hurt me – OK?'

For a second, she froze, before realising that to him she was nothing; merely an object – one with whom he had a pact. On another level, Megan knew that something inside her had touched something deep inside this man. He would never admit it – and she would never admit it to anyone else, either – but it already existed in an intangible form. It was something strange: like a whispering and lonely soul reaching out…touching…and then stunned at what it finds. So stunned, that it was immediately forced into rejection.

'Sleep now, Megan.'

He was right. She was tired; mentally exhausted from too much sharp-edged emotion, and physically weary from their explosive love-making.

Although her mind reviled and rebelled, she took mercy on herself, let her head drop on to his broad, cotton-clad shoulder, vaguely aware that he was removing her blindfold. And once again, visions of Jordan strode through her dreams; his sexy smile and warm, possessive eyes. Clinging to the thought of her husband was providing the only escape for her troubled mind. Holding tight to the thought of Jordan, was the only way she could keep a grasp on her sanity in this dreadful situation.

She woke in the light, desperate to see Jordan's image in the photographs; Zeus was in the bathroom – she could hear him moving around. Megan slipped the informal album out from under the pillow, opened it at the moment when her bouquet of freesia's and baby's breath soared into the air, her own and Jordan's backs turned to the guests…

On the opposite page, Jordan tugged her towards the lush trees, to the stream beyond, where they sat on smooth boulders, dressed up to the nines, laughing, skimming stones, like naughty kids playing hooky.

'Most people don't walk away from their own wedding reception, Jordan,' Megan had wriggled from the boulder to lie in the soft, deep grass, her head on Jordan's lap.

The water reflected in his blue eyes, a grin slanted his mouth. 'Do you care?' he'd asked, his fingers playing with copper-coloured curls, he'd picked a long strand of grass and stroked it lightly across her neck and shoulders.

In turn, Megan reached up and stroked a finger along his bottom lip. 'I reckon six hours of toasting and eating and dancing is enough for anyone, Jordan.'

Secretly, Megan wondered if Ray Blackmore had been the worse for drink? If the way he'd all but wrenched her from Jordan's side to dance, had anything to do with her husband's decision to cut and run.

'What did Ray Blackmore say to you?' His thumb smoothed across her brow, as though he read her mind.

'I couldn't tell,' Megan lied. 'He's so drunk.'

Ray Blackmore. The one associate of Jordan's that Megan despised. He'd whirled her on to the dance floor, his features heavy, distorted by alcohol. 'You've got great breasts, Megan!' he'd leered, trying to make their dance slow and smoochy, whilst all around them the guests were attempting their own interpretations of the 'Lambada'.

'I think that's far too personal, Ray. If you're trying to say you're sorry for all the rotten things you've said to me…'

'I'm not sorry 'bout any of that,' he slurred, his palm moving dangerously close to her curves, 'It won't work out between you'n Jordan – you shoulda' listened to me, Sweet Lips. It'll never work out.'

Revulsion had squirmed inside her and she'd twisted away from his groping hands, straight into Jordan's arms. 'Time we left, Megan.'

Relief brought a broad smile from Megan. 'Great!'

By the time they'd said goodbye to everyone, another half-hour had passed. They were almost at the huge glass doors which opened out on to vast, wooded grounds. Disbelief filled her when Ray soberly shook Jordan's hand, wished him well, then took Megan's hand in his and kissed the back of it in a chivalrous gesture. No one – Jordan included – would ever believe just how Ray had tried to blight their whole relationship. As two-faced as Ray himself, Megan smiled brightly, thanking him for his good wishes with brittle politeness.

Guests spilled out into the grounds behind the couple, someone calling out, 'Don't look round when you throw your flowers!'

Megan, recognising Alexa's voice, laughed up at Jordan as she threw the flowers in a great, wide sweep behind her. There was an excited cheer, and as Megan glanced back, she saw her friend waving the bouquet and blowing kisses at the newly-weds.

'Just so long as he didn't offend you, Megan. Ray can be a jerk when he's had too much alcohol.'

Megan smiled. Ray could be a jerk without any help from alcohol.

'I'm relieved you two get along better now.' Jordan drew Megan upwards so his mouth brushed hers, 'It could have been difficult if you'd held a grudge against him.'

She wondered if there was ever the 'right time' to tell a

brand-new husband that his best man was a total creep? That the ill-feeling between them would – if Ray had his way – be the kiss of death for Jordan and Megan's relationship? After all, the two men had worked together for eight years, while Jordan had only known his new wife for less than a year.

'This time tomorrow, we'll be four thousand miles away.' Jordan loosened his tie. 'You all packed, darling?'

'More or less. I've four bikinis and some shorts and T-shirts,' she laughed against his mouth. 'How about you? I hope your "pager" is staying at home in a drawer.'

'OK…' he held up his hands. 'I promise – no pager.'

'Oh, no! I can't bear it!' Megan clasped her hands dramatically at her breasts. It looks as if we'll have to spend our honeymoon in the Canary Islands – quite alone without your pager. What on earth will we do?'

'What *have* you been drinking?' Jordan shook with laughter. 'It looks as if I've married a really crazy woman.'

'Oh no!' Megan put the flat of her hand to her forehead. 'You mean you didn't realise? Jordan! I thought you knew!'

A very sexy smile slanted Jordan's mouth, the deep dimple slashing his cheek. 'Come on,' he tugged her towards the river edge. 'I'm going to…'

'You've got to wade through the meringue first, Buster!'

At the memory of her own soft laughter, the lump in her throat brought Megan sharply back to the present. She sniffed, tears filling her eyes and preventing her from focusing on the last of the photo's in the book.

And, in the same moment, she became aware of the dark form beside the bed. Dressed in clean fatigues. Black eyes expressionless. She pressed her lips together, brushing a hand across her wet cheeks.

'Zeus!' A loud rap on the cabin door saw his eyes blaze with rage. Roughly, he leaned down and shoved the album under the pillow.

'Stay there!' he hissed grimly, before turning to face the door. 'Good morning, Artemis,' he said as the woman swept inside their cabin.

'We have trouble,' she announced imperiously, while Megan watched as Zeus instinctively reached for the gun in his shoulder holster.

'No, it is stopped – the attempt to send messages is stopped.' Slyly, Artemis's eyes slid to Megan. 'I come to tell you that you must punish your woman, Zeus. Then you must bring her along to the stateroom, so the fools can see that she is "paying" for their stupidity!' She leaned her feline form against him, 'They think they are getting away with their stupidity. They must learn the error of their ways!'

Megan's mind ran up against a brick wall. Zeus was going to beat her senseless to punish others. His flat response: 'Very well,' broke through the sledgehammer beat of her heart. Slowly, a coldness began at her toes, freezing her muscles, then whole limbs. So much so, that by the time Zeus closed the door, Megan could hardly breathe with fright; raggedly dragging air into her paralysed lungs. He'd promised! He'd promised he wouldn't hurt her!

'You…you…' She tried to remind him, her whole being stiff like a corpse against the wall of the cabin. 'You…promised!' The last word left her on a rush of panicked air.

Zeus merely glanced at her, then entered the bathroom. A moment later he reached for Megan, who by then was far too stunned by panic to even flinch. His fingers touched her lips, pushed something dry and round on her tongue, then he tipped a glass to her mouth – all this in silence. Megan felt her muscles relax, her head sink into softness, then she knew no more.

Her head thumped and whirled as if she'd been drinking alcohol for a month. She couldn't get comfortable, the pillow had turned hard against her cheek. Megan didn't know, didn't care where she was – it was too great an effort to open her eyes. She was only aware of voices snapping in command, of laughter edged with cruelty, of her own discomfort caused by the hard surface she sprawled on. Lights on the far side of her eyelids were so bright, it was no spur to open them. For a while, Megan dipped into semi-consciousness, asking herself no more questions, just drifting…drifting…

'Any more attempts to contact the outside world…' Artemis' loud voice was cutting and harsh. 'Any more nonsense, and another of you will suffer like this woman. There will be no pretty faces left amongst you. You will all be guilty of murder!'

What did she mean? Megan wondered, trying to make sense of the foreign woman's chilling words. 'Suffer like the woman?' Had Zeus beaten her? Megan dared not move an inch, lest a greater punishment rain down from Artemis.

When Megan thought she'd scream out with both frustration and panic, she felt her limp form being raised from the hard floor; her ears filled with the sound of a sob and a sniffle.

In silence she could feel herself being carried down corridors that she could visualise but not see; her eyes still stuck firmly closed. It was Zeus carrying her. Apparently, those well-muscled arms and deft fingers could inflict terrible pain as well as pleasure. She felt his change of pace as he carried her down the stairwell to the lower deck and along another corridor, then she felt the slight shifting of her weight as he pushed a security card through the door lock.

Woolly, everything was so woolly and undefined. The lighting was not so bright and Megan sensed that she and Zeus were alone. Eventually daring to open her eyes, she discovered that she was in the bathroom, just the light from the main cabin shining in a triangle. Enough light to see her white T-shirt was half-black – no…she squinted down…it was dark red…

'*No!*' *Not blood*…? Her own scream echoed into the corners of her mind. Blood. Dried hard against her, stiffening half the garment; her face too was half obliterated with the sticky mass.

Cold with shock, Megan trembled with panic, with anger. 'You…you promised…' she clutched the front of his shirt, struggled to focus on his dark eyes.

He didn't reply, but turned on the shower, his hands supporting her, washing away the stickiness, dropping the T-shirt into the shower basin, then the rest of her clothes. Warmth from the water seeped into Megan's chilled shocked state.

'What did you do to me?' She gripped his shirt. '*What?*'

Again, silence greeted her, fragrant shampoo worked the stiffness from her hair, whilst Zeus held her against him, supporting her with one arm around her waist. Megan could feel control slipping away, the vision of her bloodied self and fear giving rise to a scream of terror. But it wouldn't come out, it broke on an impotent gasp, washed down the plug hole with the water.

And yet…it dawned on Megan slowly that aside from the slight residual ache of her stiff limbs and scratched cheek, there were no other aches or pains.

And was she imagining it, or was Zeus's touch gentle? If not gentle, then definitely not that of a man who deliberately inflicted pain?

Her hair was wet when he laid her on the bed; gingerly, Megan traced fingertips over her head and neck, her nose and mouth, but could find no wound.

'Zeus?' She pushed herself upright, light-headed at the too-fast movement, 'What's happening?'

He moved into her line of vision, his clothes black, dry. Those dark, emotionless eyes looked down at her. 'What?'

she whispered, so confused it was painful.

He crouched beside her, a single finger touching her lips. 'Sleep now, Lacey.'

'Please…?' She grasped his hand before he could move away. 'Please tell me?' Words spurted, 'Zeus, there's no pain, but I saw…' Had she flipped over the edge? Would she never feel anything again?

'You saw what others saw. It is enough. You can sleep alone tonight.'

Still Megan clutched his hand. 'I don't understand?'

There was a single, muted light shining over the other bunk; it was enough for Megan to see a trace of emotion in those dark, black eyes. 'I cannot be seen to treat you well. That is all you need to understand.'

The truth filtered through the woolly layers shrouding Megan's mind. *There was no pain because he hadn't hurt her*!

He'd drugged her? Almost certainly. But he'd done that to save her. Somehow, then, he'd made her appear as if he'd taken her to within inches of her life. A ridiculous surge of gratitude broke free in a small smile; she frowned then because anger flashed in his eyes.

'If we are ever amongst the others and the same situation arises, Lacey, I will have no choice. This you must understand.'

She nodded, distracted by a phial on her bedside table, eyes focusing slowly on the label, 'Theatrical blood'. 'I understand.' But she also understood that given the choice, Zeus wouldn't hurt her; not because of the pact she'd drawn him into, or because they'd made love. Quite simply, he didn't want to hurt her; there was immense, euphoric relief in that.

Slowly, as if possessed, Megan knelt, slid her arms around his neck and held him until his arms banded her waist. That contact, purely Megan's reaction to relief, sparked the strange, dark attraction between them, their souls whispering whilst they remained silent, bonding through loneliness.

Megan didn't sleep alone.

For two days, Zeus left Megan in the cabin alone when he went to join the others in the stateroom. He was never away long, leaving with the instruction, 'Stay in bed in case Artemis or one of the others comes in.'

Megan nodded, ever anxious when he left her in case one of the other hijackers came inside the cabin. Zeus she could handle, if only because she had a power over him that surprised her. She believed that although he didn't want to hurt her – he would if he had to. Yet despite his curt manner and angry black eyes, he was never immune to Megan's smile.

In moments alone, she found herself wondering what his lips would taste like – she knew how they felt on every part of her – but not against her own mouth. He had never kissed her on the lips. She was, in every way, Zeus's woman. His expert touch had her responding with increasing need. Sometimes, she craved his touch; her eyes always covered with the soft silk scarf. And sensual shivers coursed through her when his rough chin brushed across the softness of her skin. Megan was aware too, that something had happened to her emotions.

That early sense she'd had that something inside her reached out and touched something within Zeus grew; it felt to Megan like a huge, blossoming flower – trapped inside a prison of barbed wire. It could only grow and thrive so far – then no more.

Zeus made no comment, never disturbed her when she sat cross-legged on the bed, the photo album open, Megan endlessly tracing the captured moments of herself and Jordan. Neither did he comment about the tears that sometimes rolled down her cheeks. In a strange kind of parallel, Megan reasoned inwardly that whatever Zeus did to her – it could never hurt as much as the cruel path Jordan had chosen – the path away from her. The irony too sat with her – the photo album she had brought along only to cast on the waves – that single object gave her untold comfort in moments of dark, empty despair.

'Do you have a picture of your wife?' Megan asked after looking through her album late one evening, three nights after Zeus's supposed 'punishment' of her.

His frame stiffened visibly; a slight movement, but one Megan detected easily as he moved across the cabin towards the bathroom.

'No.'

'Do you have children, Zeus?'

'No.'

'Do you and your wife plan to have a family?'

She saw a trace of exasperation behind his mask as he closed the bathroom door against her.

'Zeus!' It was Artemis – she burst into the cabin just as Megan flopped on top of her album and affected sleep.

'I am in the bathroom.'

Artemis joined him.

Megan strained her ears. 'The other hostages are refusing to eat unless they see Lacey is still alive.'

'Oh, no…!' Megan whispered into her pillow.

'I'll waken her and bring her upstairs. There is no problem.'

There was a silence then, during which Megan imagined the slinky Artemis wrapping herself around her virile second-in-command. 'Here, let me,' the woman purred. 'It is a crime to cover such beauty, Zeus.'

What was she doing? Zipping his trousers up?

'Join me in the morning to get the sun on your face. Such a beautiful face!'

Megan couldn't hear Zeus's reply. But she supposed that

Greek gods, like men, needed to feel the sun's warmth on their skin now and again. And never, even by the wildest stretch of her imagination, could she see Zeus in her mind's eye as 'beautiful'. To her, he was magnificent.

'Dress yourself, Lacey.' His manner sharp, he turned from seeing Artemis out.

She pulled on jeans and a white T-shirt, dragged a brush through her hair, feeling out of sorts about something, but not sure what.

A strange burst of pleasure moved through her from Zeus's palm when his fingers spread at the band of exposed flesh at her waist. She spun around, their bodies brushing.

'You want me.' A moot question when he drew her hips against him. 'Take your jeans off.'

'But – the others…?'

'Can wait, Lacey. It is my needs you attend.'

Megan had no way of knowing that her green eyes darkened with passion as Zeus carried her to the bed, working his mythical magic on her double-crossing body.

'Close your eyes,' came the familiar command before his deft fingers slipped the soft silk over her eyes. Megan wondered if being blindfolded heightened her awareness to Zeus's touch; it certainly felt that way.

For some reason Megan couldn't fathom, Zeus seemed angry with her after they made love. Because she spoke freely, more than aware that most of her questions were evaded or ignored, she dragged on her jeans for the second time, and asked, 'Why are you in a bad mood?'

'You!' His black eyes accused her of some heinous crime.

'Me?' Megan gasped, her hair back with a scarf. 'I haven't refused you anything! I haven't fought you!'

Black eyes stared. 'Your ripe body torments, Lacey, your eyes reveal deep pleasure when we have had sex.'

Frowning, Megan finished knotting the tie at her neck.

'My shape I can do nothing about – and if you see pleasure in my eyes then…then…it is your fault!' A small smile curved her mouth, unwisely, she challenged, 'I know why you're angry. You're angry because you want me sexually. Because when this is over – you won't have me any more. Someone else will!'

'Silence!' The word broke from him like a curse, his fingers closed around her hand, he pulled her from the cabin along the corridor, up the steps to the passageway leading to the stateroom.

Before they entered, Megan whispered, 'You made me this way, Zeus, no one else did.'

'Get in there!' His deep, clipped voice carried into the room before he catapulted Megan through the doors.

The audible gasp of relief reached Megan. The other passengers looking dishevelled, pale, tired and strained were still sitting on the stateroom's carpeted floor.

'I'm OK.' Shoulders back, head held high, Megan smiled. 'Don't worry about me. You must eat. We'll be off this ship soon – I promise.'

Roughly, Artemis shoved Megan against a pillar. 'Enough! You are not in a position to make promises.'

Oh, Megan longed to slap the sleek woman, yank away her mask and fight with her – release the frustration of days of manipulation. The longing wrenched so hard, Megan clasped her fingers in front of her, eyes staring straight into those cruel black ones. She could feel colour rising from sheer impotence, anger building like heavy waves against a sea wall – any minute, it would escape, explode, drown them all.

A large hand hooked around the inside of Megan's elbow, gently lowered her to the deck, where she wriggled to lean against the pillar.

She shared a few glances with her fellow captives, reassuring them with tremulous smiles, relieved when they didn't refuse to eat. A mixture of relief and regret shone in the hostages' eyes.

One hour merged into another, the photograph album never far from Megan's fingertips when she was in the cabin. Zeus was as monosyllabic as ever; but when they were alone, Megan chattered away as if there was nothing strange about them being together. For all he didn't speak much, Megan sensed a kind of ease between them, almost, she thought guiltily, as if they were a couple.

'Zeus, do you ever get the urge to pig out on chocolate, or is that too indulgent for you?' The question accompanied a little smile. 'Whenever I get a bit low, I start craving chocolate, loads of it – I reckon it's a safe form of hormone replacement treatment.' She hadn't thought him listening, certain that Zeus 'tuned' her out when she sat, cross-legged on the bed, the photo album open on her pillow. She took no notice when he left the cabin a little later, turning the bedside light on to study a photo of Jordan.

How long Zeus was gone, Megan had no idea, she was lost in the riverside world of her own wedding day, Jordan's laughter, his sexy smile. She jumped when something landed beside her knee on the bed. A large bar of milk chocolate.

'Oh…' He'd been listening! Megan felt a ridiculous surge of emotion, but couldn't identify it. 'Zeus, that's so kind, thank you.' She gave a little laugh to hide the constriction in her throat. 'If I asked you to get me off this ship, would you?'

He didn't answer, those black eyes merely met briefly with hers, then he stretched out on the other bunk.

Always, he was abrupt; yet when they were alone, Zeus was never unkind.

She had been sitting with the others in the main cabin for the whole day, whilst Zeus carried out some work for Artemis. Philip, the steward who had passed her the painkiller, seemed strangely nervous as he handed Megan her dish of food.

'Keep this bowl for Zeus, he'll be here soon.' His voice lowered, the spare helping on a tray which Megan set down beside her.

She whispered, 'OK.' As she set down her own dish, she noticed a crack running along the base of the bowl intended for Zeus. Smartly, when no one was looking, she laid her own bowl over his and tipped the cracked one to lie atop the other, so the contents emptied themselves into her own bowl. Her eyes almost popped from her head when she lifted the damaged bowl away, there, wrapped in cling-film was a scrap of paper. A swift sweep of the room showed no one looking in her direction, she slipped the scrap of paper into her jeans' pocket. A message? Philip had mixed up the bowls? He must have. As Zeus no longer insisted on following her into the bathroom, it wouldn't be difficult to find the opportunity to read it – alone.

Megan shared the stew between the two bowls again and almost jumped with guilt when Zeus' hand touched her shoulder. 'Come.' He took the tray from her, 'I will eat in the cabin.'

Once in the cabin, Megan's fingers automatically slipped beneath her pillow for the photo album. She'd wait a while before escaping to read the note.

'Where's my photo album?' Megan threw the pillows from the bed, pulled down the covers, dropped to her knees to look beneath the bunk. 'Damn! Where did I put it?'

'It is not there.' Zeus' flat response.

'It was there this morning..!' She tore the sheets clean away from the mattress, 'It's got to be here somewhere!'

'I threw it into the sea.'

'No…!' Megan shook her head, 'you wouldn't be that cruel, Zeus, you wouldn't…!' But her words trailed away when she saw the truth glitter in his eyes. 'Why?' She flew across the cabin, grasped the front of his shirt, 'You wouldn't! Tell me you're kidding!'

Firmly, his fingers closed around her wrists, set her hands down at her sides. 'It is in the sea.' Black eyes registered only impatience. 'I do not need to explain myself to you.'

Gasping, Megan turned away; he let her go. Suddenly, without the photographs of Jordan, everything seemed too bleak. Why had she ever thought Zeus different to the others? Why? Why did he do such a senseless thing? He knew how much that album meant to her. Too angry and too upset to stay in the same room with him, Megan closed the bathroom door.

'Get a grip,' she whispered to herself. 'The man's a terrorist – nothing of mine means anything to him! He doesn't care!' As Megan undressed to shower, anger riding her, she silently admitted she'd over-estimated her imagined power over her captor.

The slip of paper wrapped in cling film stuck to her damp fingers when she eased it from her pocket. Slowly, heart pumping, Megan opened it.

It read, 'Meet me in Laundry Room at 3 a.m. Bring keys to enable communication.'

Quickly, she pulled on the uniform over her nakedness, glanced at the luminous clock hands on the cabin wall.

Megan frowned at the note. Keys? Communications? Had Philip written this message to her?

Oh, thank heavens. A chance to bring someone to rescue them? The keys Zeus had commandeered were needed to send a message. Philip was relying on her to steal them away from under his nose.

That Zeus had destroyed Megan's last link with Jordan somehow focused her energies. Somehow, she'd stay awake, somehow get the keys. He'd had her body, at some level touched her soul – but destroying the photo album just for the sake of it – that action destroyed Megan too, her caution cast aside like he'd cast the treasured album into the sea.

Much to Megan's relief, Zeus slept in the other bunk that night. She lay awake, eyes wide, anger fed – against the soporific pull of slumber. At a couple of minutes to three, Zeus breathed deeply, rhythmically in sleep.

There was only one bunch of keys in the dresser drawer; Megan swept them silently into her pocket. Holding her breath, she tiptoed barefoot from the cabin, grimacing at even that non-existent sound. Once in the corridor, she ran, the note crumpled in her palm. If anyone came near her – she'd swallow it – but her mouth was too dry, her heart jumping too quickly to swallow anything; and most unnerving of all – lights along the ceiling flickered automatically into life as she passed under them, so there were no shadows to hide in.

Laundry Room. The door opened silently, she slipped inside; it was deserted. It was exactly three o'clock. Megan stared helplessly at massive washers and dryers, the air held the scent of washing powder in its hot confines.

'Megan?' It was Philip who darted swiftly into the room, closed the door silently behind him and flicked the lock. 'You got the message?' He frowned as though the fluorescent lights were too much for his eyes. 'You brought the keys?' He looked at the bundle dangling from her fingertips and held out his hand.

'What are you going to do?' Megan whispered. 'Will it take long?' Lord, if Zeus discovered her missing…? Well, it didn't bear thinking about. She hated him, for what he'd done, for what he'd made her feel.

As she spoke, Philip moved to the rear of the laundry room and unlocked a panel, to reveal a shelf holding what looked like a radio and headphones; he flicked switches and put on the headset. 'Watch the door! Not me!'

Curious, yet obedient, Megan flattened herself where she

could see through the reinforced glass panel of the door, kept glancing towards Philip to see only his back. Yet the way his elbows moved, she guessed he was twiddling knobs and tapping keys, and forced herself to keep watch on the corridor.

Strange. Out of all the staff on board The Dream, she'd never have pegged Philip as having the nerve to take a risk like this. From the start he'd cow-towed to the hijackers, even sickened her with his crawling, 'Yes sir, no sir, three bloody bags full, sir…' Maybe it was one of those times that looks were deceptive. Being staff, maybe he was one of few who knew where this radio was kept?

Every heartbeat seemed like forever, Megan could scarcely breathe for fear of discovery. 'Hurry up, Philip!' She glanced over her shoulder at him, he was putting the panel back in place.

Soundlessly, he joined her at the door, slipped the keys into her trembling fingers.

'Did you send an SOS?' Megan whispered, 'Will someone help us?'

'I hope so.' He looked through the glass panel at the empty corridor, rocked from one foot to another and pushed his hands into his pockets in what Megan could only describe as a nervous gesture. Sweat stood out on his forehead. 'Just remember, these hijackers are killers, and they've got their own people everywhere – in the radio room, the bridge – everywhere.'

'But…I thought there were only six of them!'

'There's six you see. The rest you don't.'

Megan took a sharp breath. 'I'd better get back!'

'Don't ever come back here; don't tell anyone what you've seen.'

She shook her head, frowning. 'I'm not stupid!'

Then Philip had gone, the opposite direction to the one she must take, and Megan felt fear, danger, panic – in every damp molecule. Leaving the room was like leaping of an endless cliff, and wondering if she'd land in the sea or on sharp rocks.

The passageway was silent and eerie. Megan thought it'd be a miracle if her legs held her up another second. Zeus – the vivid image of his body over hers – the potent fragrance of him swirled around from her own nervous sweating skin. They wouldn't get away with this – he'd find out. She gripped the slightly opened door with damp palms, an image of Hades made her shake. They'd make *her* pay – her life and her sanity – Philip had risked Megan's life for everyone on board!

Turning the cabin door knob, she squealed when the door flew open, literally swinging her inside. 'Where have you been?'

'To meet my lover!' Megan shot back.

He had his back to the misty moonlight, so Megan couldn't see his expression, but she felt his rage. He reached beyond her, closed the door. 'Where have you been?'

Megan stood her ground, planted fists on her hips. 'I have a name!' Copper hair shimmered around her shoulders.

'What is that in your hand?' He reached for her balled fist, pried the keys from her grip, shoved them deep in his pocket. 'What were you doing with these? Who did you meet with? Where?' Although his voice was deep, it was oddly gentle, his black eyes glittered with restrained anger.

She shook her head, closed her lips tightly. Ambivalence, as if she'd betrayed him, yet couldn't betray Philip tore at both sides of her emotions.

'Where have you been?' He asked her over and over, and Megan clung mutely to her secret. 'Tell me!' Unexpectedly, he caught her wrist, dragged her to the bed and straddled her.

'Where have you been?' Not for one minute did he believe her excuse for leaving the cabin, and not for one minute must she underestimate his deep, husky tones as being anything but cruel.

Megan held her silence. Why had she gone to meet Philip? Was she crazy?

'Who did you meet?'

She turned away, unable to bear the sight of him, even more unable to bear what she'd done with him…that part of her cared for him.

'What did you do?'

Megan shot him a disgusted look, then turned away again. Yes, she really had called out this man's name, encouraged him, kissed every part of him he'd allowed her to expose.

'There are other ways to make you talk.'

Wincing, expecting some kind of horrific pain, Megan felt the colour drain from her.

'You have beautiful legs, Lacey.' His gloved hand toyed with her ankle, then moved slowly, scintillatingly upwards to rest on her knee. 'And your breasts are the kind men fantasise over.'

Frowning, Megan looked at him whilst his gloved hand moved up her inner thigh, fingers moving insistently against her soft skin. What the hell was he doing? What was he doing? 'You are a very sexual woman, Lacey,' his fingers moved against her, and Megan bit her lips to keep a pleasurable gasp inside. No! He knew how to arouse her – she'd practically written the handbook for him in the last few days!

Staring straight ahead as though Zeus and his magical touch didn't exist, Megan yawned loudly. But her gesture saw Zeus rip open the front of her uniform, free one plump yet firm breast and gently suckle the nipple he'd exposed; and his fingers still toyed, tormented, brought powerful recollections of the unwanted, dark desire they'd triggered in one another.

'Your body wants me.' His skilled mouth and hands drove Megan crazy. And it was somehow more erotic because she refused to respond, refused to let her body rise or enjoy his practised touch. *Never*! She'd never speak to him, or even pretend to willingly let him have her again.

'You would like me to taste you, Lacey.' His fingers increased their pressure, brought her to the unmoving brink of ecstasy. 'Where have you been?'

She shook her head, but Zeus didn't see, his dark, masked face was moving down...

The cabin door slammed open, Zeus swore vilely.

'This specimen met with your woman to send an SOS!' It was Hades, and he threw a bloodied Philip across the floor; Philip scrambled to sit up.

As though he'd never laid a hand on her, Zeus turned away from her, whilst she hurriedly fastened her dress with one hand. 'I see. And how did she know where to meet you?' This to a terrified Philip.

'I...I got a message to her.'

'Did you manage to send an SOS?'

'No.' Zeus looked to Hades who shook his head in confirmation.

'Do you realise what you have done?' Zeus's tone was cold, harsh, and he stood over Philip's weaving form.

'Have you displaced the signal, Hades?'

'Sir.'

'Why did you need this woman to send an SOS?' He fired at Philip.

'I needed her help, sir – she was the only one could get your keys...'

Megan's tormented mind was swimming and ebbing. Hades stood to attention beside the door; his eyes glinted with horrible lust and self-satisfaction. He had her now. She'd gone too far.

'Lock him in the storage hold,' Zeus shot at Hades. 'I'll deal with him later.'

'What about her?' The feral gleam in Hades' eyes made

Megan stiff with terror, real terror. She'd achieved 'double agent' status now, and in any world, there was nothing more deplorable.

'I will punish her.'

'What about the rest?'

'I will let you know what is to be done with the others.' When Hades didn't immediately respond, Zeus snapped, 'Take him to the hold – now!'

Megan shook from head to toe as she tried without success to bring her fear under control. It wouldn't be controlled, wouldn't be contained. As Zeus turned to her, pure rage glinted in his eyes, Megan spurted, 'Why don't you just shoot me and get it over with!'

'How did he get a message to you?'

Megan narrowed her eyes, looked deep into Zeus's anger filled gaze, didn't reply.

'How?'

'Just shoot me!' She couldn't bear the fear, couldn't stand it another second. By slipping away from Zeus, she'd made him look idiotic before the others.

'Maybe I will.' His voice was deep, furious, and then from somewhere, Megan heard shouts, screams of pain.

In that second, Megan changed her mind, she didn't want to die – she wanted to live. She shook uncontrollably as snap shots burst in her mind. Her handsome dad, so proud of his girl; her mother, before drink destroyed her – still complete and secure beside him; work and…and Jordan. A mewling sound escaped her then air turned solid, wouldn't relieve her lungs; her heart, starved, pounded.

The shot cracked, echoed. Megan gasped and sank tonelessly to the ground.

'What the hell's going on?' Rigid with anger, Zeus dashed out into the corridor.

At that moment, Artemis appeared from above decks. 'I heard gunshot! What is this?' She gestured with feline grace at Philip's shuddering form, looked from Hades to Zeus.

'It is Zeus' fault.' Hades narrowed his eyes, firmed his jaw. 'His involvement with that woman made him careless. She crept away and met him…' he jabbed his recently-fired gun in Philip's direction. 'They were trying to send an SOS. It's that woman! Every problem stems from her.'

'Is this true?' Artemis folded her arms, stared at Zeus.

'I was dealing with it, until this idiot fired at the steward.' He told her, his voice cold and angry. 'You just can't control yourself – can you, Hades? You're a trigger-happy imbecile.' Then turning to Artemis, he added, 'The fool was supposed to be taking the steward to the cargo hold, and leaving him there for me to deal with.'

'Where is the woman?'

Before either man could reply, Artemis stormed into the cabin, and dragged Megan by the hair out into the corridor.

Shell-shocked, winded, Megan stayed where Artemis dumped her. 'I told you she was trouble! I want this woman where we can all keep watch on her, Zeus. Take her up with the others – right now!'

A smirk twisted Hades's mouth. 'What shall I do with him?' He held the gun to the terrified steward's temple.

Megan twisted around to scream, 'N…no! No…*you bastards*! You can't kill him!'

Artemis cracked out commands in her own tongue; the look she gave Megan said she'd gladly wring her neck; and she didn't look any more pleased with the two men who served her.

Reaching down, Zeus yanked Megan to her feet, muttered something in a foreign tongue and pushed her ahead of the three of them.

Megan felt the anger of three people directed at her back as she walked shakily along the corridor, up the steps and into the main lounge, while Philip was led below.

That the other hostages had heard the gunfire was obvious

by the expressions on their faces. Guards who had talked amongst themselves and who had begun to relax with their 'tame' captives, prowled alertly now.

Artemis grasped Megan's upper arm and flung her sprawling to the deck. 'You have this bitch to thank for the near-death of one of your number.'

An audible gasp hit Megan's ears. Was it her fault? Truth to tell, at that moment, her mind wouldn't function beyond shock – the shock of seeing Philip's bloodied form. Why? Why had he taken that risk? Why had she? Would she ever stop trembling? Could she die from shaking so much? Could she die from the hostility focusing on her from all the other passengers?

The stunned silence and her own shock lasted a long time. She longed to sleep, until she could wake up in a safe time, far beyond all this danger. Then she tensed when the sound of a helicopter filled the silence; the entire room filled with a tangible mix of anticipation and dread. And the sound of safety mechanisms being released from weapons.

Had Philip sent a signal? Megan looked at Zeus who stood, flattened beside a window, shielded from the outside world, gun ready, body tensed; but she could tell nothing from his eyes. In that moment, she felt a strange, twisted loyalty to him. If nothing else, he'd managed to save her from the dreaded clutches of Hades. And in amongst the confusion of hatred, shock and fear, Megan wished herself back in the relative safety of her cabin – with him.

Oh, my God – I'm going mad! How can I think like that? she asked herself incredulously as the sound of the helicopter grew fainter and, practically in unison, she could hear the safety catches of the guns being slowly released. Tension that had gripped the ship slowly receded, and Megan didn't fight the need to slip away.

Burrowed in the warm escape of sleep, her mind and soul captured Jordan's image…

'You're asking too much, woman, you're turning me on and you won't let me near you!' The flash went off and Jordan broke his pose, strode towards her, reached out to snatch the camera from Megan's hands.

'Back off, Buster!' Megan shook her hair back over her shoulders to catch the breeze, adjusted her crossed legs in the arched window seat. She indulged her love of photography – and her love of Jordan. Naked to his jeans-clad waist, his hair tousled from their night of steamy passion, and with stubble beginning to form on his sculptured cheeks and chin, he looked gorgeous! And with his enticing smile ready to erupt into full-blown laughter any minute, Megan took another photo, muttering, 'For heaven's sake – stand still, Elliot!'

'Megan – there's only time for just one more. I've got to leave in half-an-hour…' he murmured, while his eyes devoured her, roaming over the curves of her body as she took another photo.

'Jordan – you're such a poser!' she squealed with excited, anticipatory laughter as he grabbed her up in his powerful arms and threw her down on the bed. Taking the camera from her grip, he repeated, 'I've only got half-an-hour, then I won't be back till morning.'

'That's OK,' she teased. 'I've got plenty of work to catch up on.'

Intense blue eyes looked down into hers. 'You could try saying you'll miss me.'

'It's only a day.' She wriggled as Jordan held her wrists to the side of her head, straddled her and nibbled her shoulders with mind-bending gentleness, though the fine cotton blouse.

Part of the way she coped with Jordan's absences, was filling them with work, piling up stacks of it for when he wasn't there. And for some reason, she was always reluctant to admit just how much she missed him. Yet it was always part of his delicious game to try and get her to say just that.

'And a night.' Blue eyes darkened when he spoke. 'You'll miss me tonight.'

A slow smile curved Megan's lips. 'I've never missed you before – and don't see why I should now.'

'This is only the third night since we got hitched that we won't be together. You'll miss me.'

Miss him? She'd feel as though half of herself had walked out the door! 'Maybe,' she teased. 'Maybe not.' Megan deliberately raised her knee, so her thigh brushed Jordan's buttocks, watched his eyes flare with need.

'I'll miss you, Megan.' That deep, resonant voice of his sent little shivers racing over her skin and through her insides.

'Well,' she raised herself up on her elbows so her blouse strained and watched Jordan restrain himself from pushing her back down on the bed. 'Don't go then.'

'I don't have a choice.'

'Sure you do, you're a rich man.'

For a long moment, he stared into Megan's eyes, and she sensed he was deliberating whether to tell her something monumental. 'It's not that simple,' was all he finally said, and uncharacteristically serious, he pushed himself from the bed and walked away from her.

'I've got to get my gear together,' he looked at his watch. 'I'm picking Ray up. Are you sure you'll be OK?'

'Just what exactly do you and Ray do, Jordan?'

'Routine stuff – it would bore you to tears.' He unlocked a drawer, put some things into a hold-all, zipped it up and swung it to the floor before turning to face Megan. 'Basically we scope out sites all over the free world, for anyone with enough money and the yen to build something.' He seemed troubled, and wouldn't meet her eyes. 'I won't deal with cowboys and I won't help anyone pollute the environment. But apart from that,' he shrugged, 'the world's my oyster.' Megan refused to let Jordan see that his air of unease had rubbed off onto her.

'Jordan, I was on my own six years before I shacked up with you – so of course I'll be OK.'

There was something too intense about the look in his eyes; but Megan read it as love. That's all it could be, there wasn't any other explanation – and any doubts were blown away when he kissed her, held her, dropped to his knees and made exquisite love to her – there on the floor.

'You'll miss me.' A smile twisted one corner of his mouth as he stood at the door, ready to leave, his wrists rested casually on her shoulders, fingertips toyed with her luxurious copper curls.

Megan wanted to hang on to him, cling like a barnacle. But instead she managed to give a casual shrug. 'If you say so.'

chapter five

Next day, the hostages were still shocked by Philip's treatment, the gravity of their situation spelt out in no uncertain terms – defiance meant death. Yet by the same token, Philip's imprisonment sparked a real desire to mutiny and Megan caught it on whispered conversations around her.

No one had spoken – rather – whispered to her. Megan knew what it was like to be lonely in a room full of people, to be ostracised and blamed. Suzanne caught Megan's gaze and her sympathetic hazel eyes held no blame; as before, her smile did much to rescue Megan's sanity.

As time ticked on and on, and as she remained silent and thoughtful, drawing no attention, Megan sensed that maybe their blackballing her was more to do with the fact that – given half the chance – she would do something to save them all.

Jack Hodges found himself slapped about for objecting about badly-cooked food; and from then, a silent resentment built – none of them was immune to public degradation.

At the same time too, an emotion shared by all the hostages was an almost pathetic thankfulness towards their captors – just for feeding them, for letting them live; and Megan despised herself for relating to these emotions herself.

She thought they, the captives, were like baby birds stranded in a nest, their dependence on their black-clad, faceless parents grew and bonds strengthened. It all stemmed from need and so long as they remained firmly in the nest, they were fed and kept in relative comfort.

Megan, longing to know what was on board The Dream that was so precious to these people, found her gaze drifting constantly to Zeus whilst she wondered. Was it money? Jewels? Artefacts?

Those black, cold eyes of his stared straight back at her, told her nothing. Then she was sure she must be imagining things when his eyes darted pointedly towards the bathroom. In response, a hot flush rose through her entire body, he wanted to be alone with her. She wanted to be alone with Zeus. No! Looking away, Megan's mouth went dry. The heat inside the sun-drenched cabin became unbearable. She unfastened the top button of her uniform dress and wafted her paper napkin to create a breeze over her neck. Her gaze, like a magnet, was drawn back to Zeus. And Megan had no way of knowing that she looked like some pre-Raphaelite temptress inviting her lover to do as he would. She was even unaware of the small smile tilting her luscious pink mouth, but saw heat flare in his eyes, and delicious, dangerous shivers raced through her. So hot, so sleepy, Megan sank onto the crumpled quilt beneath her, one last glance in his direction before she closed her eyes. It was a glance that said, 'If you want me, you work something out.'

And out of a need to escape reality, Megan let her thoughts slip into her time with Jordan, a time when she'd been loved so deeply, and thought she always would be.

'It's for you. Some geezer called Lucas Knight. Asking for Themes and Dreams Party Organisers.'

'Thanks, darling, You'd make a great secretary!' She took the phone, frowned slightly as Jordan slammed around the huge lounge looking anything but amused. What had she done now?

'Hello, Lucas?' Megan rested one knee on the office chair they kept beside the phone, propped the phone beneath her chin and retied her cotton dressing robe sash. 'What can I do for you this time?' She took notes on the ever-present note pad on the desk, glanced up to smile broadly at Jordan.

Lord, he was gorgeous! But he was in a hell of a mood. Did he have to hang around and make so much noise?

'Ten people?' Lucas wanted a party organising for six men and four women.

'That's right. Could you organise gifts for the women, Megan, like you did last time? And roses – single red ones?'

'That's no problem, just give me an idea of price for the gifts. What kind of menu are we looking at?'

'A lot of courses, not heavy, something a bit different, novel…' her client hesitated, and Megan turned to look out over the Thames, beautifully shrouded with early morning mist. Flowers from their window box reached up, their fragrance tantalised in the promise of a hot day.

'Have you thought of Chinese? Japanese?'

'Sweetheart, would that mean I'd get to see you in a Chemsong?' Lucas laughed, 'Now with your legs, that'd be exciting.'

Megan's soft laughter filled the air, earned another barrage of slamming around from Jordan. Tactically, she kept her back to him. 'You'd have to pay extra, Lucas, we don't have chemsongs in our wardrobe yet.'

'Come up with a figure? I like that idea.'

'OK. What'd the venue be?'

'My Hampstead house, Megan. I'd want the place decking out for atmosphere – could you quote for that too?'

'Heavens, Lucas, it'd cost a bomb.'

He laughed. 'Megan, if this crowd buys my conversion designs, and preliminary word is good – I'll make a fortune, so cost doesn't matter.'

Quickly, Megan made a list. 'Music?'

'I'll provide that.'

'Good.' She doubted if anything amongst her own rock music collection would inspire a business-like atmosphere. 'I can do some plans this evening, hopefully get everything priced up – when do you want to see the suggestions?'

'Could you meet me for a working breakfast, Megan?' Lucas asked, 'Around nine-thirty?'

'Just a moment,' she flicked open her diary. 'I've an engagement at three in Kensington. Do you think we'll get through everything by noon?'

'Sure. Look, let's make it eight-thirty. Catch a cab to my place so you can get an idea of the space involved.'

'OK, see you, Lucas, bye.'

'What is wrong with you!' Megan spun around the minute she put the phone down, planted her hands on her hips.

'I hate listening to my wife flirting with another man!' Jordan's blue eyes were darkened with raw jealousy.

'Flirting?' Megan flung her diary at Jordan's head, and missed, 'That was business, you turkey!'

'You sounded like you were a trollop, organising an orgy!'

Anger ripped through her, she flew at Jordan, hair swirling in a banner of copper flames. 'You bloody hypocrite!' He caught her wrists before she inflicted too much damage on his rock solid chest and shoulders. The air between their bodies sizzled, but Megan was too angry to be distracted by intimacy. 'How dare you talk to me like that!'

'You sounded like a tramp.' Jordan's sensual mouth thinned into a straight line, 'How did you manage to get a big-name client like Lucas Knight? Did you sleep with him?'

Stunned, Megan gasped; she pulled away from Jordan, but he didn't release her wrists. Then he did, when she shook her head and whispered angrily, 'You are the only client I ever slept with, Jordan.'

Don't let me cry! Anger had an awful habit of making her tremble, then cry – and she needed tears like a hole in the head at that moment. They'd seem so manipulative, so weak. Just as to say any more would seem defensive. Without another word, she collected the diary she'd flung at him from the floor, picked up her notes from the desk, and strode into the bedroom, put them into her briefcase. From now on, she was having her calls diverted to the Mews. If this went on – she might even move back there permanently!

Tears fuzzed her vision as she stepped into the shower, thought how nice it would be if Jordan had gone by the time she got dried and dressed. Then, she thought how horrible it would be if he'd gone…

Water, gently perfumed shampoo and steam kept her safe from Jordan's accusations for a while. Ursula – her own mother had accused her of looking and acting like a trollop…years ago. When she'd taken a night-club job waitressing to support them. And that was whilst her mother, drank herself into oblivion over the death of Megan's father.

God! It had taken eleven months for Ursula to realise Megan was going out every night until the early hours – and yes, she did look like a trollop – but it was the uniform, a short, low-cut slinky dress – all the waitresses at La Papa's wore the same. The wages were rubbish, but the tips were enormous. And without that job – she and Ursula would both have gone under. But never – ever – had Megan so much as dated a customer at La Papa's! She'd been tempted by one or two of the handsome, rich clients. But at just sixteen and lying about her age – she had too much at stake. And what thanks? 'Good grief, Megan! You can't go out dressed like that! You look like a complete trollop! No daughter of mine is selling herself like that! You slut!' But after another couple of drinks, Ursula was incapable of knowing whether her daughter was in the house or not.

All that – for wanting to support them. And now Jordan – the man she loved beyond any kind of sense – was accusing her of the same thing!

Not knowing whether Jordan had already left their flat, Megan dried her hair, twisted it into a neat bun, pulled on a white blouse and black suit. There! She faced the steamed mirror. Now she looked like a complete prude! Maybe that'd make him happy!

What Megan wasn't prepared for was that Jordan would be on their low, leather settee with his head in his hands. She had to clasp her hand over her mouth to keep from calling his name, grasp the doorframe to keep from running to him. It was shattering to recognise in that moment, that she loved him so deeply – it would never change. She could be angry – yes. Even hate him a little. But she would always, always love him to distraction.

Sensing her presence, Jordan rose to his feet. 'Megan,' his voice husky, his masculine, handsome features etched with misery as he faced her. 'I'm so, so sorry.'

She could feel anger flaring again as she recalled his words, and that battled with compassion in the face of his misery. Whatever she said would affect their lives forever – it was one of those see-saw emotional rides that had the potential to help make or break them.

'Do you want coffee?'

He seemed taken aback at her question, pushed his fingers back through his soft, dark blonde hair. 'You'll be late for work.'

'So will you.'

'I don't care, Megan.' Devastation lit his blue eyes and she just wanted to fly into his arms and make it all better. But she didn't.

She brought two mugs of coffee and sat beside him on the settee, kept a business-like distance between them. 'My mother once said something very like what you accused me of.'

Jordan set his beaker down on the low table, and Megan knew why. He wouldn't be able to swallow – she couldn't either. Then those incredible blue eyes returned to hers. He was trying not to talk, to justify, Megan felt that too. They both knew he'd said enough.

'I left home because she said it once too often, Jordan.'

'Oh, Megan…' She saw his whole body convulse, glimpsed the agony in his eyes before he closed them. 'I'm so sorry.'

Again, her softer emotions wanted to reach across, hold him, kiss his beautiful mouth until it laughed with pleasure. But she held her cup – the only reason she'd hung onto hers – to remind her they had to sort this out.

'I love you, Jordan, much more than you seem to realise…' When he faced her, frowning, she continued, 'If you knew how much, you would never accuse me of playing around.' She took a breath against a heart beating too fast. 'I was talking on the phone, not flirting. I talk the way I talk – you liked it well enough to marry me. Or at least I think you did.'

'You know I do – I love the way you are.' He was so upset, Megan couldn't bear it.

'Well,' she said, her voice gentle, husky, 'The way I am is the way I am with everyone, whether I sound like I'm flirting or teasing – or whatever – I've only ever made love with you and I don't want it any other way.'

He looked up at that, took her outstretched fingertips in his large palm. 'I don't want to lose you, Megan.'

'You're not going to – all you have to do is believe me.' Kneeling, she put down her cup and wrapped her arms around his neck, held him so tightly; and she could feel Jordan against her as his arms slipped inside her jacket, holding her fiercely. In a single movement, he pulled Megan around to straddle his lap and they kissed, savagely, desperately needing each other – and he pulled the pins from Megan's hair in the process, flung them to the floor. 'I love you,' he whispered against her mouth. 'I'll never hurt you, I swear…'

Before they each made late departures for work, Jordan proceeded to show her just how much he loved her. They were very late…

'You know, Jordan,' she'd changed out of the suit, which he hated, and now wore a soft, flowing skirt and a clinging, sleeveless T-shirt; the old fashioned, iron grilled lift made slow progress to the ground floor. 'You should come with me – meet Lucas Knight?'

'Are you kidding?'

'No – he brings his girlfriend every time. Why shouldn't I take you?'

Chuckling, Jordan narrowed his eyes thoughtfully, 'You're serious, aren't you?'

'Yup. Go on, it'll be much more fun with you there – just so long as you don't touch me up under the table when I'm trying to do sums.'

'How about when we're eating?'

'Oh, that's OK, you can do it when we're eating.'

Laughing, Jordan squeezed her to him. 'I'll see what I can sort out with Ray.'

'Brilliant!' Her smile lit up her features, bowled Jordan for six. She couldn't know that he silently vowed he'd go with her to her breakfast meeting – whatever Ray's objections. He also silently vowed that whatever it cost him, the jealousy that gripped him would be controlled – at least when he was close to Megan. He prayed he could keep that vow.

The lift reached the ground floor and they left the building; hot sun blazing down on them.

'What're you thinking?' She threaded her fingers around his neck for a last goodbye kiss. 'Are you worried about us?'

'I'm worried about destroying us. This is something new I'm dealing with, Megan. I'm not doing too well.'

'We dealt with it today, Buster – I'm not naive enough to think it's never going to happen again.'

'I'll try not to let it happen again.'

Smiling, because she instinctively knew you couldn't change the basic person – didn't want to – Megan hugged him. 'That's OK, then, I don't want us to "blow" anything this good, Mr Elliot.'

It was so hard to let go, and go their separate ways – but eventually, the pager Jordan carried in his shirt pocket let out a low level sound. 'Looks like we've been rumbled.' He switched it off after reading the message.

'Shame.' Megan's green eyes reflected the laughter in Jordan's, her copper hair glinted warm and bright in the sun, 'I was just about to drag you back upstairs.'

'Stop teasing and get in.' He swung open her car door.

'OK!' Megan raised her fingers in a little wave, 'I'm going, Mr Elliott!'

Jordan laughed; and Megan carried that wonderful sound with her to work. She dearly hoped she'd done the right thing inviting Jordan along the following day to meet Lucas.

After a frantic day, when her staff wiggled their eyebrows over Megan turning up so late, laughed because she was having trouble concentrating, and pulled her leg non-stop about the obvious cause for her lateness, Alexa just had to catch her taking the 'caller divert' from her work phone.

'What if you miss calls?' Alexa gasped, 'Megan, you've always diverted your out-of-hours calls!'

Megan plugged in the ansaphone. 'Not any more.'

'But…'

'It's not worth the hassle.'

'Oh. Jordan?'

'Let's just leave it at not being worth the hassle.'

Alexa grimaced. 'Did the phone go off while you two were…er…otherwise engaged?'

'One day,' Megan put her arm along her friend's shoulder. 'When you're an old married woman, you'll understand!'

'So you feel old?'

'Lord!' Megan laughed, 'No, I've never felt better, you twerp! Stop asking questions, will you? I need your help with this job for Lucas.'

That same evening, Megan sat up late at the desk in the massive lounge, completing all the notes ready for the following morning. She stretched the kinks from her spine and wondered why Jordan was out so late.

'Oh, well.' It wasn't unusual, and Megan made herself a hot drink, discarded her cotton wrap and slipped into bed. She barely stirred when Jordan joined her, just enough to snuggle right up to him and whisper 'night-night.' What the time was, she had no idea.

The alarm was set very early and Megan woke first the following morning, rubbed the sleep from her eyes and looked down at Jordan's handsome features. Then she frowned. On his shoulder was a large round bruise. Instinctively, she reached out to touch it with gentle fingertips. His large palm immediately trapped her fingers. 'It's nothing to worry about, I've been training.'

'Training for what? The world heavyweight championships?'

A lazy smile curved his mouth. 'I need to get fitter.'

'Well, I like you as you are!' Megan didn't add, 'I'm just getting really fed up with your job.'

'Hey!' Someone was nudging her, Megan stirred, remembered where she was and pushed herself upright. No sooner has she righted herself than the food slithered off the plate and across her lap. 'Oh, bloody hell!' The curse left her and she flattened her hand over her mouth, looked around apologetically. 'Sorry.' It was worth the warm slop on her lap to see mouths quirk with amusement.

'Zeus!' Artemis herself even sounded a little amused. 'Take her to shower and change.' Then she added, 'And bring her straight back.' A few titters of knowing laughter greeted her remark.

As Megan left the cabin, she heard Artemis inform everyone. 'You will all be taken individually to shower and change clothes over the next few hours. We are near to our destination.'

There was a chorus of something that could only be described as gratitude; and for once, none of the captors scolded with, 'Quiet!'

'There is something I must make sure you understand.' Zeus spoke in lowered tones once they made the cabin; he took Megan's clothes when she stepped out of them, then her lacy bits of underwear. 'Hurry…' he turned on the water. 'I will speak while you shower.'

There was something in the urgency of his tone that worried Megan, sent creeping shivers across her flesh. 'What?'

'Hades wants you. Artemis has given him permission to have you before we dock. She wants to leave it until just before – so no one will see what damage he inflicts.'

'No!' Megan's hand reactively shot out of the shower curtain, pulled Zeus closer, he pushed her back under the water spray, emptied shampoo on her head, 'You are no longer mine. You betrayed me, therefore I cannot stop him.'

Naked, save for ropes of foam reaching down, Megan grasped the front of his army shirt. 'You've got to make me yours again! Zeus – please?'

'It's too late for that! Will you listen?'

But Megan was panicking so badly, Zeus had to move into the shower cubicle with her to rinse the soap from her hair.

'I'll do anything – anything! Don't let him…don't let him…' Still she gripped his shirt and felt a little better when his hands moved down to rest at her waist and pulled her against him. 'Listen to me, Lacey.'

She let her forehead fall against his chest, a soft, terrified moan – just audible – keened in her throat. Deftly, Zeus washed her, allowed her to hold onto him, then he turned off the spray and pulled a bath sheet around her, led her to sit on a chair in the cabin.

'Megan…'

He rarely used her first name and it always shocked her. 'I promise you I won't let him hurt you.'

Zeus watched as the pink, just-showered glow drained from Megan's cheeks, her skin turned completely white. 'If you lose your temper, or fight him, he will hurt you. He does not like women, he likes to use them horribly.'

Lord, it was hard to take in. Megan ached for Jordan like she never had before. Why had he left her to cope with all this? 'What do I do?'

Relief stole over Zeus's features. At last, she was paying attention. 'You act submissive.'

Green eyes widened, filled with revulsion, she gasped and shook her head. Zeus crouched down and gripped her face between his wet hands, forced her to meet his gaze. 'Don't raise so much as a finger to stop him and he won't touch you – I promise you, he won't want you. He is only attracted to the fire in you.'

Again, she shook her head, so deep in horror, she couldn't speak.

'Close your eyes, Megan.'

Without question, Megan closed her eyes. Then she felt the touch of his hand at her waist, the slight pressure of his lips on hers; it was all too brief, but tantalising.

'Wasn't that against the rules?'

'Yes.'

'Zeus – is it against the rules for you to make love to me?'

As she spoke, his hand rode up her thigh. 'No.'

'If…if I die,' silent tears rolled down her face. 'Zeus, if I die, I want you to know I appreciate you trying to save me.'

His dark eyes studied hers for a long moment, his nod imperceptible. 'You will not die. Look what you have done so far to survive.'

She stood perfectly still whilst Zeus blindfolded her; what

had seemed so wrong at first, felt right now. It really was that simple. 'Help me, Zeus.' Her breast rose against the palm of his hand and Megan let the towel drop, moved into his powerful arms; and without kissing her lips again, Zeus took her on the chair, on the table and the floor, his erotic touch scintillating. It was incredible, uninhibited... Strangely beautiful. She touched his hair, it was caught back in a band at his nape, kissed the tiny stud earring at his lobe. Megan cried out in ecstasy as he brought about the cataclysmic response she needed as though they had all the time in the world. Megan wondered if Zeus had just 'made love' to her – as opposed to 'having sex' with her. She certainly felt as though he'd made love to her; and she felt as though she'd made love to him. Afterwards, he held her, but it was too brief; perversely, Megan dreaded him removing her blindfold.

'Take this.' Zeus was popping a tablet into a glass of whisky, as he threw the silk scarf to the floor.

Megan frowned. 'What are you doing?'

'It is for Hades. A kind of...tranquilliser. It will slow him down and knock him out.'

Zeus supported her against him when they went back to the main lounge, his arm only dropping away outside the doors. 'Think of it as a silent, unmoving fight. All you need to do is lie still until the drug takes effect and you will win your life.'

Despite her incredible fear, Megan smiled at Zeus; it was a warm, dazzling smile. She thought he flinched – but it was impossible to be sure beneath that damn mask of his.

'Why do you smile?'

'My husband always said my smile did things to his insides. I can't give it to him, so I'm giving it to you.'

'Thank you.' The closest emotion she'd ever seen to warmth entered Zeus's eyes, 'When I see you next, do I give it back?'

'No, Zeus.' She smiled again, more sadly this time. 'It's my way of saying thank you – and goodbye.'

Before he could respond, Megan flicked her drying hair back over her shoulders and moved through the door in front of him.

If she could have seen beyond Zeus's mask to his concerned expression, beyond that and into his mind, Megan would have been shocked beyond words. Perhaps to the very outside edge of sanity; perhaps even over that spinning, terrible edge.

A definite party atmosphere invaded both hostages and captors alike. There were even smiles amongst those who'd spent the best part of two weeks on the stateroom floor. What's more, the smiles no longer turned hard and accusing when they looked across to Megan to see how she'd fared with the second-in-command.

Matt Duprey, the man who owned the island for which they were bound scratched his prickly beard and smiled at Megan. His wife, Linda, after days of sitting, terrified, smiled too.

Maybe this would be a last chance to smile.

Murmurs, excited whispers and even low-level chat were tolerated – or ignored by their captors.

Setting her sights directly on Suzanne, the woman who'd given Megan comfort throughout the whole ordeal, she knelt beside her. Suzanne leant against her dare-devil, hunk of an action hero, Jack.

'Suzanne?' Megan whispered, not daring to raise her voice.

'Oh, you smell lovely.' Suzanne shuffled to sit upright, 'I hope I get to shower soon.'

'I'm sure you will. Seeing that they're letting everyone talk a little, I wanted to thank you for not blaming me …'

Suzanne glanced worriedly in Zeus's direction, 'Did you have to…?'

Heat flushed Megan's cheeks. Have to? Wasn't she the one who'd asked Zeus to make love to her? 'No, I didn't have to, Suzanne. I had a choice.'

Suzanne's eyebrows shot up, eloquently asked the question.

'In another life…' Megan could feel tears rising, didn't understand why. 'In another life, Suzanne, I could love him.' As she said the words, she understood why she felt so full of emotion.

Even those words weren't too much for the woman. She smiled, albeit sadly. 'It happens that way sometimes.'

Beside Suzanne, Jack Hodges snored; she giggled. 'You'll have guessed Jack's not the tough guy in real life.'

Megan laughed and it felt so good, like water on her parched and battered soul. 'At least you have each other, warts and all.' She chanced a glance at Zeus, found his eyes on her and smiled.

She had to keep the mounting nerves under control – she could see herself running from the cabin and flinging herself over the side of The Dream. 'I'll chill out for a bit. Think about my husband.' Fear battled with a heavy sleepiness inside her. She closed her eyes, drew Jordan's image into her mind; but as though the balance of her mind had already been upset, the vision that came to her was the last time they'd been together. Everything was so normal; it was a fantastic, warm day, and the high, arched window was wide open to let in the balmy breeze whilst they ate breakfast…

'Morning, gorgeous.' Jordan's smile made her heart twist, Megan wondered if it always would.

'You are badly biased, Buster.'

'I've got 20–20 vision. You're gorgeous.'

'You know, if you could have seen me just ten years ago, you wouldn't say that.'

'Do you know…' he raised his coffee cup. 'I've never seen any old photos of you. You should dig some out.'

'You're not ready for that.'

'You got any?'

'Mmm.' Her mouth was full of scrambled egg. 'You're not seeing them though.'

'Where are they?'

She shook her head. 'No way, Jose, no – never!'

Unexpectedly, he stood, pushed away his plate and started systematically pulling out drawers and messing things up the way only a man in earnest can.

'Stop that! You'll mess all my stuff up!'

'Where?'

'Can we finish breakfast?'

'If you get them soon as we're done.'

'Mmm.' She shot him a disgusted look. Sometimes it was best just to give in gracefully.

He saw them all. Megan at all ages – with her parents, then the child of eleven and twelve, wearing braces on her teeth, thick, pink-rimmed glasses, hair in bunches, and a smile that couldn't care less. But as she grew older and the braces remained, the smiles became closed-mouthed; and the school photo of her just before her sixteenth birthday was hauntingly painful. Her father had recently died and she tried to smile at the patient school photographer. The effect was heart-rending. 'Baby, that's just so sad.' Jordan whispered, obviously moved.

It wasn't the best time.' But Megan had learned to cope, bringing out the memories of her father now and then, revisiting the fun times. She'd learned very quickly that life went on – and someone had to pay the bills. After a long time, Jordan turned to the next picture, almost choked on his coffee. 'Bloody hell!'

Grimacing, Megan said, 'That was my waitressing get-up.'

The photo was of Megan at sixteen in a very short, low-cut, clinging cream dress and high-heeled cream boots. Her hair cascaded around her shoulders, her smile broad, flirtatious.

'You don't look any different now.' He shoved his fringe back when it flopped onto his forehead. 'What'd you do? Go to bed a girl and wake up a siren? Megan, your legs are sinful.'

'I kept myself under wraps till I had to work.' She shrugged one shoulder. 'And my legs keep my feet on the ground.' Megan didn't add that they didn't have the money for anything other than cast-off and charity shop finds – even with her working.

'You could have worked as a model with a shape like that, darling, you didn't need to serve drinks.'

'No chance. Skinny was in.'

'Hell, now that's a crime.' He gave her a sexy grin, made her blush, pulled her gently around the table and on to one long, jeans-clad leg. 'We should take a day off together.'

'We should.' Megan gave him a naughty smile, wound her arms round his neck and let time ride in his sensual, beautiful kisses. 'We could decorate, or shop...' she teased him. 'Or we could make babies or something.'

'We've already had the decorator in – and I sure as hell not shopping.' A grin hiked one corner of his mouth, 'How about we work on that baby idea?'

Megan laughed against his mouth. 'You call that work?' Putting her palms on his shoulders, she sat astride his long legs, leant back against the table on her elbows, laughed when, a low curse erupting from him, Jordan swept everything from the table in a single movement, then draped her across it

Later, Megan grimaced at the scattered remains of their breakfast. 'You know, Jordan, maybe we just ought to stay in bed another hour in the mornings.'

'Hell, I'm telling you, it wouldn't make any difference – I still wouldn't get through breakfast without wanting you.'

They groaned in unison as Jordan fastened his jeans, pushed his fingers back through his soft fringe – and his pager sounded.

'Don't answer it,' Megan challenged, whisking it from his palm.

'*Megan!*'

'I'm fed up with Ray Blackmore ruining our lives!' Her thin robe billowed with the breeze as Megan stood on the windowsill, held the pager out into the air.

'Go on, drop it.' Jordan shrugged, blue eyes twinkling at his outrageous wife. 'Ray won't like it, but I don't give a damn.'

'He can't do that!' Megan's fingers closed around the little black pager, 'I'll report him. He's a rotten bully!'

'Whatever.' He shrugged, moved towards Megan, then in a lightening movement, his arm snaked out and caught her round the hips, his fingers taking the pager from hers. 'You're a crazy woman,' he glanced at the message, and grimaced. 'You should have dropped it.'

Megan wrapped her legs round his waist, her arms round his neck, watched his eyes darken as he felt her nakedness against him, her robe floating lightly around them. 'Here.' He gave her the pager. 'Chuck the bloody thing.'

She didn't need telling twice and sent the little black gadget sailing out of the window. 'What was the message?'

'We've got maybe two minutes before Ray gets here.'

'Come on – into the shower. I'll leave the outside door open.'

A slow smile slashed Jordan's face. 'Think maybe you need more practise?' He carried her towards the bathroom whilst he spoke.

They soaped one another, made exquisite love in the

shower, then eventually, Jordan stepped out, leaving Megan to luxuriate. 'Better go face the old bastard.'

She could hear raised voices as she dressed in the bedroom; it was still before seven a.m. and Megan had arranged to go straight to Thames Ditton, meet Alexa and the rest of the staff there to set up a garden party. With the forecast of high temperatures in mind, Megan pulled on a gauze thin green cotton sun dress, a flick of mascara, and a thin film of bronze lipstick; she tied her wet hair into a top-knot with a pale green scrunchy and put in a pair of gold and emerald drop earrings which Jordan had bought her earlier the same week.

'Hello, Ray.' Barefoot, Megan padded into the vast lounge, but Ray didn't hear her, he was waving the broken pager around under Jordan's nose.

'Man – you're brain's permanently in your freaking trousers since you got married!' A plate crunched under Ray's heavy foot as he stepped towards the table to put the pager down with a slap. 'You need more training, Jordan – you're getting sloppy!'

'I said, 'Good morning, Ray.' Megan shot him a dazzling smile she didn't feel, wondering which charm school Ray had been to. He should ask for his money back. 'Would you like a cup of coffee, Ray?' Kill the snake with kindness, don't loose your temper.

'Yeah…' He barely glanced at Megan. Directly in Jordan's line of vision, she winked at him, made a rude gesture with her hand in Ray's direction; and she loved the amusement that lit up Jordan's stunning blue eyes. Did Jordan feel this way when her friends turned up to visit? It wasn't so bad now that they'd moved. But whilst Megan had still been in the Mews, Alexa or one of the other girls were always 'just popping round'. It didn't matter how much you loved your friends – it caused frazzled nerves after a while.

Ray certainly made Megan feel frazzled. He'd no

manners; he called round whenever he wanted – no less than four times a week he disturbed their precious breakfast times.

Lord! Soon they'd have to stay awake all night to get any time together. As Megan stirred three sugars into Ray's coffee; it occurred to her maybe she was jealous of her husband's partner.

'Crazy…' She'd run that by Jordan, he'd laugh like a fool!

The men had moved into Jordan's study. 'You've got to be out of your mind!' Jordan's deep voice permeated the door, 'No! No way, man.'

'You're the only one she trusts, there's no choice. You're the one got so thick with her.'

Ray sounded so damned serious. Didn't he realise there was life beyond work?

They could be in there for hours, discussing whatever it was they discussed. Sighing, Megan set down the coffee on the tiny round table outside the door, rapped loudly, 'I'll leave your coffee here.'

'Yeah…' from Ray. There was no reply from Jordan.

She shrugged, left the two of them to talk and cleared up the mess she and Jordan had made earlier. At eight, Jordan and Ray were still in deep discussion. Resigned that she wouldn't spend any more time alone with Jordan before work, Megan packed her briefcase with plans for upcoming parties she could work on later at the Mews and tapped lightly on Jordan's study door.

'What now?' It was Ray – gracious as ever.

'I want to speak to Jordan.'

She heard a low muttering from Ray before Jordan snatched the door open, his eyes saying how much he loved her. Silently, he pulled the door closed behind him. 'You going, Megan?'

'Yep,' she put her briefcase down, 'I'm leaving you with

that miserable sod you call a partner.' She smiled and Megan noticed the way Jordan's eyes softened. 'You'll probably still be holed up with him when I get back tonight.'

'Do you reckon?'

'Yes.' Megan rose onto her tip toes and Jordan tilted his mouth down to cover hers in a long, lingering kiss. 'Why does he have to come here all the time?'

'It's the way we work, Megan.'

'I'm jealous.' She wriggled against him, then skipped away, grabbed her briefcase, loving the soft, deep sound of his laughter.

'I love you.' His words in response to her cheeky good-bye wave held a wealth of meaning.

As Megan pulled back the heavy iron grill of the lift, she thought how much she'd changed. Once work had been the driving force of her life – it still was vital – but she could never get through a day without anticipating the excitement she'd share with Jordan when she got home. Maybe she was getting obsessed too? She smiled, didn't care, felt too good to care.

Over the next three weeks, Megan was her busiest ever; more and more bookings were filling her diary, plans filling all her free time. During those three weeks, there were just two short messages on her ansaphone from Jordan.

Short was an understatement. One time, he said, 'Megan' then hung up; the second, 'It's OK...' Both were cut off immediately and Megan played the tape over and over, uncertain in the end if it really was Jordan's voice. On about the twentieth time, the tape mangled, and in a fit of temper, Megan jerked it out of the machine and flung it across the room. Where the hell was he?

Why'd he been away so long? He'd told her the job would only take a week. Another of those 'scoping' jobs? Had he had an accident? Was he lying in a ditch somewhere, bleeding to death? And almost worse, the stomach churning thought…was there another woman?

She couldn't eat. Couldn't sleep… Two days later, Megan strode into the local police station. 'I'd like to report a missing person, please?' She wasn't quite sure whether to be upset or angry.

The desk Sergeant spoke amicably to Megan for a few minutes, then asked, 'Does he often go away? Working? Recreation?'

'Well, yes.' She frowned. 'But not for this long. Not without getting in touch…'

'Has he tried to contact you at all, Mrs Elliot?'

'Very briefly – he left a couple of short messages on my ansaphone.' She just didn't tell the man how short.

'Well, then, don't you think he's just got delayed? Maybe there's a perfectly logical explanation – you know what the business world's like?' A couple of drunks were being hauled into the tiny station behind her, the arresting officer kept signalling to the desk Sergeant. 'I'd really like to get these gentlemen sorted, Sarge,' he finally interrupted. The phone rang and a WPC popped up from nowhere. Everyone was talking at once.

'What sort of business is he in, madam?'

'He's a Civil Engineer.' She lowered her voice urgently. 'He went to Cairo a few weeks ago.' One of the drunks lunged towards Megan, 'What you 'ere for, Doll? No business on the streets so you've to come in 'ere looking for trade?' His hot, sour breath hit her in the face.

'I shouldn't worry, madam. There's probably been a break-down in communications. He'll likely be back home when you get there.' The harassed Sergeant spoke gently, but Megan couldn't cope with the place any longer.

'Just forget it!' She ran out of the building. There was still Jordan's father – why hadn't she thought of him before? And there was Ray. 'I'll have to be bloody desperate before I try and contact him…'

Over the following months, Megan spent hours on the telephone trying to track down the Elliot of 'Ponsonby and Elliot' first. A cold trickle went down her spine to hear, 'No, dear, I'm afraid Mr Elliot retired to Australia two years ago.'

Jordan's father had been retired in Australia for two years? No wonder he hadn't made the wedding! 'Oh, Lord. What if he's not really that 'Elliot'? What if she'd married a shady character with a name like Smith who'd be impossible to trace? What if he made his money illegally? What if he'd gone off to marry some other poor gullible woman – and given his father's name as Ponsonby this time?

'Megan – can you get off the phone? Lucas has been trying to call you all day,' Alexa burst into Megan's office, 'Now he's here in person! He's not in a good mood!'

'I'll be right out.' Megan bit at her bottom lip, caught sight of herself in the tiny wall mirror just as she opened her door. Mauve smudges sat deeply beneath her eyes; her pale skin was unhealthy looking. And her hair – that glorious coppery mass of soft curls – was lacklustre.

'Lucas!' She tried for a broad smile, it worked…sort of.

'Are you ill?' He frowned. 'Or pregnant?'

'No, I'm fine, just didn't sleep that well.'

'You haven't returned my calls.' Lucas didn't believe her excuse, but nodded, closed her office door. 'I've an idea I want to discuss – it needs to be put together pretty quickly.' He carried on talking and Megan didn't register a word he was saying, her mind still tangled up with her husband.

'Sadly, Megan, it may be time I took my business elsewhere.'

'What?' That snapped her from the mire.

'You haven't heard a word…'

'Lucas, I'm sorry. Please, run it by me again?'

Impatiently, Lucas looked at his watch. 'I really don't have time now.' He rose to his feet and shook his head. 'So, it's true, then? I thought I was seeing things – months ago – during that blistering heat wave.'

Puzzled, Megan frowned up at Lucas as he rose to his feet. 'Sorry?' Had she missed another entire conversation? Was she losing her mind?

'Jurgen…he's got another woman.'

'Who's Jurgen?'

'No! That's it! Jordan! Your husband – sorry – your ex…!'

'My ex?' Megan shot to her feet; then slumped back to the chair; moved purely by Megan's shock, Lucas was forced to explain. 'I saw him. When was it? Yes, that's it!' He slapped the desk. 'Hottest day this year.

Terribly striking young woman – not as lovely as you, I might add – but all over one another…'

Megan could feel herself slipping close to the brink. The hottest day of the year, was when she'd organised the garden party in Thames Ditton? Concentrate! Concentrate on what Lucas is saying!

'…at Flavio's – you know?'

Yes, she knew. It was just about the most exclusive club in the City. Exclusive, expensive, extravagant. Snatches of Lucas's words filtered through the pounding in her ears.

'She was all over him.' Megan could barely breathe. 'My girlfriend said he must be drunk; but I don't think so.' If she clamped her lips tight together, could she manage not to be sick? 'We were both shocked, damned shocked, I tell you – especially because my girlfriend and I were both struck by how he seemed to idolise you.'

Megan held herself tense so she wouldn't fall off her chair and scream. 'And dressed all in red leather, she must have climbed straight off a motorbike! It's hardly the thing, is it? Flavio's have dress codes. They'd obviously slipped the manager a back-hander…'

No! This all sounded so sick! Her head spun with mixed

up visions, words, the final truth. It really was over. There'd been another woman all along. It was that simple. Jordan wasn't lying in hospital somewhere with amnesia. He wasn't working as a missionary in a foreign country, or visiting his retired father in Australia and losing track of time. He wasn't using Smith as an alias. He'd been as close as Flavio's with another woman. A 'striking, all over him' woman.

Lucas stood without Megan even registering as his parting words settled around her. 'You're damn right throwing the charmer out, Megan – you'll meet someone else. I'm sure you will.' There was no way – no way could Megan pull herself together to say more than goodbye to Lucas. She wanted him to leave so she could get drunk – scream with pain at the top of her lungs...throw herself out of the window.

She scowled grimly across at the lead-light window. 'That'll do you a lot of good, Megan, you're on the ground floor!'

As far as she could tell, her lungs hadn't worked since Lucas dropped his bombshell. Could she cry? Maybe, if someone stamped on her foot – hard. But she doubted she'd feel that; for some reason, she was trapped in an emotionless vacuum. Oh, the emotions lurked all right – but she didn't know yet whether they were anger, agony, grief or hysteria. Maybe even madness? Fear? Quite of what, she wasn't sure. It was like trying to identify each separate ingredient of a stew – a well mixed one from which no single flavour leapt forward and unmasked itself.

The fear – yes, the fear was the one emotion which charge over all the others. Yet it was a physical reaction that had Megan shooting to her feet and dashing for the bathroom with her palm clamped over her mouth.

A month followed then, where Megan could only function at the end of the telephone; she had Alexa overseeing every aspect of their parties; whilst Megan worked behind the scenes from the Mews – where she could retreat to her office at a moment's notice.

Still though, Jordan haunted her thoughts – he *had* loved her – he had! He haunted her nights too with vivid memories. Mornings were cold, chilly things, a tear-drenched pillow her only companion.

What Megan couldn't ignore was that he'd never been back to their Docklands flat – or she'd never seen him return. Some of his things were still in the wardrobe but a lot of his things had gone. Enough for him to set up with another woman…?

Three months after Jordan's desertion, Megan was driving to the Mews and she saw Ray talking to a skinny young man in a baseball cap. In a lightning second, she'd pulled up beside him, the man he spoke with slipping away. 'Ray?'

'Ah, Megan, I haven't seen you in a long time. How are you?'

'I'd be a lot better if I knew where my husband was.'

Megan left her car, stood before Ray, heart in her mouth as the man spoke. 'Jordan gave me a message to pass on if I saw you around.'

A message! Her insides flooded with warmth, all the agony of the past three months sank away.

There'd be a good explanation for the woman in red leather too…

'He did?' It was her first spontaneous smile in a long time.

'Yeah.' Ray pulled his collar up against the sharp October wind. 'Said to tell you he's left you. You can stay in his flat or sell it, he doesn't care.'

Ray would just love it if she blew her cool. He'd love it! She could see it in his eyes – he'd had that news saved up since Jordan had left and hadn't even bothered telling her! Megan kept the smile – it was frozen in place in any case, she could do nothing about it. But she chose her words carefully.

OK, Ray, thanks a lot.' And Lord only knew why, she winked at the man. 'Been nice knowing you.' No, she didn't know why she said that, but she'd seen the flare of surprise in Ray's eyes – he'd definitely expected histrionics!

Megan drove straight to the Mews and organised a van to move her belongings out of the 'marital' home. Then she cancelled it. What the hell did she need a van for? Everything was Jordan's except her clothes and personal items.

Ray's insensitive message had a cataclysmic, metamorphic effect on Megan. The mourning was over, the anger began. Oh, and it felt so much better. If anyone thought she'd be skulking around from now on – they'd better watch out – Megan, angry, was stunning. And Megan channelling that anger into energy was incredible. During the following weeks and months, she pulled herself back into shape, used make-up to disguise her pallid complexion and called up every contact she'd ever made, met with clients and prospective clients. She answered enquiries about her husband with, 'We've gone our separate ways.'

The name 'Elliot' was dropped as her surname, Megan Lacey reinstated. She couldn't find him to divorce him – but Megan didn't need the constant reminder of his name. She managed to hold herself together with a mixture of anger and nervous energy, that saw the mauve smudges beneath her eyes deepen even further; but also saw the laughing, passionate, fiery, copper haired flirtatious woman she'd always been, re-emerge. And only she knew that behind the façade her heart was breaking every time she thought of Jordan.

'Lacey!' It was Artemis who spoke, breaking the painful recollections, 'Stand up!'

The previous goodwill pervading the atmosphere vanished; the obvious enjoyment the woman derived when her eyes challenged Megan was blatant. 'You are to go with Hades.' To make matters worse, Artemis moved towards Zeus, spread her long, gloved fingers over his shoulder and writhed sinuously at his side. 'I think you will take care of his…needs.'

A moment of desperation paralysed Megan; she beseeched Zeus with her wide green eyes, but his were diverted to Artemis.

Instead, she heard his words, 'Look what you have already done to survive.' And Suzanne's words, 'You'll get through it…'

Megan silently said goodbye to the two people who she owed most too and allowed Hades to push her through the door.

chapter six

The cabin Hades dragged Megan to was tiny; there was just a curtained bunk and wardrobe. She saw the wild, unholy relish in Hades' evil eyes as he flung her from the door, straight onto the bunk. His breathing was laboured and he trembled with lust-filled excitement.

Every fibre of Megan screamed that she defend herself, roll from the bed and try to escape. 'We're locked in. You will not get away now!'

She rolled onto her back, her stomach curdling with revulsion as he flicked his fingers at his chest as would a tormentor looking for a brawl. 'Come on.' She'd love to scratch his eyes out! Megan gripped the bed cover to keep herself from moving, bit the insides of her lips to keep herself from yelling obscenities. 'Please, please,' she chanted silently, 'let Zeus be right…'

'Zeus said you were red-hot!' Still, his fingers beckoned her to fight. Still her responses begged her to fight. 'He slapped you about good – you enjoyed that, didn't you, babe? Come on, show me what you've got. Show me what made Zeus crazy for you.'

Blanking her stare, Megan clung harder to the bed cover. She closed her eyes and yawned. Lord, she was so tired.

'What are you doing!' He was enraged, Megan could feel it even with her eyes closed. She heard his breath buckle rattle with the strength of his anger.

'Getting comfortable.' What had Zeus said? Submit? She stretched her reluctant-to-move arms above her head, stretched her legs out to their full length. And lay motionless.

'No!' Hades sounded panicked.

Her eyes opened to see his features twisting under the mask, his teeth were bared. 'Fight me!'

If she died, she'd go down fighting, but Megan could see the truth of Zeus's words in Hades's eyes. Try it this way first. If it was live or die, then she could do it this way. 'I'm bored with fighting.' Megan sighed, pushed the stray curls from her cheek, prayed he couldn't see her hand shake, even that small movement an effort.

His eyes sparked with disbelief. But Megan hung on grimly to the cover and pretended to sleep.

'Give me what I want!'

He reminded Megan of Rumplestiltskin, she prayed he'd tear himself in two with fury – like the bad-tempered creature in the fairy tale.

'Do it!'

Heavy tiredness, so overwhelming tugged her, Megan didn't know if she would be able to fight if she had to.

Suddenly, Hades moved as if flooded in strobe lights, jerky, uncontrolled. Even the sounds erupting from his mouth seemed other-worldly. Megan didn't know if it was her own senses involved in some half-insane trickery, or whether his eyes really did roll back so she could see only the whites of his eyes, the hand jerking as it reached towards her.

She tried to move, but some strange lethargy had invaded her limbs, could only stare at Hades. So tired... Megan detached her mind and side-stepped into darkness, just seconds before Hades crumpled.

Back in the stateroom, Artemis was raising a glass of champagne to the remaining hostages, 'The waitress should be keeping Hades amused. No woman has ever survived his...' she hesitated cruelly, 'passion.'

'No!' Suzanne gasped, shook her head at Artemis' words,

'No, he can't hurt Megan!'

Suzanne, put her hand over Jack's as they both stared, horrified, at Artemis. The 'leader' merely shrugged. 'Forget her. She is finished.'

'We have much that is good to think about.' Artemis sipped the champagne, turned to stand squarely before Zeus, ran her fingers over his well-muscled shoulders. 'Are you sorry Lacey didn't live? You could have reclaimed her.'

Zeus showed no emotion, he just refilled the woman's glass. 'It matters not.'

'Wait until we dock to remove her. There are other, more important matters for us to deal with now. Kronos!' Artemis called to the man, 'Is everything secured for disembarkation?'

'Yes, Artemis.'

'Good! Zeus. You can be responsible for getting rid of the woman and Philip's bodies once we reach land. Make it look like an accident. I suggest you issue Hades with another gun. Use his to finish off Philip and put it into the waitress's hand. Then go below and stay with the caché. I will join you in a half-hour. Kronos, take charge of these people – I need to go and change.'

Suzanne gasped involuntarily. 'Please! Please, let us see Megan once more! Please!'

Zeus shook his head, spoke quietly. 'It is better to remember her as she was.' His eyes held the message: 'remember her how she was before Hades got his hands on her.' And as Suzanne closed her eyes on shocked tears, Jack's comforting arm supported her.

As soon as Zeus left the stateroom, he broke into a run, he was breathing hard by the time he reached Hades' tiny cabin at the far end of the ship. Pushing Hades' sleeping form away from the side of the bed with his foot, he frowned down at the dishevelled, fully-dressed, lifeless form on the berth. In a single, gentle movement, he rolled Megan onto her back and felt for the pulse in her neck, looking at his watch as he did so.

He wafted a tiny bottle under her nose and took her pulse again.

'Megan…' he grimaced, fingertips tracing the freckles on her cheek 'Fight back, Lacey, come on!'

Deeply asleep, Megan could feel the blood in her veins trying to pump again. A strong smell hit her nose, shocked through her in waves, a beautiful, resonant, familiar voice pulled, coaxed at her.

'There isn't much time.'

Suspended beneath the thick fog of unconsciousness, soft, barely audible laughter broke from her. 'There isn't much time…' echoed from another lifetime. From Jordan…

They rode up in the old-fashioned lift to their flat, kissing, laughing, 'You're turning me as damn crazy as you are, Megan,' Jordan's eyes turned from bright blue to dark, 'I couldn't concentrate all morning for needing you.' He kissed her until the lift stopped, swung Megan up into his arms, dashed for the privacy of their flat.

'You know, Mr Elliot,' Megan teased, slowly unfastened his tie, undid his top button. 'Dropping by the Mews and announcing you need me to "come home and sign something", didn't convince anyone.'

'Yeah, well I never was much good at lying.' A totally, masculine grin lifted one corner of his lips. 'I hate this suit, Megan, it makes you look so damn prim.' Jordan's impatient fingers battled with the neck to hip buttons. 'Hell! You undo them, darling, I don't have time…'

His fingers tugged up the hem of her short, tailored skirt and he whispered, 'Thank goodness!' when he found her wearing stockings, kissed her, wound her shapely legs around his waist, filled her, wasted no time undressing. 'Megan, I love you so much, it's killing me.'

She'd abandoned the buttons to hold on to his shoulders, drew his mouth down to hers, thrilled at his incredible need.

They made exciting, tempestuous love. Jordan looked up at Megan, astride him when the storm was over.

He ran a flat palm up her thigh, those smouldering eyes of his flickering with lust again.

Laughing, Megan flicked his dark tie. 'You didn't take a damn thing off that time!' She wriggled a little, jerked his shirt from his trousers and spread her fingers beneath its fabric, over his chest, before she sank down to kiss his sensuous mouth. Whilst they kissed, her eyes opened to meet Jordan's blue gaze.

Megan – what are you doing to me?' He gripped her wrists, held them still, grew hard inside her. A low curse broke from him, he grimaced and rolled Megan onto her back, took her again, muttering, 'You could at least have lost that wretched jacket…'

'When you're in this much of a hurry, Buster, you've got to take what you can get.' Then she whispered against his mouth, 'But if you tug really hard, the jacket comes off over my head.'

In a second, the jacket flew across the room and Jordan feasted on her softness, made love to her with such skill, that Megan ended up a boneless wreck.

Jordan's curse dragged Megan back from the warm afterglow of love-making. He staggered to his feet, tucked his shirt in and ran his fingers through his soft, mussed hair. 'I'm supposed to be some place else!' A couple of tweaks to his tie and he looked as immaculate as ever. No one would ever know he'd spent his lunch break making up for lost time.

'Listen.' He pulled Megan to her feet, pushed her wild hair back over her shoulder. 'Sweetheart, I've got to dash!' He kissed her briefly, firmly on the mouth. 'Can you grab a cab back to the Mews?'

'Do I have a choice?'

He shrugged, grabbed his briefcase, raised his other hand. 'No. Sorry…' Jordan's smile devastating, apologetic as he hurried out the door.

Megan laughed. She felt deliciously naughty – more like Jordan's mistress than his wife. He just had to have her when his need got too hot to handle. If that was what happened when they both slept through the morning alarm, and didn't have the time to make love – maybe she'd set it a bit later on purpose some mornings!

'Alexa…' Megan contacted her partner. 'I'm running behind because of that business Jordan had to take care of. I'll go straight to my appointment with Open Seas from here.' As she spoke, Megan pulled on a shower cap, stepped out of the rest of her clothes. 'I'm going to push for them to keep our details on file in case of an emergency. They're so committed to their regular catering contractors, I think that's the best approach.'

'Yeah, and we'd better not hold our breath.'

'Well, we've got some pretty good testimonials these days, more than we had last time I tried to get in there.'

'Go for it!' Alexa chuckled. 'We've nothing to lose.'

'I'll do that.'

'Sure. Oh, Megan, don't be late, you haven't got much time…'

'I don't have much time.' He was tapping her cheek, the smelling salts burst under her nose again, this time, the sharpness of them opened her eyes.

'Can you hear me?'

'Y-yes.' Megan frowned, she'd lost the script somewhere, her gaze fixating on a masculine hand moving close to her face.

'When I take you on to land, play dead. You got that?'

'Dead?' He pulled on his glove, Megan was confused.

'Why?'

'Safer that way.' Her mind was trying to grasp reality, but fluffed and tricked in its befuddled state.

'Did Hades…?'

'No. As I promised you, he was unconscious before he could touch you. Look, you've got to pretend to be dead a while longer.' He said something else, but Megan caught only, '…when we disembark.'

'Mmm.' Megan's eyes closed. Zeus swore, shook his head and slipped silently from the cabin; the antidote to rouse Hades from his drugged state remained in his pocket for a little longer.

Play dead? Why? And why was he going to disembowel her when they landed? Different. He was the same, but different. His speech…yes, his speech was different.. Or did he say he'd take care of her when they disembarked? What did he mean? Her cotton wool brain played tricks, drugged…? Why?

'You will all be taken to a small building overnight whilst we unload our 'cargo' from The Dream.' Artemis walked amongst the hostages confidently, flourishing her hands. 'Tomorrow, your crew will be returned to you and I strongly advise you *all* to continue the short journey to your island destination.' She hesitated, cocked her finger at Matt Duprey. 'It is your island, Duprey, is it not?'

'It is.'

'I *also* advise each and every one of you to forget everything that happened and will happen, until you are returned to The Dream tomorrow evening. You have been allowed to live – but you must live mutely. Our organisation has a long reach. Speak of this and you will endanger the lives of your families. Your fate will be the fate of Lacey and Philip. Put it behind you and you will be safe.'

Then, she swept the hostages with her pistol, her voice hard. 'Do you all understand what I say?'

With military precision, the hostages were moved from The Dream to a large, airless bungalow on the sloping beach. It was dark, and they were told to move silently and quickly.

Megan didn't even move when Zeus returned to the ship after everyone else had left, to carry out her 'body'. He'd convinced Artemis that it would be best to bury both Philip and Lacey deep.

'I'll use the lifeboat to take the corpses ashore, taking some supplies at the same time. It will be quicker that way.' They had enough to worry about with the illegal cargo they carried, getting it ashore and hidden rapidly.

'A good suggestion, Zeus.' As always, she touched him whilst she spoke, then snapped the order to begin unloading the cargo, pointing to the beach bungalow it was to be taken to.

Lights were set up to shine down on the long, thin jetty that reached out to The Dream. There was only room to move single file along the rickety wooden platform. Hades, Eros and Kronos were to unload whilst Artemis and Thor guarded the hostages.

Balmy, the air was balmy...

It felt as though she was still on honeymoon, and Jordan was carrying her to their beach apartment in Puerto Rico, Gran Canaria. The sound of crickets filled night air; a dog barked somewhere. Waves lapped the shore. Megan sighed and snuggled into his chest. 'I love you,' she murmured, the sound of her own voice brought her further up the ladder of consciousness.

'Shut up. You're supposed to be dead!'

She frowned, her mind clearing quickly in the fresh air.

'Hell!' Megan gasped completely awake when Zeus dunked her backside in the sea as he climbed out of the small boat.

'Will you be quiet!' His tone rough. 'If you don't button it – right now – we'll both be pushing up daffodils!'

'Uh?' Pushing up…? 'Where'd you learn your English?'

'Shut your mouth!'

'You're not foreign!' Moonlight burst from behind dark clouds. Megan grabbed the bottom of Zeus's woollen face mask, yanked upwards, backwards over his head. Blond hair. '*Jor-dan*!' she gasped in a shocked, choking breath.

'*N-n-oo*!' A scream exploded in her chest, couldn't find release, insanity clawed her mind. '*No*!'

A second. Two. Neither of them moved or breathed. Just stared. A large hand clapped over her mouth, his other clamping her waist.

'Don't make a sound, Megan. We're behind schedule.'

The air trapped behind his hand made a gurgling sound as Megan struggled and flailed, her eyes hating, loving, disbelieving, believing. Her insides freezing, her mind flipping and weaving like a crazy, trapped bird.

'Zeus!' The call came from the gangway. She bit his hand, hard. He drove her under the water, held her under so bubbles rushed to the surface until Megan thought her lungs would burst. 'You all right?'

'Yes, Kronos, I am fine.' He laughed, added dryly. 'I dropped the woman's corpse. I have it now.'

Laughter rang around in Megan's head, she took a breath against his chest where he smothered the noise. 'Trust me,' he whispered, coldly. 'Or die.'

'Trust you?' So hoarse, barely audible, Megan swung her fist at his stomach; he caught her hand, held it fast. 'Jordan, I wouldn't trust you enough to wipe my feet on your face. *You swine*!'

'I don't have time for this…' He threw her over his shoulder, knocking the air from her stomach, ran from the shallows up the beach, towards the bungalow. 'Make a sound and they'll shoot you. I haven't got time to baby-sit you any more.'

Baby-sit? She grabbed hold of his belt to keep from swinging around, glanced sideways to see a long stream of people being helped along the jetty. People? 'Who're they?' she spluttered.

'Terrorists. The precious cargo.' The sound of a helicopter throbbed loud in the air – suddenly – appearing from nowhere.

Big, conical lights, smoke, shouting, whistling, firing, the massive noise and draught from the helicopter, stirring, whipping sand; men dressed darkly wearing bright yellow strips, dangling, dancing on ropes from the airborne craft.

Megan thumped Jordan hard on his back. 'Put me down! Put me down!'

She wriggled and twisted, glimpsed something written on the back of the men's boiler suits in huge letters; but she couldn't open her eyes properly for the sand the helicopter blew up. One of the bright beams of light broke over her, then a tiny red dot shone on Jordan's thigh, Megan gasped, 'No!' before his entire body jerked, and a sound – more a hiss – broke from him, and she tangled with him as they hit the soft sand.

'You stupid bastards!' Megan staggered to her feet, her yell lost in the mayhem. Smoke, coughing forms spewed from the low, white bungalow further up the beach; she heard that horrible ratchet sound of weapons being armed. Someone was running towards her.

She took a step towards him, thumped him in his chest. 'You stupid bastards! I wanted to kill him!' But the tall man in the woollen hat, face blackened, a tiny microphone leading from an earphone just smiled condescendingly. 'You're safe now, Miss.'

He kicked Jordan's form so he rolled onto his back. 'Oh, sheesh!' The man murmured something into his microphone, something like, 'Elliot down and wounded, we need a Medevac.'

She saw the man wince at the loud reply that threatened his eardrum. 'Keep the floodlights away from East of the beach, repeat…'

'Will somebody tell me what's going on?' Megan slumped to the sand beside Jordan, the man pushing a thick pad against the wound on Jordan's thigh, looked across to the spot-lit bungalow. Against the outside wall, a woman – Artemis – dressed in red leather, was handcuffed hand and foot.

Red leather? Megan felt sick.

'Jordan?' It was her 'hero rescuer' leaning over Jordan, bringing him round, 'Where the hell's Phil?'

'Still in the boat – playing dead – nasty head and chest wounds. But he'll live.'

'Suzanne? She all right?'

'Far as I know, she's cool.'

'Man, I'm sorry, you didn't have your 'colour' on – and this woman looked like she was having trouble with you…' He grimaced apologetically. 'We had her on the hostage list with an excellent description. Megan Lacey?'

'Megan Elliot.' Jordan's eyes were still disguised behind black contact lenses, his overlong, layered, soft blond hair clung to the sweat on his face and neck.

'Megan Lacey.' Megan glared down at Jordan. 'Don't you dare call me Elliot!'

Jordan's mouth quirked into that unbelievable, masculine smile of his, a dimple slashing even deeper in his unshaven face. 'Craig, this is my lovely wife, Megan.'

'I am not your wife anymore – you double-dealing, sleazy b-b-bigamist!'

Megan wanted to hit him – *hard* – but Craig sensed that and moved between them. 'Oh, sheesh. The one McRoss and Blackmore gave you a hard time over?' Craig looked

Megan up and down, not insultingly, just interested, 'Man, I ain't surprised. Dull, she isn't.'

'I'm not putting up with this!' Megan planted her hands on her hips. 'Just go to hell! I never want to see you again!'

She wanted to slam a door – preferably in Jordan's face – and punch him into the middle of next week! She trembled from head to toe with fury, and it jerked up another notch when Jordan said sardonically, 'Yeah, I reckon she preferred Zeus.'

Megan spun around. 'Just what the hell do you mean?'

'You got so you really wanted him.' Even blackened behind the contacts, Megan saw the fury in Jordan's eyes.

She flung herself towards him, couldn't take any more. 'You bloody hypocrite!' Craig though, was quicker, pulled Megan firmly away. Still she struggled, kicked out at Craig, at Jordan. 'How can you accuse me of that, when you were always making up to that sleazy cow in her red leather get-up?'

Copper curls flew around her face as she fought to free herself from Craig's bear-like grip, 'The things you called me! Made me do! Now you're jealous because I slept with you to survive?' She got one hand free in a great surge of fury, almost caught Jordan's head before Craig pulled her back.

'Sorry, ma'am,' he murmured, before in a smooth movement, he handcuffed her wrists behind her. 'Jordan's one of our top undercover agents, can't have him beaten senseless by his…er…wife. Wouldn't look too healthy on his CV.'

'Get these off me!' Megan tried to free her arms, but soon stopped when she almost lost her balance. 'I'm not a criminal!' Again, her hair flew everywhere, her uniform poppers unfastened half way down exposing flawless, creamy flesh. 'And I'm NOT his wife!'

'I believe you could be dangerous.' Craig sounded almost serious.

She ignored him. 'How could you let Hades come any-where near me? Never mind being jealous of Zeus, Jordan!' she yelled, so outraged that she couldn't think straight. 'Maybe Zeus wasn't the only one!'

His face darkened, features taut with anger and agony such as Megan had never witnessed. And she felt perverse satisfaction that she'd thrown the bomb straight in his face.

'Megan – I told you I'd drugged him. I'd have killed him if I had to. No way would I have let him ...'

'Just don't say you're sorry, Jordan. I won't believe you. I won't believe anything you say to me – ever again. I don't want to speak to you ever again. I'm Megan Lacey now, I'm divorcing you and citing mental and physical cruelty as the reason! I'm going to tell all the newspapers...'

'Ah, Megan!' It was Ray Blackmore, and his voice stopped her in her tracks, her stomach lurching sickly. He frowned down at her handcuffs, shook his head. 'Been fraternising with the enemy?'

'Oh, get lost, Ray!'

A strange choking sound broke from Jordan and Craig simultaneously.

'Medevac's on it's way, Jordan. You idiot, you should have had your colour on!' Ray bit out.

'Well, hell,' his eyes flashed in anger at Megan. 'I got distracted bringing my wife's 'corpse' off The Dream.'

Ray shook his head. 'What were you doing on The Dream?' He was angry – coldly angry. 'Did you stowaway because Jordan was on board?'

'Get stuffed, Ray!' Frustration grew in Megan because she couldn't lash out. 'Tell your bloody action man to take these handcuffs off me! I haven't done anything wrong.'

'No. I asked you a question, Megan.'

'Miss Lacey to you, jerk. I won't answer!'

'Jordan, while you and your wife are in the Medevac, kindly explain to her that she has to be debriefed.'

'Debriefed! No!' Megan got so mad, flailed about so much, she lost her balance and fell over. 'I am not ever again – sleeping with a man!' It was only after she'd landed awkwardly on her side, knocked the wind from her lungs, that Megan realised what Ray meant. And she hated all three men for practically choking themselves with laughter at her expense.

'Right.' Ray pulled himself back in line. 'Craig, get in touch with her office. Find out what she was doing on The Dream – get straight back to me. Find out if anyone from her company knew Jordan was on board.'

'They won't tell you anything!' Megan yelled defiantly, earning herself a mouthful of sand.

Ray gave Megan a look which said he thought she'd be better off dead; she stamped on the urge to stick out her tongue at him. 'Do you honestly think I'm so desperate, that I'd stowaway…?'

Ray held up his hand. 'Save it, Megan.' He leant over Jordan, put a fresh handkerchief over the bleeding wound. 'I think we've established you're alive.'

'Jordan…?' She gasped, his eyes were closed; he was very, very pale. 'For pity's sake, Ray, undo these handcuffs.'

'Craig put them on you, Megan. He must have had good reason.'

'Look – my husband is lying there dying – and you've got me handcuffed!'

'For your own safety.' He scanned the beach for Craig who ran towards them.

'OK. Lacey was on The Dream to handle the catering and on-board parties. She didn't have a clue about Jordan being on board. In fact, the girl I spoke to said that if she'd known he was there, she'd have refused the job!'

The sound of a helicopter landing in the distance distracted Megan. 'It's for Jordan.' Ray nodded to Craig, who helped Megan to her feet.

'I'm not going with him!' Megan tried to dig her feet into the sand, but got pulled along by Craig. 'I want to go with everybody else!'

'You have to go with Jordan,' Ray said flatly, clearly fed-up with her.

'Why? I'm not married to him anymore! I told you that!'

'Yeah, and the minute you thought he was dying, you swung a line about him being "your husband".'

The stretcher bearers ran to Jordan's side, moved with incredible efficiency, a drip-bag line inserted into a canula before Megan could blink. He was so pale, so devastatingly handsome… and Megan hated him so much for what he'd done to her.

'I told the other hostages you were going to a 'specialist' hospital for treatment because there may be psychological damage. You can't see any of the others till you understand the position.' Craig put his arm through one of Megan's, Ray her other.

'I'm not going with him!' She struggled against them, but against two large, fit men, she had no effect.

'There's some things you've got to hear before you see your friends again, Megan.'

'You! I can't believe how nice you were to me in front of Jordan on our wedding day!' Megan snarled at Ray. 'You're a slimy, two-faced pig!'

'Yeah, well, all this just proves what a mistake your marriage was, doesn't it? You're a disruptive influence on Jordan's work.'

'Me!' Megan jerked to a halt; the handcuffs on her wrists as both men carried on walking. 'You were the disruptive one, you…you jerk! Do you know how early we had to get up to get any time together?'

'Yeah, well I warned him that getting hitched wasn't a clever move.'

'You had no right to interfere!' Megan was careful to keep

walking, these two obviously didn't care if her hands fell off and dropped to the sand. As it was – her feet hardly touched the ground they moved so fast.

'Mind the propellers, Megan.' Ray jerked a thumb at the idle objects. 'Craig, get her inside.'

'I don't want to go to the hospital.' Megan gritted her teeth. 'I'll complain to your superiors, Ray, for making me!'

'Do that.'

'Pig!'

She didn't want to look at Jordan as they loaded his stretcher opposite her. Wouldn't have. But he let out a low moan. Involuntarily, she moved slightly towards him, but Craig kept her firmly in her seat. Another of her buttons popped open – and there wasn't a thing she could do about it. She certainly wasn't going to ask Ray or Craig to do up her uniform. Let them see, the creeps, she thought; what the hell do I care? The fact that her breasts were threatening to spill right out of the uniform didn't seem that high on her priorities at that moment.

'Why is it so important that I come with you and not join the others?' Megan forced civility into her tone, figured she might get more out of these two goons that way.

'Every hostage has to be physically checked out and debriefed in detail.' Ray's eyes flicked to Craig, they'd both enjoyed the earlier joke at Megan's expense. 'Not till then can we be certain Jordan's cover stayed intact. You broke through it – despite his best efforts.' Ray sighed. 'Maybe someone else did.'

'I don't think so.' Megan considered, still as angry as ever, but it seemed that appearing civil was the only way to get anywhere. 'He had me fooled until he said we'd be "pushing up daffodils".'

'You must have freaked him out big time – just being on The Dream, let alone trying to cope with you mouthing off.'

Megan shot Ray an angry look but managed to keep silent.

'See, now you know what Jordan does – in particular what he did – on The Dream, we need to keep you incommunicado until he's one-hundred-per-cent certain he can trust you not to blow his cover. Because you know who he is, and what he does.' Ray emphasised, 'You can't tell anyone. You'll put the whole Organisation in jeopardy; particularly your own and Jordan's lives.'

'I won't tell anyone a damn thing…' Megan began to realise the enormity of the issue she was caught up in. 'Just let me go.'

'We can't. It's Jordan's decision.'

Megan tipped back her head. It was HER decision. And she'd learned a few things on board The Dream. Let everyone think they were getting what they wanted – then walk right out the hospital doors…

'The other hostages have been taken to St Luke's Hospital on the mainland.' Craig spoke to Ray. 'We should be at Maquippa in half an hour.'

'Won't the other 'Greek gods' notice Zeus isn't with them?' Megan shifted in her seat to ease the discomfort of her tight handcuffs.

'As far as they're concerned, Zeus is dead.'

'If they think he's dead, how can Jordan be in any danger? Or me.' Despite herself, a cold shiver raced through Megan. She tried to distract herself. 'I don't see why I need checking over. I'm in one piece.'

Craig and Ray exchanged a strained look. Craig grimaced. Ray spoke. 'You still have to be checked out.'

One of the paramedics was working on Jordan's leg wound and she stared at the man's back, blinked back the rise of angry tears. For heaven's sake – not now! Not in front of those two hard-nosed pigs!

The faceless paramedic moved aside, adjusted the drip on

its pole; Megan felt the force of Jordan's bright blue eyes on her. Lord! Those tears still sat unshed in her eyes and he'd think they were for him. But challenged by his gaze, Megan couldn't back down. She stared right back at Jordan. No relationship could survive this! Megan didn't want it to. She'd loved this blue-eyed man passionately, then grieved, spending months in so much pain. And yes, her cheeks flamed at the self-admission, the last time with Zeus – she had wanted him. Why, she didn't understand. Maybe she'd just needed to know she was still alive – because Hades might kill her.

If she was completely honest, and Megan had to be, Zeus had triggered the same incredible sensuality in her that Jordan always had. She'd asked him not to hurt her, and he hadn't. He'd excited her even as she'd fought against his blatant sexuality. *I'm not going to feel guilty for that, you rat!*

Her eyes flashed with anger, an anger magnified to Jordan by the tears still sitting, unshed in her beautiful, forest green eyes. Suddenly, his blue gaze dipped to her breasts, a muscle spasm twitched in his cheek; he took a breath between gritted teeth and let his eyes close. 'Fasten your dress, Megan.'

'Certainly.' She cooed, 'Just as soon as you tell these goons to take my handcuffs off!'

'What?' Jordan tried to move, then stopped on a shaft of pain. 'Ray, you must be mad! What's she doing in cuffs?'

Ray nodded towards Craig. 'It's Craig's shout.'

'Take them off her, Craig. That's an order.'

'Jordan!' At the flash of anger in Jordan's eyes, Craig winced and amended, 'Sir, Ms Lacey tried to attack you.'

'Mrs Elliot…' Jordan ground out, 'Won't try it again.'

Megan couldn't believe her ears. Of course she'd try it again! Jordan and Craig shared a knowing look. 'If you're sure, Sir.'

'Yes.' Those blue eyes captured Megan's disbelieving

ones, sparked when he added. 'You can always put them back on, Craig. Once Mrs Elliot has fastened her dress.'

Craig gestured for Megan to move forwards on the bench seat and unfastened the handcuffs.

'You condescending jerk!' Megan lurched forward on the seat so her knees were close to Jordan. 'What do you mean, Mrs Elliot?'

'Must have been a Freudian slip of the tongue, Megan.' He smiled, but it didn't reach his eyes.

Megan heard the slap in her head – the great, loud, resounding sound as her palm swiped his cheek. But that's the only place she heard it. Her wrists had been cuffed so tightly, her arms were like lead, and tingling – useless.

'I said fasten your dress, Megan.'

'Where do you get off telling me what to do!' She still couldn't move her arms and his arrogant command really ticked her off.

'You're my wife, darling,' he said coolly. 'And I don't "get off" on telling you what to do.' Those blue eyes hardened. 'I don't want everyone else looking at you now.'

Even Ray cleared his throat at that. Megan thought she would explode with pure fury. And she felt all three men tense, ready for the inevitable explosion.

Megan sensed Jordan wanted a fight as much as she; and because of that, she smiled, crossed her legs so the tops of her stockings just peeped from the uniform, and took a deep breath so the remaining two buttons at the waist strained. 'I like the way I look.'

'Oh, sh-oot.' Megan heard Craig beside her.

In an instant, Jordan's large hands spanned the gap between them, pulled Megan clear of the bench seat to drop on her knees beside him. 'Stop that!'

Perversely, it thrilled Megan to see Jordan so out of control. She hated him, and wouldn't let him get under her skin again. He was damn well going to suffer for what he'd done. 'Oh, Jordan.' She bit her bottom lip, let her tangled hair fall around her cheeks, recognised confusion in his eyes when she whispered, 'I've been mauled so much these last couple of weeks, I can't think straight.'

Disgust, jealousy, quiet bubbling rage lit his eyes. Megan loved the way his fingers trembled as he snapped her uniform poppers together. That was, until his wrist brushed the fullness of one creamy breast when Megan swayed towards him slightly. The contact lasted less than a second, but its impact frazzled every single nerve end in Megan's body. In that second, she glanced into Jordan's eyes. And saw every beautiful moment they'd ever spent in one another's arms, their souls reaching out – touching.

'No!' The denial to herself, but Jordan had seen it, felt it too.

'It's not over, Megan.' Jordan said the words as if he wished it was.

She slid back onto the bench, tidy again, her arms aching a bit, her wrists sore where she'd struggled against the cuffs. Trying for dignity, she wriggled down her skirt, folded her fingers together in her lap, stared straight ahead. When her pulse slowed to something like normal and the electric shock from his touch receded, Megan announced calmly. 'It will be over when you let me go.'

'When I what?'

'When you let me divorce you.' Continuing to look out of the window, she explained. 'Your friends here said I can't divorce you unless you allow it.' Megan said that as though she'd do whatever she wanted – whether Jordan 'allowed it' or not.

'It's not that simple.' Jordan said, his mouth in a taut line, 'What grounds would you cite?'

'Whatever you fancy, Jordan, take your choice! Desertion, mental cruelty, physical cruelty, lying, cheating, adultery…'

'Adultery! Now hang on a minute…'

'That – that slug in red leather!'

'Artemis?' Jordan gasped. 'How'd you know about her?'

'Someone saw you "devouring" one another.' Megan wanted to throw up just saying that.

Jordan diverted his attention to Ray. 'Do we need containment on that?'

'Haven't got any details from "Ms" Elliot yet, Jordan.'

Frowning, Megan looked from Jordan to Ray and back again. 'Do you mind talking so I can understand?'

They both ignored her. 'Soon as I get the info we'll assess it.'

Lord! They were so infuriating! Then a secret smile curved Megan's lips. She'd damn well ignore them the next time they asked her anything!

'Are you in a lot of pain, Mr Elliot, Sir?' The paramedic eased a gauze pad over Jordan's thigh wound. 'If it gets too much, we can give you something else for the pain.'

'Better not.' Jordan winced at the applied pressure. 'I need my mind sharp, that last shot made me woozy for a bit.'

'Certainly, sir.'

'What do you mean, lying?' Jordan impaled Megan with his blue eyes. 'I didn't lie to you.'

'You lied plenty.'

'For instance?'

'Your father, for instance, has been in Australia for the past two years!'

'I never said he lived in Britain.' He frowned, glanced at Ray, 'How'd you find that out?'

'About a thousand phone calls.' Megan remembered the pain, the callous hurt he'd caused her. 'Come to think of it, Jordan, I didn't know if you were dead or alive for months!'

'Megan…'

'Civil Engineer indeed! Just let me ask you something!'

she interrupted. 'If it'd been me just walking out one day –
what would you have thought? Oh, she's just off somewhere
enjoying herself? She'll be back when she's ready!' Megan
gave the pain free rein, 'Was I supposed to forget you ever
existed?'

'No.'

'You are cruel and heartless. You never loved me, or you
couldn't have treated me like this!'

Megan folded her arms, sat back. Being this close to him
was like vigorously rubbing salt into an open wound – a big
open wound. For the sake of her sanity, Megan visualised
herself walking off the helicopter, running for freedom,
away from the husband she'd loved so much – too much.
Even when he'd married her, he must have seen her as dis-
pensable. The way he'd been – so intense – so much fun. So
sexy. Had any of it been real? Silently, she shook her head.
The most wonderful part of her life was reduced to a sham.
Jordan had never loved her. Lust that's all it ever was. He
couldn't have loved her and treated her so badly.

They landed and Jordan was whisked away by the
paramedics, met at the swishing doors of the brightly lit,
Gothic style building. She could smell salt in the air – they
were somewhere beside the sea. But there was no sign of an
ocean – no sign of any kind of landscape beyond the flood-
lit, perfectly manicured lawns. The walls were higher than
any she'd seen and Megan's despondency increased. Impris-
oned. That's how she felt.

'I can't stay here…' She shook her head, shivering in the
night air. 'What is this place?'

A familiar-looking woman walked towards Megan, her
round face wreathed in smiles, her eyes kind. 'Suzanne!'

'Megan – thank goodness you're all right.'

'I thought you said the hostages were going to a different
hospital?'

'Suzanne works for us.' Ray gave Megan a gentle shove

towards the front doors. 'She'll stay with you and help with your debriefing.'

'Oh, hell!' Megan shook her head. 'Is anyone who I think they are?'

'I imagine you're feeling pretty angry right now.' Suzanne linked arms with Megan, smiled that wonderful, sympathetic smile, and walked briskly towards the old building. 'We've got to get you checked out, love, it shouldn't take too long – the staff here are fantastic.'

Megan was confused because Suzanne was as kind as ever – she hadn't changed into Attilla the Hun and started saluting the likes of Jordan and Ray...

'You know, I'd heard a rumour Jordan was "very married", Megan, that he'd gone against the Organisation's code. But I'd no idea it was to you.'

'We're getting divorced.'

'Oh, dear.' She smiled, showed Megan into a large examination room, 'The Organisation usually insists on retirement when an operative's cover is blown.'

Suzanne said it lightly, as though it was no big deal. 'Could you get in the gown and put your clothes into the plastic sack?' she added. 'I'll get you something new to wear from the stores, for after you've been examined.'

The medical examination was thorough; every sample it was possible for a human being to give was taken.

The questions which followed were endless, relentless. What had Jordan given to Hades to knock him out?

'Some kind of pill.'

Suzanne, who'd stayed to take notes, shook her head, gave some long name.

'Ah, yes. That little jewel.'

When Megan frowned, the female doctor explained, 'It eventually slows the heartbeat to the point where the uneducated could mistake death. Useful – in the right hands.'

She smiled kindly from behind her large, clear glasses. 'I

imagine you gave your husband quite a scare.'

How did they all know so much that she didn't? 'No. I think he'd have preferred it if I'd died.'

That earned her a shocked glance from both women. The female doctor cleared her throat. 'Right, then, Mrs Elliot, I'll do a pregnancy test just in case.'

'This is just so awful.' Megan sat up and pulled the gown down around her knees. 'Is this really all because I recognised Jordan?'

'Yes, Mrs Elliot.'

'And if I hadn't? No one would care whether I was pregnant or – or anything?'

'Oh, you'd still have undergone this examination, but at a different location.'

'I see.' But Megan wondered whether she really did see.

'If you'd like to shower, or bath, Mrs Elliot, you can now, the humiliating part of this is over for you.'

Megan smiled out of politeness, grateful about that. But she wouldn't have if she'd any idea of the humiliation to follow.

chapter seven

'How are you doing, Jordan?' It was the Organisation director, Frank McRoss. 'Just relax,' he held up his hand when he saw Jordan start from sleepiness to full alert.

'Fine, sir.'

Frank was small, wiry, his hair thinning. He wore round, wire-framed glasses with such thick lenses, his eyes appeared big and gentle. He was the most powerful man Jordan knew.

'Try again.'

'I feel like hell. I blew this one, big time.'

Frank laughed. 'I don't call securing eleven terrorists 'blowing it big time'. It's a good result. I came by to congratulate you.'

Frowning, Jordan fought the sleepiness caused by pain killing drugs, 'That's not all you came by to say, is it?'

'No.' Frank pulled a chair up to Jordan's bedside. 'I know you haven't been fully debriefed, but I'll bring you up to date on what we've done.'

Jordan had an uncomfortable, sinking sensation. For Frank McRoss to visit his hospital bed, something must have hit the fan.

'Not a single person on board The Dream thought you were anyone other than Zeus. We've put out the story to the news agencies that one terrorist and one contracted employee on board the ship were killed, and all credit is going to the security services. What you have to do is get back into your real identity for now; we'll use you for desk work, information gathering and backup for a couple of years.'

'That's cool.' Jordan enjoyed collating information, as opposed to the 'deep cover' operations which could take months, or as with Zeus, years to bring to fruition. At least he now had the freedom to remain himself and retain some kind of life.

'I thought you were going to brief me on another long job, Frank,' Jordan smiled, 'I don't expect a visit for a bullet in the leg.'

'Ah, well…there's something the doctor thinks you should know. I'm not sure your wife will tell you voluntarily.'

Jordan paled – visibly.

'They'll run another test tomorrow. It looks like Megan could be in the early stages of pregnancy.'

'How – long?'

'Megan likely became pregnant two weeks ago. It had to have happened on board The Dream.'

'You shouldn't be telling me this.'

'No. Your wife doesn't know yet.' Frank sighed. 'I'm telling you in case it colours your judgement as to whether to let Megan walk or not. Hades didn't touch her.'

'I know that. I put enough tranquilliser in his coffee to knock an elephant out for a week.' Jordan shook his head, 'Hell, Megan and I are both so ticked-off with one another – ' he shoved his fingers through his hair, 'I know how I felt about Megan, Frank.' He couldn't even begin to think about picking up the pieces of their marriage right then. 'I got to tell you, this is one big mess.'

'It is. We've got Suzanne and our best interrogation team with Megan at the moment – and she's said diddly-squat!' He laughed. 'She says that she's not telling anybody anything until you agree to divorce her.'

Jordan's stomach lurched sickly; all the colour drained from his features, his voice a deep whisper when he replied. 'I guess if there's no other way, I'll have to tell Megan she can have a divorce.'

'Do you mean that?' Frank Ross's eyes were quizzical.

'Hell, no. It's the medication talking. You get what you need to know from Megan, then I'll tell her I didn't mean it.' He ran his fingers back through his overlong, layered hair, looked uncomfortable with the thought.

'Rather you than me, Jordan. I really don't know if you'd manage to pull that off.'

'Have you got a better idea, Frank?'

'Maybe. I'll have Suzanne bring her up to see you, and we'll make sure that Ray is here. Try talking her round – encourage her to lose her temper with you if it helps. I'll give you a list of questions we want answers to.'

'You want me to debrief my own wife?'

'It might just be the only way.'

'Did you tell her anything before the two of you got married?' Frank was at the door, rubbing his chin.

'Only that I played for keeps and I wouldn't be letting her off the hook anytime down the line. Nothing about the job.'

'The exact words?'

Darkness stained Jordan's cheeks. 'I said, I love you, Megan and I don't want you to marry me if you have any reservations.'

'Mmm. If you want to keep her, Jordan, you might have to stoop to emotional blackmail. You already know the organisation's stance on marriage, so it's no good me preaching that at you.'

'If I'm honest…completely honest, Frank, I'm so angry with Megan that I don't know whether I'm capable of trying to pull our marriage back together.'

Pregnant? Jordan thought, that'd be ironic. They'd tried so hard those first couple of months to make babies. He'd have been over the moon then. But now? She'd be having the child of a dead terrorist. His alter-ego.

If he could have kept his hands to himself, everything

would've been fine. But he just hadn't been able to resist touching Megan whilst she slept – he'd needed to comfort her because she called out his – Jordan's name. Lord, she'd sounded so tormented, so agonised. But as soon as he'd touched her, the dreams became more vivid and Megan had woken sobbing.

The vision stuck in his mind of moonlight spangling her green eyes, and she'd whispered so longingly, 'Kiss me...'

He couldn't be so close to Megan and stay away from her. The persona he'd spent a year working on before he'd met Megan – the case he'd thought had died along with Artemis' husband, the former leader – had revived with the vengeance of a demented phoenix rising from the ashes. And that persona – Zeus – had threatened to crumble just at the sight of Megan.

Not for anything would he have chosen to leave Megan after just two months of marriage. But there had been no choice. He was an agent. It was his job.

'If Megan is pregnant, can you persuade the Doctor to hold back from telling her?'

Just silence for a moment, then Frank said, 'I'll fix it. But if she is...'

'A day, Frank...?'

'Guess a day wouldn't do any harm.'

'Appreciate that, Frank.'

'They're a damned nosy bunch.' Megan exploded, 'I need a kip and they just keep on and on asking questions!'

Suzanne laughed. 'It seems like that when you're not used to the way things work in the organisation, Megan. But they're only asking you about what they need to know.'

'I'm not telling them a damn thing till Jordan agrees to divorce me.'

'Sure. That's OK.' Suzanne couldn't believe how close-mouthed Megan could be, or how fixated she was on divorcing Jordan. She wasn't unpleasant to any of the highly trained debriefing team – quite the opposite in fact. But no one had learnt a thing from her.

'You'll feel great once you get into some decent clothes.' Suzanne tried, but Megan's keen eyes just stared blankly at her.

'I'll feel great when I can get out of this place – and back to work.'

It wasn't the response Suzanne expected. 'Jordan's asked if you'll go and see him, Megan.'

'If he agrees to a divorce first.'

'Well, maybe he wants to agree in person.'

'I don't want to see him.' Megan shoved aside the cream eclair, the nervous, fluttering butterflies in her stomach couldn't face anything that rich. Not now, anyway.

'Fair enough.' Suzanne grimaced, somehow, she had to trick Megan into visiting Jordan. 'Let's go and see what Jan sorted out for you to wear?'

'It's nothing fancy, just a room I use while I'm at the base – along here on the right,' Suzanne gestured towards the white door, a little later, having offered Megan the use of her own room, so that Jordan's wife could change and freshen up.

'Will you get in trouble for spiriting me away?' Megan whispered, looking both ways along the silent, broad corridor, nervous that someone would see them and stop them.

'Don't worry.' Suzanne turned into the door and released it, 'Come on inside, quick.'

Unquestioningly, Megan darted into the room, the door clicking shut behind her.

'Ah, thank you, Suzanne.' Ray Blackmore's voice.

'*No!*' Megan spun around.

To her left, Jordan was sitting up in bed, with Ray Blackmore between her and the door. Suzanne had moved to

Jordan's side and sat down, her face averted.

Megan threw her case at Ray and darted past him for the door, grabbing the handle and rattling it. 'Let me out of here!'

'The door's locked.' Ray folded his arms.

A soft breeze broke over Megan's sweat damp skin. The window! Wrong-footing Ray, she dashed for the large open window, had one foot on the frame, and about to launch herself into thin air…two floors up.

Ray yanked her backwards, 'You stupid woman, are you trying to kill yourself?'

Still flailing, Megan was only peripherally aware of an intermittent buzzer – of two more men entering the room. 'I want to leave!'

'You aren't leaving until you tell us everything.'

'Ray, for Pete's sake, let her go.' It was Jordan and his words stopped Megan's fight dead. She spun to look at him and wished she hadn't. She could see him clearly now…soft blonde hair falling across his forehead and curling into his neck; a small, stud earring glinted in the sunlight. His skin had a lightly tanned look and his beautiful blue eyes were sleepy. Jordan's torso was far more muscular than it had been, the white bandage around his ribs in stark contrast to his brown flesh.

The impact of seeing her husband in full daylight was devastating. You couldn't just turn love on and off. It was there – all the time – and Megan gripped a chair back to stop herself from running over to him; kissing him, loving him. But the logical side of her mind reminded her that she couldn't have this man again. He'd betrayed her twice. A spear of pain pierced her heart at the thought of just how cruelly he'd treated her,

She raised her chin, copper curls shifting against her shoulders as she looked directly at Jordan. 'Divorce me and I'll tell your friends what they want to know.'

'It's not that simple, Megan.' Jordan clenched his fingers into fists on top of the bedcover. Damn! She was the only woman in the world who could make him feel a thousand emotions at once.

'Believe me, it *is* that simple.' She shrugged and smiled, but Jordan didn't miss the anger blazing in her eyes. She was clearly going to blow up any minute.

'No, it's not, Megan.'

She clenched her fists at her waist. 'Don't try telling me you love me, and that it's all been a big mistake, Jordan. I'm not going to buy that.'

'No, I'm not going to do that.'

His tone was deep and soft, tingling all the way to Megan's toes, leaving her wanting to scream with pain. *He didn't love her. He never had loved her*!

Swiftly picking up a vase of flowers, she tossed them at Jordan's head. 'I hate your guts! All I want from you is a divorce!'

'No!' He fielded the vase – had seen it coming.

'Right then, your so-called "friends" can clear off. I'm telling them nothing!'

'Megan, they…we only want to know everything that happened on board The Dream. What's the big deal?'

'The big deal – *you jerk*! – is that you could have told me who you were, right from the start! You could have protected me better from Hades…!'

'He didn't touch you, Megan.' Jordan told her steadily. 'I would never have let that happen.'

Green eyes glittered in reply, colour flooding her cheeks at the inference behind his words, but she reined her temper in. 'It's so nice of your "friends" Jordan, to tell you the test results before they told me.'

'We thought you'd like to hear them from me.'

'Oh, sure. But they're all here in case you hadn't noticed! Oh, what the hell difference does it make? I don't know whether I hate you most – or them!' She glanced at Suzanne and regretted those words; Suzanne was obviously upset at the way things had gone, but now Megan had no one to trust.

'Do you know what really ticks me off?' Jordan let rip, saw Megan's eyes open wider, startled; he was being unfair, irrational, but couldn't help it. Raw jealousy, her declaration of hatred tore him in two.

'I really don't care what "ticks you off" any more, Jordan.'

'The way you really came on to Zeus – you couldn't get enough of him, could you?' Dark jealousy ripped across Jordan's features.

Megan was shocked – so shocked that she laughed out loud. 'You're right. And you, Jordan, you're nothing but a hypocrite. It's fine – just fine for you to take off with that snake in red leather, when we've been married for only two months. I'll tell you something, shall I? Our marriage was one big mistake – and I want out!'

'Artemis was business, Megan. I didn't make love to her.'

'What I did with Zeus was business.' A husky edge touched her words. 'I wanted to stay alive.'

'You seduced him.'

'Is that what you really think?' Megan shook her head. 'I had good reason for that first time.'

Jordan's look of disgust somehow fuelled Megan's determination to stay calm – he was further out of control than she was. 'It was to hide the note,' she added. 'The note which Philip had slipped inside my dress.'

He'd had no idea of what Philip had done – she read that much in his eyes, before she realised that she was telling this room full of people *exactly* what they wanted to know. OK, if they wanted some details, she'd give them a few more.

'I didn't notice you objecting! You...Zeus...didn't exactly back off! Right?'

Scowling, Jordan pushed, 'What note? What did it say?'

Megan shook her head. 'I can't remember.'

'You'll remember if I say I'll divorce you?'

'I'll remember *everything* – if you agree to divorce me.'

'I think you'd regret that.' It was all Jordan could do to speak past the devastation lashing him.

'What you think doesn't matter. You can't just waltz out of our marriage one day, and then think we'll pick up where we left off the next. I don't want you. In fact, I don't want anything to do with you!'

'You know, Megan, we might still love one another.'

'Yeah, right!' She gave a shrill laugh. 'I don't think so.'

'Will you sleep on it, darling?' The gentleness of his tone caught her unawares, provoking a strange trembling feeling in her chest. She hesitated too long – the sadness overwhelming her was much worse than the anger.

'Thank you, but I've made up my mind.' She dragged her gaze from Jordan's, before moving over to the window, her eyes misty with tears.

'Megan, just tell us what we need to know, then you and me can take time to see if we've got anything worth saving?'

Keeping her back to him, Megan shook her head. She could hardly speak for the lump in her throat. 'No…!'

She sank down on to the windowsill, trembling and crying. There was silence in the room as Jordan caught his breath, and reached for his crutch. Using that and his good leg, he struggled out of bed, making his way across the room and put his arm around Megan's shuddering shoulders, 'I'm so sorry, darling.'

'Don't touch me!' She jerked away from him, 'Being sorry doesn't mean a damn thing!'

For a split second, Megan had longed to sink against his powerful torso and cling to him. But her mind was whirling and swirling and she couldn't let Jordan's physical appeal overwhelm her. Unshed tears shone in her lovely green eyes as she drew herself upright and gazed up into his face. 'Please, let me go. I can't take any more of this.'

All Jordan wanted to do was to pull her to him; to kiss her and absorb all the hurt he'd caused. But when he put out a hand towards her, she flinched.

'Is this really what you want, Megan?' How the hell was he managing to stand this close to her and not touch her? Jordan clenched his fists, willing himself to step back.

She saw the pain etched in his features, but she couldn't let herself care. She'd been in that same state for so long…too long. It was too late – for both of them.

'Yes. It's what I want.'

'There's something you should know…'

Megan held up her palm. 'Don't tell me anything. Just let me go.'

'OK, have your divorce,' his voice was unsteady, then he managed to pull himself together. 'I'll make a generous settlement.' A nerve twitched in his cheek, accentuated by his five-o'clock shadow.

'Thank you.' Before she could dwell on the agony inside her, Megan turned to Ray. 'What exactly would you like to know?'

'Mainly details concerning Philip. He was working with us…and he's still on the critical list, so can't tell us himself.'

Megan explained how she'd slipped and fallen, how Philip had dashed over to her when she'd supposedly passed out, and slipped the note inside her belt. 'It fell to the floor in the cabin later. That's why I…ah… seduced Zeus.' She grimaced, remembering. 'There was no way to hide the note, other than to drop my uniform over it.'

'Until you could read it – later?'

'Yes.'

'Do you recollect what the note said?'

'The first note said nothing, it was a piece of paper

wrapped around a pain killer.' She went on then, to tell them about the second note, found beneath the food and wrapped in cling film.

'The note was meant for Zeus.' Ray's expression hardened. 'How in hell did you let her get away from you, Jordan? You fell asleep?'

'Don't tell me you wouldn't have done the same thing after almost a year of living like a monk!' Jordan retorted. 'I wanted her – she's my wife, for pity's sake!'

'Was.' Ray said pointedly. 'You shouldn't have taken a lover – any lover, Jordan.'

'He had to, you idiot!' Megan snapped, springing without thought to her husband's defence. 'I'd got Hades so worked up, that it was the only thing Jordan…Zeus…could do! He did it to save my life.'

'He should not have got involved with you!' Ray told her grimly. 'The whole operation was jeopardised. Who was with Philip when he was shot?'

'Hades. I heard some screaming, then the shot,' she explained, before going through the events that had followed, looking regularly to Jordan who reinforced her recollections with those of his own.

Megan wondered if she looked as exhausted as he did. She also found herself wondering if he was in serious trouble over what happened to Philip? Which compelled to say, 'You know, Jordan couldn't have done anything to save Philip. Hades is one of those people who lives to hurt and terrorise people. He's utterly sick.'

'So, how come you survived a night with him, Megan?' Ray's tone invited anger.

Her eyes flicked towards Jordan, a muscle twitched in his cheek, his blue eyes clearly signalling that she should tell the truth.

'Jordan…Zeus…' she amended, 'told me on no account to fight Hades.'

'Did you not think it strange that Zeus should care what happened to you?'

'I wanted to stay alive, Ray! I hoped Zeus was right, but I didn't question what he said. I could only hope it worked.' She shuddered. 'When I passed out, I didn't think Zeus's advice had worked.'

'All the same, didn't you think it strange that Zeus should advise you?'

'No.'

'Why not?'

Megan shook her head, 'Does it matter?'

'It may.'

'I…I don't know how to explain it. I was grateful that Zeus never hurt me. Sometimes, we talked and he was kind of…I don't know…gentle. I felt something for him.'

'You had no idea – even when you started to feel something for Zeus, that he was actually Jordan, your husband?'

'Of course not! He was completely different. Even the way we made love…had sex…was different.'

'When – exactly – did you discover Zeus was Jordan?'

'Something he said, when he was carrying me ashore from the dingy. He was angry and he dropped his accent.'

'There was only yourself and Zeus present?'

'Yes, the other hostages were in a small bungalow on the shore. Craig came over – he really flipped when he realised that he'd shot Jordan. Apparently, Zeus hadn't put on the "colour" everyone was wearing to identify himself.'

'Yeah, that ties up with Craig's version. He also said he had to handcuff you, to keep you from slugging Zeus.' There was some amusement in Ray's tone and Megan sensed they were winding up. She'd told them all they needed to know.

'Can I go now, Ray?'

'One more thing. Who's Lucas?'

'Lucas Knight…? He's an architect and an ex-client of my company.'

'I believe Lucas Knight is the one who saw Jordan with Artemis?'

'In a club, Flavio's. Apparently, they were all over one another like a bad rash.' Megan sighed. 'Can I go now?'

'Tomorrow. The doctor wants to re-do one test, Megan, a culture got contaminated. I'm afraid it'll have to be in the morning.' He grimaced apologetically, 'It happens sometimes. And before you leave, we need you to sign a document affirming Zeus died on the beach from a bullet wound; and another Affidavit swearing you won't reveal Jordan as an agent, to anyone.'

'I'll do that.' Freedom was a whole heap closer and she felt the panic inside receding.

'Thanks. The documents will be ready for your signature and witness in the morning.'

'OK.'

'The only other thing you need to do, is for you and Jordan to sit down and come up with compatible stories as to why you're getting divorced. Oh, and Megan, you can use the room next door for tonight.'

Even Megan could see that the need to get her story straight with Jordan's. If she said adultery and he said desertion, it might be a bit weird.

By the time she'd considered that, everyone, except Jordan, had left the room.

'So, how's your leg?' she muttered. Lord, he was still the most handsome man she'd ever seen, with the bluest eyes and the softest, sun-bleached hair.

'The bullet went straight through it. The problem's the fabric the bullet took into my leg. There's a bit of an infection. And then, of course, there's the injury to my ribs …'

She stared at him; wondered why people always did

what they were doing now – making stupid, inane conversation because everything else hurt too much. Megan took a deep breath and swept straight to the point, 'Do you honestly think that I would have married you, Jordan, if I'd known you were connected to this bloody organisation? I thought I was getting an engineer, not some macho secret agent!'

'Yeah, and I didn't know what I was getting into, either. *I* should be the one citing adultery!' Jealousy got the better of him again, tearing with claws at his heart; driving words from his mouth which he didn't really mean.

'*You swine!*' She flew at him, yanking on his overly-long hair – until he grabbed her wrists, 'You *know* that you encouraged me!'

'You didn't need much of that.'

'What gives you the right to be so guiltless? Men don't have the monopoly on need!'

'You know what it makes me wonder?' He grated, jerking Megan against his torso. 'It makes me wonder just how many lovers you had while I was away.' His blue eyes blazed with anger. 'You were so turned on by Zeus. If you weren't so all-out to get a divorce, I'd divorce *you*. Just how many other men did you sleep with?'

Dizzy with rage, Megan gasped, wriggling to free her wrists, but he wasn't letting go. She was badly tempted to say that she'd lost count! But there was no point in making the situation any worse than it was already.

'I can't believe how stupid I was! I can't believe how much I loved you, and how hard I grieved after losing you. I spent months ringing hospitals, terrified of discovering that you might be dead; months when I was almost out of my mind with grief, not knowing what had happened to you. I…I loved you so much, I almost wanted to die myself!'

Angry tears coursed down her cheeks. 'So don't you *dare*

try to accuse me of being unfaithful to you!'

Regret, pain, and yes...anger, flashed in Jordan's eyes. 'You let Zeus do whatever he wanted to you.'

For a brief moment, her mind was flooded with memories making love with Zeus – who'd been so tuned to her needs...knowing so quickly what she craved. The shame she'd known; the pact which she'd silently made with herself, that no one would ever know just how sensational it had been with him...? That pact was now nothing but a joke. The one man whom she'd never wanted to know...now knew everything!

'I'm not going to apologise for that. You knew who I was. You didn't have to touch me. You could have just pretended...'

'I did pretend! But you took care of that, didn't you, Megan?' Colour stained his cheeks, 'Stripping off and telling me you'd make sure I was the most satisfied man who ever lived?' Disgust darkened his eyes, 'Did you have to go *that* far?'

'Yes! I didn't want Zeus...but I didn't want the others punished. And I *certainly* didn't want Hades!'

'I might have believed you, Megan, if it hadn't been for that last time...'

He was right. The last time had been something special. Possibly because she'd truly believed it would be the last time a man would ever make love to her.

'If you'd been wrong about Hades, it would have been the last time I'd ever be with a man who knew how to make love to a woman. Don't tell me you wouldn't have done the same.'

Jordan couldn't think straight. He was holding her wrists, but what he wanted was her smile and her soft, supple body.

'Spell-binder,' he murmured, silently cursing his obvious arousal. She always did this...she always made loving her the single, most important thing in his life. The last rays of sunshine glinted against the soft, cascading copper curls and were reflected in her anger-brightened eyes. He let go of one wrist and caressed her hips, pulled her against him, watched her full, pink lips part in a gasp of disbelief. A moan of need escaped him as he crushed her full breasts against his naked torso. The heat of her skin through wispy fabric tormented him; he couldn't remember why he was so angry with her, couldn't think of anything beyond Megan…her fire and his need of her.

'You want me.' His fingers spread, pressing her delicious warmth against him.

Megan's hand slipped to his chest, neither pushing him away nor encouraging him. Before Zeus, they'd both instinctively known that to get this close met only one end. And as they both know, eventually the same thing had happened with Zeus. Blue eyes, smouldering and needy, tempted Megan to let go – not of Jordan – but of her anger. It was crazy and it didn't make sense. But right there and then she needed Jordan, even though she knew that it wouldn't change anything. So, she had nothing at all to lose, she told herself as his mouth closed over hers, not coaxing, but claiming. And when she didn't fight him, he released her wrist, freeing his hand to crush her into him, to mould and knead her delicious body.

He kissed her, touched her until Megan slowly wound her fingers around his neck, increased the pressure of his mouth on hers; he was familiar…so familiar and yet different. Oh, Lord – she'd forgotten just how exciting he could be.

'Did you wear this to turn me on?' His palm slid up inside the wispy skirt, over her thigh and up over her silky panties.

'Yes,' she murmured, because they both needed her to lie. This wouldn't ever happen again, and she had to make it as wonderful as it could possibly be.

'You knew that I wouldn't be able to stop this…?'

'Shush…' She kissed the corners of his mouth, his eyes, his cheeks. 'Yes, you're right. I knew.'

He whispered against her ear, 'You'll have to make love to me this time, honey.'

'I can do anything you want.' She smiled, helping him to lie down and watching his fingers tremble as he unfastened her wispy blouse, removed her bra and pulled her forward so he could take her into his mouth.

'You taste like sin.' He licked, sucked, savoured her breasts whilst she sat astride his hardness, her skirt and panties still in place. All the time, she watched him. His blue eyes were darker than they'd ever been, his hands more skilled. When Megan thought she'd shatter, she rose slightly, clasped his fingers in hers. 'It's my turn,' she smiled, 'don't worry, Mr Elliot, I'll mind your wound.'

She kissed every centimetre of his thighs, his stomach, gratified at the insistent, straining manhood inside the boxer shorts. Lightly, she traced the bulge with her fingertip.

'So help me …'

'What's the rush?' She shimmied down to kiss him through the fabric, heard his deep groan of need, 'We both know this won't happen again, and I want you to enjoy it.' For some unknown reason, Megan wanted him to never forget this last time they would have together. She wanted any other lover Jordan might have, to seem as nothing when compared to her. Out of some perverse self-preservation, she added, 'Besides, it's going to cost you a fortune.'

When Jordan's brow rose in question, the corners of his mouth twitching with the beginnings of a smile, she added, 'I want to make sure that "generous settlement" you mentioned, keeps me in luxury for the rest of my days!'

In fact, she didn't care whether he gave her any money or not – but it was more important, just then, to actually believe that she was still his wife.

A deep chuckle escaped him, convincing Megan that he

understood her mood and motivation. The delicious sound of Jordan's laughter turned into a lustful groan as she held him, then took him into her mouth. When she knew that he couldn't hold on much longer, she stood, wriggling out of her underwear but leaving the skirt in place, so that it splayed enticingly over her luscious, curvy legs as she took him inside her…so slowly…sweat glistening his brow. How could she forget just how far they could take one another? The pleasure – so intense that everything else ceased to exist? She laced her fingers with his, held his hands beside his head, swayed, moving tantalisingly so that her breasts brushed his sensual mouth, feeling his fingers tightening around hers; his size increasing inside her.

'Dear heaven, Megan,' he groaned. 'What are you doing to me?'

A smile slanted her mouth, as she increased the pace of her undulating movements. 'I'm earning a fortune, Mr Elliot,' she gasped when he caught her nipple in his teeth and sucked hard, before releasing his fingers to balance her palms against his shoulders, and his freed hands clamped over her buttocks as he rose violently into her, spilling, twisting, the half grimace, half smile of fulfilment contorting his features.

'*Jordan*…!' she gasped, shuddering as she responded instantly, and for a few seconds, letting herself rest against the rise and fall of his rock hard chest, lost in the forgotten landscape of afterglow.

She was surprised when his arms cradled her there and his fingers toyed with her damp hair, spread lovingly over her shoulders and back. She supposed it was just a parting gesture to soften the reality of what they'd done. OK…this was their last time together. But if he wanted to hold her for a minute, did it really make any difference now?

Yes, it probably did. Reluctantly, Megan pushed herself

up from his chest. 'Do you want me to help you into bed before I leave, Mr Elliot?'

An intense look entered Jordan's eyes. 'I'm paying enough for you to stay where you are, all night.' Megan knew unwanted arousal when he added, 'There are things I want to do with you.'

'I can't stay any longer.' She couldn't. Because if she did so, she might never be able to end this. Slowly and reluctantly she eased away from his prone form, and pulled on her blouse.

'That's a shame.' Jordan pushed himself into a sitting position, 'Maybe you could help me stand up?'

'Maybe I could.' She stood his crutch beside him, offered her hand to balance him as he stood.

Megan turned away and gathered up her clothes. 'How long will you be here?'

'A couple of more days. How about you?'

'I'm leaving tomorrow, as soon as they let me go,' she told him, taking a deep breath, uncertain just how to end this episode, before realising that there was only one way. 'Goodbye, Mr Elliot,' she added, throwing him a dazzling smile.

Too busy getting herself to the door on a wave of brashness, Megan missed the flash of fury in Jordan's eyes. She didn't wait to see if he replied, but ran all the way back to the room set aside for her.

'Sorry to keep you waiting,' the doctor breezed into the room, 'I just wanted to be certain of the results before you left, Mrs Elliot.'

'Everything's OK?' Physically, she felt fine. Tired. Emotionally shattered, but physically she felt great!

'Yes. You're in the very early stages of pregnancy, Mrs. Elliot. Congratulations!'

'Ah.' Somehow, Megan managed a smile – a false one, a

shocked one – but it obviously passed muster with the doctor, who clearly expected delight and wasn't looking for shock. 'Thanks for taking care of me. Am I free to leave now?'

'I believe Suzanne is coming to collect you shortly. She'll brief you on all the arrangements we've made to help you adjust.'

Megan was tempted to ask which university they planned for her unborn child to attend, but bit her tongue.

'Does Mr Elliot know I'm pregnant?'

'We're leaving it up to you to share the news with him. I insisted on that.'

'Oh, thanks.' Megan nodded as the doctor left the room and Suzanne entered.

'Everything all right, Megan?'

'Couldn't be better,' she retorted, feeling confused, ambivalent, angry and very, *very* upset.

'Good, the plane's waiting.' Suzanne lifted Megan's bag. 'Obviously, the Organisation doesn't expect you to work while you're taking care of Jordan,' Suzanne said pleasantly. 'We'll provide your colleagues with some trained help. We've explained to Alexa that your husband has turned up again, that he isn't well and that you're staying at home to care for him.'

'Hmmm.' I'll look after him all right, Megan thought viciously. I'll buy the divorcée's handbook and study it while I eat grapes and watch him suffer. One thing she hated was being manipulated, and whoever had come up with this latest twist in her marriage had a whole heap to answer for.

'Naturally, if you and Jordan really do want a divorce once he's fit again, you can easily set the ball rolling.'

'It all sounds so simple.' He had promised her a divorce – that was why she'd co-operated. Now they'd put her squarely back where she didn't want to be. If the Organisation thought that just by throwing them together, she'd suddenly become an obedient little wife – they had another think coming! And another thing: she *was* going back to work, and she didn't intend to discuss her plans with *anyone*!

'I want you know that I don't blame you for being mad with me,' Suzanne said as they started to climb the metal steps to the aircraft. 'But I was ordered to get you into Jordan's room.'

'You were just doing your job,' Megan dismissed brightly. 'Forget it.'

'Jordan feels dreadful about everything that's happened.'

Megan frowned at the other woman., 'He's not the only one.' She knew Suzanne had just said that in an attempt to pour oil on troubled waters.

Pregnant. She was *pregnant*! As though the realisation had waited to hit her until she reached the top of the steps, Megan staggered for a moment before forcing herself to stifle a heartfelt groan. Jordan was at the front of the plane; and that lowlife, Ray was beside him. They were laughing. Well, she'd show them. Straightening her shoulders, she settled in a seat at the rear of the aircraft – as far away from the others as possible.

A line of gleaming limousines met the passengers at an RAF airfield just outside London. Megan, a bit shaky, but otherwise fine, was just relieved that Jordan wasn't in the same vehicle as herself and Suzanne.

'I'm so tired,' Megan said with a yawn, wondering if she'd actually manage to reach home without collapsing.

'That's OK, Jordan's nurse is going to settle him in tonight, and you'll be left to relax until lunchtime tomorrow. If you can't cope, just give me a call.'

'Mmm.' Pregnant? Was she really? Why hadn't it happened before now, when she and Jordan had been crazily in love? A hot tear rolled down her cheek and she was too weary to wipe it away.

Somehow, Megan found herself installed in the Docklands apartment, but it all happened whilst she felt strangely detached, and so tired that she really couldn't have cared less. Then she was floating. It was beautiful – a soft pillow and a comfortable bed. And she didn't have to listen to anyone any longer. With a sigh, she closed her eyes and escaped into oblivion.

Sun streamed in through tall arched windows outside, boats chugged along the Thames. Megan stirred sleepily, stretching languidly and then nestling against the strong, familiar shoulder; her soft thigh slipping between his hard-muscled legs.

Everything was right. Exactly as it should be. Jordan's body against her back and his hand slipping from her waist to caress her breast. Megan sighed, wriggled sexily against him, then images flew through her mind to fast forward. The full force of harsh reality crashed into her tired brain and she rolled quickly away from him. Swiftly springing up off the mattress, she spun around to face him.

'What the devil are you doing in my bed?'

Jordan didn't look any happier than she. 'This is *our* bed, Megan.'

'What were you trying to do just then?'

'Dear me!' His eyes were lazy, his manner sympathetic, 'You need me to tell you?'

Megan gasped and couldn't speak for the anger sweeping through her trembling body.

'I thought you were an expert in this field,' he murmured, smiling sardonically at her obvious fury.

After taking a deep breath, she eventually managed to say, 'I'll get the nurse. She'll want to check your dressings.'

'That's it, Megan. Run away.'

She'd reached the door, proud of herself for controlling her normally explosive temper – but now it glowed red hot. Gripping the door handle, she managed to say sweetly, 'Oh don't worry, I'll be back.' And then, as she closed the door behind her, she added, 'But I won't be running!'

By the phone, Megan found a note saying the nurse had been called away, but would be back later. She had left a small bottle of capsules and some dressings, with instructions that his wound would need dressing as soon as he woke, but the bandages around his ribs should be left alone.

Megan took a long, deep breath and entered their bedroom again. 'Time for your tablet,' she told him, unscrewing the lid that was more 'adult' than 'child' proof and handing him the pill.

When he'd taken it, she folded the covers down to his waist, feeling him wince as she tore off the plaster – and some of the hair – from the wound on his thigh. 'I'm sorry about that,' she muttered, touching the area surrounding the wound; keeping her head down so that he wouldn't see the anguish in her eyes.

'I hope you know what you're doing.' His tone was unemotional and even, a sure sign to Megan that he was fighting his feelings.

'Yes I do. But even if I didn't – I'm all you've got at the moment! The nurse will be here at 10 a.m., so you can get her to check my handiwork if it's not up to your exacting standards!'

She cleansed the wound, and pressed a fresh sterile dressing over it, both hands soothing until she was sure it adhered to his skin. Her breath caught as she saw the tell-tale sign of arousal. Spontaneously, her eyes rose to his.

'Don't flatter yourself, Megan,' he gritted. 'It just happens.'

'I'm not flattered,' she sighed, able to feel him trembling

with anger through her fingertips. 'You're right, it happens all the time.'

Calmly and fully aware that she had lit the blue touch paper, she smiled and stood well back. Slowly peeling off the sterile gloves, she disposed of both the dressing and the gloves, before walking slowly and calmly out of the room – and out of Jordan's life.

chapter eight

It was an idyllic autumn, majestically beautiful. Megan took a deep breath of the crisp air, her gaze moving between golden trees and a lake that reflected a clear blue sky. For two weeks she'd walked and climbed some of the easier slopes, spending her evenings reading and ringing Alexa, to keep in touch with the business.

'I thought that I might come and see you this weekend,' Alexa was saying now on the phone. 'I could just do with a couple of days to unwind. Where are you staying?'

'I'm staying in a gorgeous little stone cottage near Windermere. It's totally deserted and when it's stormy outside, the wind whistles through the old windowpanes – it's perfect.'

Alexa laughed. 'You're idea of "perfect" always was a bit warped. Give me the address, and maybe I'll come and stay with you.'

Megan did that and the friends said 'goodbye' soon afterwards.

'There you are.' Alexa held the piece of paper out to Jordan. 'Don't ever say I don't do anything for you.'

'Thanks, Alexa. If you ever need anything…' He shrugged. 'Just ask me, OK?'

'I've more pride than you.' She grinned at the shocked expression on Jordan's drawn features. 'Besides, I only took pity on you because you look like hell.'

When he grinned at that, Alexa saw a brief emergence of the former, carefree Jordan. 'And don't go walking too far with that gammy leg,' she added firmly.

'Yes, ma'am.' His leg was still painful, and any movement of his damaged ribs still seemed to make him breathless. 'I don't think there's much danger of that for a while.'

Alexa accompanied him as he left her houseboat. 'I hope…well, I hope something good happens – for both you and Megan. Maybe the two of you could at least manage to be friends again?'

'Who knows? Thank you, Alexa.'

Jordan waved as he drove off, reflecting that he'd told Alexa more than any other person. She and Megan were close – yet at the same time, they gave one another room to breathe. Alexa had told Jordan that Megan was thinking of moving out of her business address, because she didn't feel that she belonged there any more. He wondered if it was because she had the urge to run from pain, that she needed somewhere new to start over again?

The journey north took a long time. As he drove, Jordan cursed the injuries which had prevented him from running after Megan that last morning in their apartment.

Frank and the medics had washed their hands of him this morning, after he'd told them that he wasn't waiting any longer to find his wife.

It had taken him two hours to persuade Alexa to contact Megan, and he cursed again when he was forced to waste yet more time by stopping for a while at a service station. Although only half way to his destination, the pain in his leg and shattered rib dictated both a rest and a change of position.

As Jordan drew up alongside the cottage he noticed that a lamp had been switched on inside the house, its reflection shining light out through the dusk, spilling soft light on to the wide dirt track.

'Come in, it's open!' Megan sang out when he tapped on the door.

But would she say that if she knew it was her husband?

He hesitated, sudden apprehension gripping his stomach and causing his hands to shake. What the hell was wrong with him? He wasn't the nervous type! He dealt with terrorists, criminals, double-dealing low life – so why was he nervous of Megan?

Because she mattered. She always had. The urge to turn and run struck him as he heard her nearing the door.

'Sorry, did I lock it by accident?' She whisked it open, a broad smile on her face, an old smoky-blue T-shirt and ragged jeans the perfect foil to her cascading, copper-coloured hair.

'Jordan!'

She looked afraid of him, too. That made him feel better.

'Were you expecting anyone?'

'Just someone from the farm with milk and eggs,' she said, instinctively reaching out to touch his forearm. 'Come inside.'

The brief contact startled them both. Jordan cleared his throat. A wry smile curved his mouth as he said, 'I'm really not sure why I'm here.'

Having settled him into a chair, Megan pulled up a tiny, sturdy wooden stool. When she sat down on it, he realised that he was looking straight into her clear forest-green eyes.

'I'm glad you are. I need to talk to you,' she told him slowly. 'I thought that maybe you could help me to try and understand what's happening to me. I can't seem to concentrate or settle down to anything. I...I don't feel as though I belong where I used to belong...' Her words tailed away as she added helplessly, 'It sounds so stupid...'

'No, it doesn't. The counsellors were supposed to help you unload all those sort of feelings. It just isn't easy sometimes. I think that probably too much happened to you, in such a short space of time.'

'That's exactly how it feels.' He really *did* understand, Megan told herself, pressing her hands to her forehead. 'The problem is that just as I think I've grasped one part of the puzzle and made sense of it, then I lose hold of another bit.'

'The difference…' Jordan hesitated, unsure how to word this, but intent on trying to explain. 'The difference, Megan, is that you couldn't remain emotionally detached. So everything that happened to you took its toll.'

She gave a slight nod as Jordan continued, 'Everyone else involved was trained to deal with what was happening.'

'I so much wanted you to hold me after…after…'

'The rescue?'

'Yes. I felt so alone, so empty, as if I'd nothing left.' She glanced up at Jordan, to see pain flicking over his features. 'I thought I'd lost you. It was all so big – so much to deal with. In fact, I still don't know how to deal with it all. I tried to go back to work but I couldn't do anything,' she added helplessly. 'Everywhere I turned, people were asking questions and I didn't answer because I couldn't remember "who" was supposed to know "what".' She gave a heavy sigh. 'I sometimes think that I'm going mad.'

He smiled, leaning over to touch her fingertips. 'If you are, you're not alone.'

'I don't know…I couldn't talk to the counsellor very much. I couldn't seem to open up. Maybe I didn't trust her enough…?'

'And you trust me?' It seemed incredible after everything that had happened, and he found himself feeling strangely touched.

'I think I must. It's as though I can't go on with my life until I'm able to talk everything through with you. I know we have to divorce, but I don't know how I feel about it.'

Jordan nodded, his expression grave. 'Do you know how you feel about me?'

She smiled widely at that. 'I really hate you so much for lying to me. Then I love you beyond any kind of sense, for having saved my life. And then…then I hurt for your wounds, and I hurt for us…'

She shook her head, blinking back the prick of tears. 'It just goes round and round,' she continued, looking disgusted with herself. 'What about you? Tell me what happened to you?'

'You want to see my scars?' He smiled, his eyes glinting with wry amusement. Megan clearly needed to have laughter back in her life – it had been gone for so long – and he knew that was one of the problems which was upsetting her emotional equilibrium.

'I suppose so.' Megan grimaced. 'However, if I suddenly dash off, it's because I feel sick, OK?'

'The scars won't bite you, darling,' he laughed and, as Megan smiled at his words, the ice was finally broken between them

Whilst they talked, easily, with no holds barred as they filled in the missing pieces in each other's stories, Megan felt something like ease descend on her. She smiled, because Jordan had instinctively known what she needed to talk about; knew exactly what she needed to hear from him.

'It was Alexa who helped me find you,' he admitted. 'I'd have found you eventually, but it was quickest to ask the friend you trust the most.'

'Alexa wouldn't have told you nothing!' Megan chuckled, 'Your head must have been spinning with her questions.'

'Hmm. She does have that effect!' His lazy smile turned Megan's heart over. 'I hear you're thinking of moving?'

'Yes.' Megan rubbed a finger nervously over her denim jeans. 'I think maybe it's all somehow tied up with you. I'm considering a change of career, too.'

'Why is it tied up with me?' he asked gently, a slightly husky note in his voice.

'It's another one of those things that I don't understand.

Maybe I'm running away?' She shrugged, her green eyes confused. 'There are things I want apart from work. I've just got to fathom out how to get them.'

A smile slanted Jordan's mouth. 'What is it you want?'

Megan shook her head, her voice a whisper as she said, 'I can't cope with having to tell you that – not yet, anyway.'

'Why?' He took hold of her hand, rubbed his thumb along her knuckles. 'Surely, we can tell one another anything?' he added, trying to encourage her into letting him know about the baby. Although, he suspected from the sight of her still slim figure, that she had almost certainly lost it. No wonder the poor girl was so unhappy and confused.

She looked steadily up into his blue eyes, regretting the love they had shared, because nothing else would ever come close to the feelings which they'd had for one another. And she regretted knowing that she was going to sell out – to settle for second best. 'I don't know if you'll understand.'

Jordan felt sick. Physically, violently sick. He knew, as sure as the fact that the sun rose in the East, that Megan was going to tell him there was someone else in her life. How in hell was he going to be 'civilised' about that?

'I'll light the fire,' she said, kneeling down before the hearth and setting a match to the wood-burning stove, with it's cosy glass window through which you could stare at the flames, imagining shapes and images.

He couldn't stand the suspense any longer. 'You've met someone else?'

There was a long silence, before she sat back down on her stool again and said, 'I intend to. But not yet.'

Frowning, his worst imaginings swept aside, Jordan felt strangely elated. Until she turned sideways on the low stool, staring into the flickering orange flames.

'I don't think most people find what we had, Jordan,' she continued. 'And, if they do find something special once – I'm sure they won't find it twice.' Green eyes glistened as they rose to meet his. 'I don't believe that anything which happened to us was our fault. We were simply star-crossed…'

Megan shook her head, her voice husky with tears. 'I know that one day I'm going to settle for something less than we had.' A tear slowly trickled down her cheek. 'And that will be because I can't bear the pain of loving someone as much as I love you. *It's too bloody awful*!'

There – it was out. She'd bared her soul and the world hadn't stopped turning on its axis. But Megan could feel hot tears rolling freely down her cheeks, the sight of the flames in the fire blurring to a mass of orange. There was no euphoric sense of freedom to welcome the admission, just deep sorrow.

And Jordan's silence. She glanced up at him and saw his head tilted back, his features strained and taut, as though he sought to physically absorb his own pain. She wiped her eyes, and as they misted again she dashed her sleeve across them.

'Oh, Jordan!' She slipped off the stood to kneel beside him, wrapping her arms around his shoulders, her cheek brushing against the roughness of his unshaven face; her tears taking a slow route through the day's growth.

Slowly, his arms closed about her, his mind absorbing exactly what it was that Megan had said: 'I can't bear the pain of loving someone as much as I love you'. *Love you* – not *loved*. Hope, like a brave winter snowdrop raised it's head.

'You still love me?'

'When I don't hate you!' Megan sniffed, and he felt the warmth of her breath against his neck.

'You're crazy!'

'I know. I'm also much happier when I hate you.'

He laughed huskily. 'Why is that?'

'It's simpler.'

Whether Jordan drew Megan across his lap or Megan wriggled there herself, neither was entirely sure. But they both knew that once their mouths touched, there would be no going back. For a delicious moment of anticipation, blue eyes met green, both needing each other so much: the touching, tearing at clothes, and then stopping for the simple pleasure of looking, before kissing and holding one another. It was such a fragile, bittersweet moment, and they were both frightened that this might be their last time together…

Pain assailed Jordan; both physical and mental. Megan's wild hair spread over his shoulder as she snuggled into the plump settee; her softness nestled against him, her hands spread on his chest and her leg tucked familiarly against his uninjured one.

He realised that she was going to settle for a Mr Nine-till-Five, somewhere in her vague plan of a future. Not because she wanted to. But because she couldn't stand being so much in love, and the pain it had caused her. Firelight danced against her warm skin, flaming her hair into myriad shades of copper. Absently, he lifted a soft curl which sprang to life in his fingertips.

Strangely, it wasn't jealousy that twisted in his gut – although he knew that would come one day. But as yet, Mr Steady-and-Safe had no physical form. He was still in Megan's imagination, lurking somewhere in her future. What would this man do to her? Would he make her happy? And would Megan struggle to dampen her free spirit? That part of herself that offered freedom open-handedly – and expected the same indulgence for her own spontaneous nature?

The shadowy figure in her future might love her, and might think he knew her – but he wouldn't. He wouldn't know how to free the hidden facets inside the vibrant young

woman. He wouldn't know how to smile at her shortcom-
ings – or learn to love those imperfections. He'd more likely
keep her trapped her until dust gathered over her gloriously
vibrant personality. Only making love to her once a week –
on a Saturday night after the dinner party which she'd
thrown for his stockbroker friends and their wives. She'd be
comfortable, carrying babies where his own had flourished
first…

God, that hurt! Why hadn't he been able to save that little
life? Why? A deep groan broke from him as tears ran down
his cheeks.

'Jordan?' She leaned over him, lowering her head to kiss
his damp cheek. 'What's the matter?'

Those beautiful blue eyes, that never failed to cause her
heart to quiver with desire, turned to meet hers, his hands
moving slowly over her stomach. 'I wanted to save you
both, Megan.'

For the first time, she realised that Jordan had cared about
the baby, and that he now thought she'd lost it. She saw in
his eyes that he felt he'd failed – and she couldn't let him
carry that burden.

'But you almost got yourself killed saving me. You
couldn't have done any more.'

He didn't look convinced, even when Megan traced her
finger down his cheek and said, 'You know, they say babies
are very tough.' He frowned slightly as she added in a whisper, 'It might have…'

'I'll never know, Megan, and neither will you,' her interrupted gruffly.

'No.' She choked, catching her lip between her teeth as a
tear rolled down her cheek to land on his chest. 'It all hurts
so much, losing you…'

A sad, wry smile twisted his lips. 'Darling, you didn't do
a very good job of losing me!'

'Oh…' Megan smiled through her tears. 'You shouldn't

make me laugh. It's cruel.'

He put his arms around her. 'It's more selfish than cruel,' he said, his hoarse, deep voice sending waves of pleasure through her. 'I need your smile to make me feel better.'

'Does it really help?' She grinned, witnessing the changing light in his eyes – a light that answered her question.

'Well, it's yours.' Megan kissed him lightly on the chin, then, at the same instant, they were both struck by the similarity of what she'd said – to something she said to Zeus…after they'd made love for the last time.

Everything see-sawed emotionally, Jordan closed his eyes, looked away. 'Suzanne told me what you said about Zeus.'

'Suzanne has a lot to answer for,' Megan said quietly. 'What exactly did she say?'

'That…that you could have loved him in another life.' His gaze flicked back to hers, then turned to stare blindly at the fire.

Knowing him so well, she recognised the grim note of jealousy in his voice. But what was the point in defending what she'd done? At the end – the very end – she'd chosen to make love with Zeus. OK, that decision had been driven by fear: fear of never being able to see Jordan again, and of witnessing the end to her own life.

'You're right, I did say that.' She pulled Jordan's discarded denim shirt over her nakedness. 'And I meant it.'

She had no idea why it was important to make Jordan understand the truth of the situation – especially when they were clearly on a road to nowhere. But she had to try and explain.

'He made love to me so exquisitely…' She paused, her voice wavering at the sudden hardness in his eyes. 'I…I thought we might have met in another life, because he seemed to know me so well.'

She smiled briefly at him, but Jordan's expression didn't

alter. 'I know you feel I've been unfaithful,' she added. 'And I understand why. But, I also want to know if *you* felt as though you were being unfaithful? After all, you had the luxury of knowing who I was.'

A muscle jerked in his cheek. 'Every time I made love to you, something perverse took over. I wanted…I wanted to see just how far you'd let another man take you.'

'But…but don't you see…?' Megan gasped at his frank admission. 'Haven't you realised that it's because you already *knew* how to reach me, that I responded to you. Somewhere, in my heart, I must have known that it was *you*! After all, I've only ever made love with you. So, I'm no damn expert on the subject!'

She shivered, pulling his denim shirt tighter around her shoulders. 'When we made love – whether you were Zeus, or that laughing rogue I married – we were obviously still attracted to one another. Doesn't that tell you *anything*?'

For a long time he studied her, weighing her words. However, she took heart from the fact that the light in his eyes had warmed a little.

'OK – you didn't look remotely like Jordan. Your build appeared to be heavier and more muscular; you spoke differently, you used strange gestures – you even smelled different. In fact, you appeared so different that even your own wife – who knew every inch of your body almost as well as she knew her own – even she didn't connect the two men.'

Megan was relieved that Jordan remained silent, waiting patiently as she searched for the words to explain the extraordinary situation..

'Everything…absolutely *everything* was different about you. But there *must* have been something…something which touched a cord within me. Think about it for a moment,' she added urgently. 'I was virginal when I first met you. You didn't push me into a physical relationship, you left the pace to me. But we always wanted each other – that, at least, was never in question.'

He gave a slight nod, as though he was beginning to understand.

'It's not our appearance – the way we look. I mean…I know that I'm no oil painting. I bet there's loads of women who'd beat me hands down when it comes to looks. And you've probably been out with most of them!' She laughed at the sardonic amusement glinting in his eyes. 'And even if it was the other way round, and I was totally unrecognisable to you – I reckon that something of me, Megan Lacey, would still reach you at an instinctive, sub-conscious level. Something in our souls would recognise and know one another.'

'I don't know, Megan.' He raked his fingers roughly through his hair. 'Frankly, I can't imagine a situation where I wouldn't recognise you. I understand what you're saying, but I'm afraid that I can't go along with it.'

Megan gave a deep, heavy sigh of bitter disappointment. She didn't seem able to get the message through to Jordan. He still clearly believed that she had conceived their baby during her 'affair' with Zeus – so how *could* she tell him that his child was still growing inside her? She had a sensation of sinking into black darkness and hopelessness, only just managing to pull herself together before the descent became terminal.

'What about you, Jordan? How do you see your future?'

'I've been far too busy trying to get well, to worry about that far ahead.' He shrugged. 'I've still got a few months off work to get fitter and stronger.. After that – I've no idea what is likely to happen.'

'You're talking about work. I'm talking about your personal life. Are you going to drift in and out of casual relationships for the rest of your life?'

'Like I did before I met you?' His smile was slight – and

it didn't reach his eyes.

'Yes,' she forced out. 'Just like that.'

'I guess so. Being married doesn't exactly fit in with my line of work.'

Megan wanted to yell: *Well, change your 'line of work'. Fight to keep me*! And she wanted to get up from his side to punish him for his words, but she didn't say, or do that. Instead, she coolly agreed with him. 'No, I can see that marriage clearly "doesn't exactly fit in" with your work.'

He frowned at her. 'You really are going to throw away what we've got between us, aren't you?'

'I'm not throwing it away, because it's been over for a long time.'

She heard his sharp intake of breath and added softly, 'The fact is that we never had a chance. I may have stood up to Ray – but even I'm not dumb enough to try and take on the whole Organisation!'

Slowly, Jordan nodded. 'Ray had no right to tell you that I'd left you. He's been transferred overseas. I can't work with him again.' He shrugged. 'Not that that helps now. I thought we could have it all, Megan. But it looks as if I was wrong.'

Megan shrugged, trying to sound flippant, but not really succeeding. 'I always said that I'd never ask you to give up your work. If we *could* have it all – it' would be perfect. But life isn't like that, is it? Sometimes you have to chose – and sometimes there is no choice.'

Pushing himself to sit up against the arm of the chair, Jordan tried to read Megan's expression. He wished he knew what thoughts were going her mind. 'Do you want me to leave?' His stomach knotted with tension as he asked the question. 'If so, I ought to go and find a hotel for the night.'

'No.' Her expression was open again. 'No, I don't want you to go.'

'What do you want?'

'I want to get over you! And I want…I *really* want you to understand what happened with Zeus before we…before we divorce.'

'I don't know if I'll ever understand that.'

Megan wanted to clobber him – how *could* he be so dense?

'I want to see if we can be friends again – real friends, Jordan. I don't know about you, but I've missed all that fun we had, almost as much as our lovemaking. I mean…do we have to give up everything?'

'*You want to be friends?*' he asked incredulously. Was he hearing right?

'Megan – there's no way I have any "friends" that turn me on like you do,' he told her, his lips twisting with grim humour as he slowly levered himself to his feet. 'I'm sorry, darling, but I've got to take some painkillers. And they have the effect of… Well, they tend to knock me out.'

Gathering the quilt in her arms, Megan gestured towards the bedroom. 'Crash out in there – you're too big for the settee.' He looked so tired, she suddenly had the urge to surround him with cushions and spoon soup into his sensual mouth.

'If I wasn't feeling so wrecked, I'd try and get to a hotel. But…'

'There's no need – I want you to stay.'

'There's just one thing,' he said as he took the painkillers. 'If…if we ever manage to be "just friends" – for God's sake don't ever ask me to check out your next husband. OK?'

'OK.'

'And don't…' His eyes glittered. 'Don't *ever* tell me about your sex life with him. I'll try to be your friend, Megan, but I'm not making any promises!'

She smiled, a warm, sexy smile which made Jordan wish like hell that he hadn't taken his sleep-inducing pain-killers.

'On second thoughts – if you smile at me like that,' he said as he lay down on the double bed, 'I'm *never* going to be your friend!'

The sound of soft laughter reached him as she covered him with the quilt, letting his denim jacket drop to the bedroom floor before she climbed into bed beside him.

'Megan…?' He frowned as he felt her snuggling up to him. 'What are you doing?'

'Keeping warm.'

'You do this with all your friends?'

'Nope. You're forgetting something.'

'What's that?'

'We're still married, So, this is OK.'

'Mmm…' he muttered drowsily as he pulled her closer and the warm, woozy world of sleep began taking hold of him. 'I love you, darling.'

Did he even realise he'd said that? Megan lay awake, her thoughts whirling. *This was all so bloody silly*! They loved one another, yet they couldn't stay married. Why? Because of the stupid Organisation? Was that really all? His breathing was shallower now than it had been in what seemed like a lifetime ago. Was that the bullet which he'd taken for her? She propped her cheek on her palm and studied his moon dusted features, forced herself to be honest.

No, it wasn't just that. If only she could make him see that he had no reason to despise her, for making love with Zeus. That it had been the strong core of fundamental, basic feelings between them, which had transcended the differences in his physical appearance. But Jordan had always been a jealous man, not able to bear even the idea of her flirting with another man. So, what chance did she have? And what was the point? Hadn't they both agreed that the marriage was over? Too much had happened, despite the fact that they were totally compatible, both mentally and physically. And yet, if they ever tried to fight the Organisation – which, of course, Jordan wouldn't – could they ever hope to escape the spectre of the hijack? Or of her own lack of faithfulness?

Questions still whirled in her brain as Jordan moved in his sleep. And then, a drastic solution to the problem began forming in her mind. It was scary, very risky, and just about the craziest thing she'd ever contemplated. But it looked as if it might be the only answer to her problem.

By unspoken mutual consent, neither Megan nor Jordan spoke of the hijack; they stayed in the cottage, making love, laughing and playing together like new lovers. All the while, Jordan worked to recover his strength, and they took long, frosty walks over the craggy hills.

After that first night, they dropped all mention of the hurtful, painful issues. He did find Megan crying more than once; holding her for a long time although neither of them spoke a word. And it was on one of those occasions that he handed her a photograph album, which was a duplicate to the one Zeus had thrown off the yacht. She understood now why he had done that, since he couldn't have allowed the album to fall into the wrong hands. But staring at their wedding photographs again, gave them both a sense of time running out; as if at any moment their former lives would reclaim them, and separate them for ever. It was going to happen, of course, but until then they concentrated on losing themselves in one another; not needing to spell out the reasons why they'd always revelled in one another's company.

When the last day came, fat rain clouds hung low on the peaks, threatening storms and snow. Megan peeked through the window from beneath the sumptuous duvet, wishing that the sun was shining.

'Megan…?' His voice hoarse from sleep, Jordan's sparkling blue eyes lit up with a smile.

'Hi.' She shivered and pulled the quilt up to her nose. 'Let's stay in bed till midday. It's too grim out there to go walking.'

'You reckon?' A small smile tilted his sensuous mouth as it moved to cover hers in a languorous kiss.

'Hmm…' She slipped her arms around his neck as he began making lover to her, amazed that he still found new ways to drive her insane with need and desire.

Afterwards, holding her more tightly than before, Jordan seemed more reflective and less inclined to talk.

'I feel like there's a "Goodbye" coming,' Megan whispered, half-leaning over him, her hair tumbling down to brush his shoulders.

There was a pause of one or two heartbeats, then the sound of his deep voice seemed to reverberate through Megan. 'How do you know?'

'I know.' She smiled to hide the sharp stab of pain – wanting to hit out and scream out loud… and doing none of it.

'I've got to leave in a couple of hours.'

She nodded. So soon? *So bloody soon*? In three hours, then, she'd be speaking to Frank McRoss. Her fingers clutched at the bedding just at the thought.

'What are you going to do?' Jordan's knee-buckling blue eyes shone with intense light.

'I'm going away for a month, somewhere warm.'

'Don't you have to get back to your business?'

Megan shrugged. 'No, Alexa's having a great time running things. She's taken on four more permanent staff, which has helped to spread the load.'

'Have you decided where you'll live?'

'I'll think about it while I'm lying in the sun.'

'You'll let me know, Megan? Where to find you?'

How the hell could she go through with this? How? If she begged Jordan here and now to give up his career, he would – she could see it in his eyes. But she'd always been against that kind of manipulation.

She hesitated for too long, allowing Jordan to add, 'Megan, we could maybe work something out…?' And then he felt as though his guts were being ripped out, when she gave a slight shake of her head.

'No, we've both known all along this ends with your recovery – and mine.'

He looked away, a flicker of so many different emotions playing over his hard, masculine features. 'Megan, will you do one thing for me?'

'Sure.' She gave him a sexy smile, deliberately aimed to carry the message: 'You're an absolute crackpot if you let me go'.

'Don't contact Frank for a while – give it a few months? I want to see if I can work something out for us.'

Megan wavered, tempted to leave all the emotional problems under some magic carpet. As though testing whether it was possible, she sat up. 'Do you still feel I betrayed you with Zeus?'

It was still there, that fierce light in his eyes; he couldn't hide it any more than she could avoid seeing it. It would always come between them if they tried to hold their marriage together. Not to mention the problem of his work for the Organisation.

'Yes…yes, I do.' He shoved his fingers back through his soft blonde fringe. 'I wish to God I didn't, but I just can't see things your way, Megan.'

'And you don't feel as if you could ever wholeheartedly forgive me?'

He shook his head. 'I only wish I could.'

'Everything's got to be one hundred-per-cent with you, hasn't it?' Megan's softly spoken words concealed a sting which clearly hurt him.

'Yeah. Where you're concerned, it does.'

'I'm not perfect. I'm a freckle-faced, knock-kneed imperfect human being, who wore braces on her teeth and had the figure of a dumpling until I was fourteen! It's twelve years on now, Jordan, and I'm still as flawed as ever. So, I'm *never* going to regret making love with Zeus. He…he moved me…and he gave me his baby. Unfortunately, you're the only person I can talk to, about what happened. So, I'm sorry…' She shrugged. 'But if you can't come to terms with that, then I've no choice but to contact a divorce lawyer, the minute you drive away.'

He stared at her aghast, shattered and stunned as time seemed to expand and contract around them, pressing the harsh truth into his mind. Megan would take nothing less than 'one hundred-per-cent' from him, either.

'You'd better do that then, Megan.' He flinched as he threw back the cover, pulled on his jeans. 'I'll get packed.'

They shared a too-quiet, hard to swallow past the pain breakfast-cum-lunch, before a still-shocked Jordan grabbed his hold-all. 'Megan, if you ever need anything, you know where I am, OK?'

'You mean like sex? Or money?' she demanded grimly, almost out of her mind with pain and heartbreak.

Clearly shaken, his eyes glittered with a kind of amused, wry anger. 'I meant friendship. But if you need…'

She quickly raised a hand. 'No…please…I didn't mean it. I…I was just trying to hurt you,' she added helplessly.

Emotionally, Megan was on her knees. Only an enormous effort of sheer will power was allowing her to let Jordan walk away, keeping her silent as he opened the front door on an icy wind that seared through her jeans and warm sweat shirt. Every step he took towards his car tore cruelly at her heart-strings.

'*Stay – turn around, and tell me you forgive me…*' she yelled silently at him. Even as Jordan fired up the engine of his car, Megan knew that she could stop him with lies. She could swear blind that she'd made love with Zeus purely to save her own skin. He would believe her – if only because he wanted and needed to do so. But it wouldn't be the truth. She would be lying. And they were both worth more than that.

He raised his hand in a farewell salute and Megan smiled in response. But when he drove off and she returned to the cottage, she knew that she was also symbolically closing the door on her marriage.

epilogue

Megan was right. They couldn't stay married. He just couldn't live with the knowledge of how his wife had responded to Zeus.

Jordan repeatedly told himself that, on the two hundred-and-fifty mile drive South. He told himself that, over and over again, yet part of him couldn't understand exactly they couldn't carry on as they had during the past two months? All she had to do, was to tell him that what she'd experienced with Zeus had meant nothing.

'If you were anyone else, Megan, I couldn't have cared less,' he growled above the noise of the car radio. 'So, maybe you are right, after all?'

He was too aware that in his character of Zeus, his treatment of Megan had been diabolical. Yet had he done any more – or less – than taken her as his lover, she would have likely paid with her life. 'It wasn't your fault, Jordan, and it wasn't mine,' Megan had told him. And by doing so, she'd lifted the gut-churning guilt from him so easily with that sun-filled smile of hers. Which somehow had the result of making him feel even worse about what had happened.

By the time he drew up outside the Organisation's London Headquarters, Jordan felt utterly worthless as he eased himself out of the car. For the first time, he seemed to have no roots or direction in his life. He was almost fit again, of course – probably as fit as he would ever be. But some vital elements were missing. Excitement, laughter and…and Megan.

Taking a deep breath, he pressed the entrance buzzer – hoping against hope that work would help fill the void.

Because, without anything else of value in his life, he'd *have* to make damn sure that it did.

Jordan found that burying himself in work did help to fill his empty life – for a few weeks. But, if he'd learned nothing else during that time in Windermere with Megan, he'd finally realised the devastating effect that his work had caused to his marriage. And following a long talk with his boss, the Organisation had reluctantly agreed to release him – recognising that as far as they were concerned, Jordan was now in some ways a burned-out case.

However, if he'd expected to find himself living a life of leisure, he'd been doomed to disappointment! Almost immediately after his resignation from the Organisation, he'd been approached by an old friend who'd offered him a partnership in a new company, primarily offering courses for businessmen and corporations in the detection of fraud in the work place. And, since it had almost immediately proved to be a roaring success, Jordan now found himself far too busy to think about *anything*, other than his new business.

For the past week, he'd been teaching a course on computer fraud at the conference centre of one of the top London hotels. With the last of the delegates heading for home, on Friday night, Jordan turned to his young assistant. 'I'm taking a break for a quiet drink in the bar, Nigel. But, give me a call on my mobile if anything comes up that I should know about. OK?'

'Sure, Jordan – no problem.'

'Double whiskey?' the bartender murmured, slipping a mat on to the bar. Jordan nodded, scanning the early evening customers purely out of habit.

The woman who'd piqued his curiosity every evening for the past week, was sitting in her usual seat, drinking coffee and reading carefully through a massive portfolio of some kind, making notes. He glanced at his watch and wondered if she'd leave in ten minutes – as she always did. Just ten minutes after he ordered his first drink.

She was a creature of habit – that's what he instinctively studied. She always wore dark trousers and jackets, expensive-looking black framed glasses with slightly tinted lenses; blood red nails, that may or may not be false, being the only relief from her dark colour scheme. Strange – but any man who approached her was gently turned away – and for some reason, that intrigued him. He downed the double rye whisky and enjoyed the burn, nodded to the barman to refill his glass. Maybe, if he drank enough of these, Jordan told himself, he could stop feeling, and then perhaps that miserable document in his room would quit bugging him. Maybe he could turn this day from one of the worst – into one of the numbest…?

'Megan Lacey,' she wrote on the paper whilst silently scolding herself. 'You are a prize idiot. Every night – as soon as he looks at you – you take off! Now – for heaven's sake, stay put. You can't have a sordid affair in ten minutes. And you especially can't have one if you don't even speak to the man!'

She pushed the glasses up her nose, knew a panicky rush when her imagination threw up a horrible scenario. Another woman coming to meet Jordan. How the hell would she handle that? Stupid woman, she answered herself, you just get up and walk out; go up to your room.

The hotel room was costing a packet. But then Jordan had left her a cheque for a small fortune in the cottage bedroom, along with a note: 'Megan – please don't be offended, it's a gift. I love you, Jordan.'

It seemed right to use the money to prove this to him. It would have been easier if she hadn't kept losing her nerve. And then, what Megan had been dreading the most, suddenly happened – swiftly propelling her into action.

A woman, who must have been a generation older than Jordan, suddenly appeared and was sidling up to him at the bar. Megan shot to her feet, remembering just in time to school her movements to those of the person she was now pretending to be: a French woman called '*Nicole*'.

Rather than leaving the bar as was her first instinct, she moved fluidly towards it and ordered another coffee, adding, '*S'il vous plait,*' to the barman who smiled broadly back at her.

She felt, rather than saw Jordan's attention turn to her from the woman who was struggling to take 'no' for an answer. Megan could feel colour shooting up her face, and prayed that clever make-up would hide her reaction.

Just as she was about to turn tail, her nerve sinking without trace, Jordan's familiar voice stopped her in her tracks. 'Don't I know you from somewhere?'

Bloody hell! What kind of a line is that, Elliot? Jordan asked himself, wanting to sink through the floor as he cursed his own stupidity.

No…no! You shouldn't know me from anywhere! Megan panicked, whispered, '*Non…*' and turned gracefully to bolt from the bar.

'I apologise,' he stuffed his fingers back through his hair, 'I…ah…that was dreadful.'

'*Pardon*?' Her heart bumped, thumped and Megan thought she'd pass out there and then. I shouldn't be doing this!

'A dreadful pick-up line.' He spoke in French – and far more fluently and accomplished than Megan's own small knowledge of the language.

Oh, Lord! Let me out of here! Quaking, she hurried from the bar, hampered because the high-heeled boots she wore beneath the black trousers were no substitute for plimsolls, particularly when it came to running.

She reached the lift, before taking a deep breathe and seriously considering bolting up the stairs, because the lift doors didn't open immediately.

You go upstairs, collect your things, Lacey, and you get out of here – fast! This is too damned scary.

A glance at the decreasing blue numbers reassured Megan the lift was moving at last. Downwards. Very slowly.

At last the doors swished open. She moved inside the carpeted, prettily-lit and mirrored box, shocked at her unfamiliar reflection as she gulped air with relief. Escape was hers and the decision was made – she definitely couldn't go through with this. She'd leave later. When it was very, very dark.

As the sliding doors closed, a hand shot between them, forcing them apart. 'Miss…?' It was Jordan. 'You left this behind,' he told her, setting the portfolio against the mirrored lift wall – and as he did so, the doors closed behind him.

Megan panicked, lurched for the 'open' button, but Jordan shook his head, 'No, don't worry, I'm headed for my room. What floor are you on?' His hand hovered over the panel of buttons.

'Seven, thank you.'

Jordan smiled and leant against the mirrored wall beside the computerised operation panel, gesturing towards her portfolio, 'Are you working in London?'

Megan merely nodded in reply, faced the doors with a grim expression, as if facing a firing squad. She wanted nothing more than to escape this lift…to escape Jordan – and chuck away her whole stupid, crack-pot scheme.

The lift gave a violent jerk, sending Megan bowling into Jordan's side.

His hand shot out to steady her. 'Oh, great.'

'What is it?'

'Unless I'm mistaken, we're stuck between floors.'

Megan reached for the alarm; it gave a pathetic bleep, then fell silent. The lights died and complete blackness swallowed them. 'Oh…!' Panic gripped Megan. Would the lift plunge to the ground floor and kill them?

'It's all right.' Jordan's hand rested on her shoulder. 'Emergency lighting should kick on in a minute.'

'Ah…!' She rescued her 'borrowed' voice, it worked, if a tad tremulously. 'Will we drop?'

'No, there are fail-safe's…' Jordan had spoke the word 'fail-safe's' in French, and it took Megan a silent minute or two to work out what he'd said. Even then she wasn't sure.

'Please, speak in English. It is what I am here to improve, *Monsieur*.'

He chuckled. 'You could be fluent by the time we get out of here.'

Pink-tinted emergency lighting flickered on, and only then did Megan realise that she was gripping Jordan's jacket sleeve. 'Ah …sorry.'

'It's my pleasure.' That smile tilted his mouth, she saw a brief sparkle in his eyes and let her hand drop to her side. 'Since we could be stuck here a while, we'd better introduce ourselves. I'm Jordan Elliot.'

'Nicole Lafitte,' Megan said, smiling broadly and holding out her hand, which he shook politely.

'I usually use the stairs.' Jordan shoved his hands deep into his black trouser pockets, grimacing ruefully. 'The lifts in this place have been dodgy for the past month.'

'It is too closed up…' She couldn't stay in there for any length of time with Jordan! Just shaking his hand had been electrifying, nerve-wracking.

'You mean "too closed in",' he corrected gently, amusement glinting in his gorgeous eyes. 'My wife isn't keen on confined spaces, either. I used to have to practically make love to her in the lift, to get her downstairs!'

'She will report you gone?'

'No. I'm not with her.'

'Oh, *pardon.*'

'Sorry – not pardon.'

Megan gave a little smile and repeated, 'Sorry.'

She pushed the tinted specs up her nose, understood how Jordan, as Zeus, must have tensed against hearing ill of himself. She longed to tell him who she really was, but she was trapped in the deception as surely as she was trapped inside these mirrored walls. And inside these walls, Megan had the opportunity to prove what she'd longed to prove to Jordan – that it was the essence, *the souls of two people that whispered and fell in love*, that mattered in life. That whatever disguise either of them hid behind, it would make no difference. They would always find one another.

Jordan studied Nicole in the dim light, such an aura of sadness shrouded her. Yet her smile lit up like a shaft of sunshine on a gloomy day. For some reason, he had a compulsion to see that smile again – but he needed to break through the sadness first.

Nicole, though, was the first to speak. 'You look not happy, *Monsieur.*'

'Unhappy,' a small smile twisted Jordan's mouth, his tone so deep, so familiar. 'I was thinking the same thing about you, Miss Lafitte.'

'Ah…' His blunt accuracy took Megan aback. 'Things happen. We have no control sometimes.'

Jordan touched her forearm. 'I know what that's like.'

For a month, he'd worked hard and hadn't spoken about Megan to anyone. On a good day, he had a severe ache inside – on a bad day like this one – pain gnawed and devoured like a hungry beast, ravenous for more and more of him.

Instead of drawing out the enigmatic woman as he intended, Jordan hunkered down to sit on the lift floor. ' My wife was pregnant.' Megan looked at him as he drew a ragged breath. 'We were involved in a hostage situation.'

Unexpectedly, tears pricked her eyes, the force of his sorrow moving her to kneel beside his outstretched legs, facing him. 'I'm so sorry.'

'My…my wife lived, thank God!' He gritted his teeth to stem the agony, but that raw pain shone in his darkened blue eyes. 'We lost…' his voice thickened. 'We lost the baby.'

Jordan couldn't take his eyes off the woman. Her pale face wet with pink-lit tears…tears for him, for Megan, the baby. She was so still, so silent; a stranger, yet she shared his pain so completely. Only in Megan's eyes had he ever seen that same, boundless understanding.

'Oh, God…' The words broke from him on a husky whisper.

The French woman moved closer, wrapped her arms around his shoulders, gentle fingers stroking his soft hair. 'It will be all right,' she soothed, aching because they'd both loved so deeply, but Jordan couldn't forgive her.

Trembling at the contact, her cheek against his ear, his potent masculine scent surrounding her, his hard-muscled body against the softness of her own. A gasp broke from her when his arm clamped around her waist, bringing her closer.

'*Souls whisper when we're not looking*…' Megan's words broke free in Jordan's mind. In that instant, Jordan understood everything she had tried so hard to explain. That given the right circumstances and unsteady emotions, need could overpower anyone. He needed Nicole, held her more tightly, his face buried in her neck. 'Oh, God, she wanted me to forgive her…' Pain clutched and twisted inside him. 'To forgive her for something that wasn't wrong.'

Biting her lip, Megan stifled a sob. Her heart broke when he whispered, 'It's too late…I let her go.'

'It's never too late,' she soothed, closed her eyes, felt his shuddering breath against the delicate skin of her neck and held him, fingers twined in his soft blond hair. After a long, silent time, light flooded the small space, and the lift jolted and bore them upwards.

Devastation etched Jordan's features as they stepped into the broad, carpeted hallway.

'Nicole…' He reached for her hand, but she pressed her finger across his lips.

'It will be all right.' Confusion burned in his eyes when she slipped away from him, hurrying swiftly for the stairs without a backward glance.

'It's too late,' he shook his head, stared at the carpeted stairway long after Nicole had disappeared, wishing to a blue moon and back that he'd known what he knew now…a month ago.

Megan flung the wig across the room, and then flew into the bathroom to cleanse away the thick stage make-up. The brown contact lenses she carefully returned to their special case, before turning to face her reflection in the mirror.

After flicking out the network of pins that held her own hair close to her head, and shaking it into a mass of tumbling waves, she pulled off her suit and then stood hesitating by the phone, her heart pumping madly. 'Could I have room service, please?'

Jordan stared at the legal envelope's contents – the words 'Decree Nisi' leaping up at him, their effect as physical as a punch in the guts. It had been bad enough, earlier this morning, when he'd first received the envelope. And now, after his experience in the lift, his life seemed dust and ashes. He heard the tinkling approach of a room service trolley and shoved his hand into his trouser pocket for a tip.

He threw open the door – and froze to the spot.

'*Megan*…?'

With her heart banging against her ribs, she witnessed Jordan's unguarded look of total shock. The stunned blue eyes staring straight into hers, before gradually taking in her white maid's uniform…and her bare feet!

Visibly shaken, Jordan moved towards her, fingers trembling as they touched her hair, palms moving slowly down to caress her cheeks.

'Are you real…? he muttered helplessly 'Or are you a mirage…?'

She smiled, slipped her arms around his waist, her head tilted back so she could gaze up into his eyes.

Jordan's soft blond hair fell onto his forehead, that beautiful smile of his still a little sad. 'Megan, something happened just now…'

She put her finger across his lips, rose up on to her tip-toes, anchored her arms around his neck and kissed him; fired by his hungry response and the way his arms trembled when he held her, his hands greedily moulding her against him.

'I need to tell you something…' he whispered, his sensual mouth so close, his hands at her waist.

'You don't need to,' she whispered back, smiling when he frowned in puzzlement. Trailing her fingers over his chiselled features, she said gently, 'You need tell me nothing…*Monsieur*!'

'*Nicole*…?' Disbelief flickered in his eyes; only slowly replaced by a smile as everything gradually fell into place. '*You* were Nicole…?'

Megan's green eyes sparkled with laughter. 'Well, I'm me now!' She gave a delicious wriggle against his powerful body. 'About those fantasies of yours,' she whispered against his lips. 'What happens next?'

'Ah…' He grinned. 'Well, there's this man…this husband…who took a very long time to realise that his wife was the one, very precious thing in his life. So, he gave up working for his Organisation, and…'

'Oh, Jordan…' she sighed happily, almost unable to believe her ears. 'You really don't work for them any more?'

'Nope – I've got…sorry, I should have said this "husband"…' Jordan grinned, his blue eyes glinting down at her. 'This "husband" finally saw the light, and is now a partner in a new company, offering courses in security to business and corporations.'

'Oh…oh, that's *wonderful!'* she cried, her arms tightening about him.

'And, although this husband was heart-broken to receive his divorce papers, this morning, he's now hoping that his wife – a very sexy woman dressed all in white – will forget the divorce…and make love to me.'

'How about…' Megan leant back slightly in his arms so she could see his reaction, tracing his lower lip with her fingertip. 'How about a very sexy, *pregnant* woman in white…making love to you?'

'You mean our baby's OK?' Tears magnified the sheer happiness in Jordan's eyes, then he smiled, clearly astounded.

'Megan – *that's perfect*!' he said, laughing with sheer happiness as he lifted her clean off her feet, whirling her around as he kissed her. 'That makes our life just damn perfect…!'

We're sure you've enjoyed this month's selection from Heartline. We can offer you even more exciting stories by our talented authors over the coming months. Heartline will be featuring books set in the ever-popular and glamorous world of TV – novels with a dash of mystery – a romance featuring two dishy doctors – and just some of the authors we shall be showcasing are Margaret Callaghan, Angela Drake and Kathryn Grant.

If you've enjoyed these books why not tell all your friends and relatives that they, too, can Start a New Romance with Heartline Books today, by applying for their own, **ABSOLUTELY FREE** copy of Natalie Fox's LOVE IS FOREVER. To obtain their free book, they can:

- visit our website @www.heartlinebooks.com
- *or* telephone the Heartline Hotline on 0845 6000504
- *or* enter their details on the form overleaf, tear off the whole page, and send it to:
  Heartline Books, PO Box 400, Swindon SN2 6EJ

And, like you, they can discover the joys of belonging to Heartline Books Direct™ including:

- ♥ A wide range of quality romantic fiction delivered to their door each month
- ♥ Celebrity interviews
- ♥ A monthly newsletter packed with special offers and competitions
- ♥ Author features
- ♥ A bright, fresh, new website created just for our readers

Please send me my free copy of *Love is Forever*:

Name (IN BLOCK CAPITALS)

_____

Address (IN BLOCK CAPITALS)

_____

_____

_____

_____ Postcode _____

If you do not wish to receive selected offers
from other companies, please tick the box ☐